Coyote Laughing

S.R. Ruark

Indies United Publishing House, LLC

ISBN: 978-1-64456-061-7

Library of Congress Control Number: 2019948936

Indies United Publishing House, LLC
PO Box 3071
Quincy, Illinois 62305-3071
www.indiesunited.net

I would like to take a moment to thank those who have helped me make this book possible. Lynn Riley and Kirby Kerr for doing the original read through. Patti Tattum, Katrina O'Keefe and Karen Rodgers for helping work on some of the editing. Scott Reed for information on vaults.

Table of Contents

Chapter One...1
Chapter Two...19
Chapter Four..31
Chapter Five..49
Chapter Six...59
Chapter Seven...68
Chapter Eight...79
Chapter Nine..89
Chapter Ten...95
Chapter Eleven...113
Chapter Twelve...125
Chapter Thirteen...129
Chapter Fourteen...136
Chapter Fifteen..140
Chapter Sixteen..146
Chapter Seventeen..153
Chapter Eighteen...159
Chapter Nineteen...166
Chapter Twenty...169
Chapter Twenty-One...177
Chapter Twenty-Two...194
Chapter Twenty-Three...211

Chapter One
Cactus to the Rescue

The man felt the dream forming from the fog of heavy sleep. He saw unbroken prairie before him with stars brighter than any he had ever seen in the city, he heard the gentle rustle of the wind through the unending grass. There were rocks behind him that looked like a giant child's blocks knocked over... blocks that could be built into towering heights or knocked down again into tumbling ruins. The fire in front of him was small yet his skin could still felt the heat. He looked down with a frown. He remembered going to bed in boxers, but was now wearing a leather breechcloth, leggings and fringed moccasins with geometric patterns done in dyed porcupine quills. He ran a hand down the side of his leg. The leather was soft to the touch. Not like modern leather pants but softer almost cloth-like. He closed his eyes and took a deep breath. The smell of smoke, grass and air, without a hint of gas or asphalt, filled his lungs.

"Today is the start of the rest of your life."

Jason opened his eyes, making out the outline of a medium sized yellow dog with a very fluffy tail. The dog sat just outside of the light cast by the crackling fire. Jason raised an eyebrow at the creature, refusing to flinch in the dream.

"Coyote." Jason was not naming a type of canine but one of his gods, the god of mischief.

A playfully chaotic god in children stories but a seriously scary bad ass of chaotic mayhem. The scary tales were told by the People after the children had been put to bed. Children would grow up soon enough. Coyote was not a god to mess with. Things... tended to happen to those who tried and Jason was not a stupid man. His great grandfather was a shaman and talked to Coyote on a semi regular basis, but Coyote had never deigned to visit Jason.

"Until tonight there was no reason." The deity said. Coyote moved closer to sit by the fire wrapping his tail around his front paws cat like, across from Jason. Coyote acknowledged the man with a flick of an ear and a large open mouthed canine smile, wider than a normal dog's toothy grin. The fire light made his teeth seem white, wet and very sharp looking. A scary smile.

Jason waited. His father had taught him patience while hunting. Information, he had found was just another type of hunt and Jason was very good at getting information.

Coyote grinned again. "You'll need that patience young one."

"I am not young." Jason was not going to be baited even if his mouth was dry.

"You are not a wise old man nor starting the decade of learning by the People's reckoning either." The tone was amused but slightly condescending.

Jason waited. Young was not an insult; however, the implied insult of stupid did make him grit his teeth, bunching the muscles in his jaw. He blanked his mind from thinking rude things. Gods weren't known for their tolerance with impudent "children".

"Today is the start for the rest of your life." Coyote repeated, looking at him intensely.

"Every day is a start."

"For a new day. Today your life changes."

"I die." He said flatly. The wind blew cold up his spine.

Coyote yipped in laughter. "If you were going to die, I would not be here. No need to tell a dead man to pay attention." A sly look, through narrowed yellowed eyes.

"Thank you for your words of wisdom, Coyote." Jason tried for a calm response.

"It's not for you that wisdom is needed."

"It's not?" Now that piqued Jason's curiosity.

Coyote seemed to smirk. "The one with the sharp teeth." was all he said with a gleam of white teeth.

Jason winced. He hated being bitten. Never knew where some one's mouth had been.

"You'll do, child of stone." Coyote grinned; he rose to his feet and stretched. His paws almost touched the fire as he yawned with his ears back flashing a long jaw of canines at Jason again. The open mouth yawn was wide enough to have unhinged the jaw of a true coyote. With that Coyote turned, his tail wagging slowly as he took a step away, stopping to look coyly over his shoulder at Jason. "One more thing, take tweezers with you today."

With that, the dream splintered and Jason was tossed awake, like a leaf in a strong wind, tumbling back into the real world. Jason sat up in the motel bed smelling of stale smoke and spilled beer, with a taste of smoke from a cedar fire in his mouth and nose.

Tweezers? Jason got up to check his medical kit.

"Hey. Just saw the extra water lily in my pond today."

"Yep. The fish needed some extra feeding."

"Think there has been enough feeding. You've left a few other plants that need to be cleaned. They've started to turn into compost."

"I'll get to those in the next day or two."

"Sooner would be better. Hard to run a business without you leaving your broken toys in my garden."

"As long as my bank is supplying payment for your business I think you can tolerate a toy or two out."

Silence for a moment.

"A day. The heat here makes the…plastic melt."

"A day it is."

The lines clicked dead. A long finger tapped the top of the cell phone. Yep, clean up was a bitch, and sometimes toys just shouldn't be allowed at all. Time to do some house cleaning.

It wasn't the vaults themselves that were the issue; it was the first attempt at maneuvering them through the warehouse that pulled a muscle in the tall man's back. Each vault weighed 2,474 lbs and stood at 62". The floor pallet jack he had rented couldn't handle the load, causing him to tear a muscle while trying to un-stick the pallet jack from underneath the T30.

He didn't swear or kick the vault, but settled for glaring at the damn thing for a full 5 minutes while his back spasmed. He had to go back to the rental store for a pallet jack truck, not just a damn floor pallet jack, putting him behind schedule. Three hours later he was finally back on schedule with a rental truck and a rented pallet jack.

He joked with the sales guy that his wife's new garden stone fishpond was more then he and the boys could carry.

"Yeah, those women. Always wanting the biggest and heaviest they can get." the counter guy said with sympathy. "Tell the slave driver she better be putting out some good laying for the work you're doing."

"That down payment was paid this morning!" the man said with a self-satisfied grin.

They both laughed while the pallet jack truck was loaded into the rental van.

"Have it back by 5." the counter guy said "And I hope your second "payment" is as good as the first!" the sales guy called out laughingly.

"It will be, it will be!" He waved out the window, heading towards the highway. The naproxen was wearing off and he would need to find something stronger. He had 6 safes to arrange, then wire up with explosives. Some things needed to be wired right to counter the people wired wrong.

"Carrie, are we almost there?" I asked, flicking the cigarette butt out the open window, not quite yelling to be heard. Carrie's car was a small blue thing without AC and rattled like a monkey in a cage, hopped up on speed. The CD player had been stolen 3 months ago so there wasn't even music to relieve the tedium of a boring drive in a bad car. The ripped vinyl seats were not the most comfortable, either, but Carrie loved her car more than any of the many boyfriends and one-night stands she's had since getting it. She even nicknamed the POS, Little Blue.

"Almost! If your directions are right we should be hitting the greenhouse in another minute or two." Carrie's hair was blowing all over her face and shoulders. The sunset was turning her hair more strawberry then blond.

The road shimmered in the heat of the desert sun, making the car hotter and stickier than usual. The sun was to our backs, yet nothing had cooled down. The open windows made talking in anything other than an almost shout pretty hard, but the blowing wind didn't cool us much either. God, I hated her car but anything flashier was sure to attract unwanted attention, so small and crappy, but running, is what we used.

"Those directions are accurate, slut." I gave an off-handed wave, breezily dismissing her need for minute directions.

"Look bitch, just 'cause..." She tried to laugh, talk and spit out hair at the same time. I grinned back, reaching for another clove cigarette in my deep pockets. The lighter I pulled from my sleeve like a magician with a handkerchief. I loved doing that trick, made me feel like Houdini. The trick was useful in picking up and hiding things as well.

My hoodie was black, long sleeved and had deep front pockets. Comfortable and concealing, enough I could ignore being hot and sticky in favor of those pockets and the arm coverings. Black was just a plus. Besides, it matched my nail polish. I was styling hard as I sucked in a mouth full of the sweet flavored smoke.

"Greenhouse!" I shouted as what looked like an abandoned warehouse complex came into view. I waived my cigarette to the left side of the road, triumphant in being right.

"That?"

"Yep." I shouted smugly. The building looked vaguely promising from far away. The back part of the warehouse was huge, being close to 4 stories tall and about 3 blocks wide. The front had a sloped roof made of the green panels used in greenhouses and only about 20 feet tall; short compared to the back end. Parts of the larger back structure had areas of green panels as well. The very large greenhouse looked abandoned. Yep... we were in the right place.

Now if the guy would sell to us, we should be set for at least a month and would be able to pay next semester off in one big chunk instead of pieces. That meant more time for studying and not trying to hustle the next decent sale. I liked my 3.4 GPA, but it was a bitch to maintain while having a regular job, a side job and still going to school full time. I was almost salivating at the thought of just being able to study most nights and not hit the clubbing/frat party scene.

The gravel was loud under her not-quite-balding tires. There was only one battered truck to the left of the front building, almost hidden behind the towers of leaning pallets and the fading light. It was hard to tell the color from the road, but I was betting black, maybe dark blue.

"See any cameras?" She shouted.

"Do I look like I can see 100 yards into the distance bitch? And, no!"

"Yay!" Carrie pulled in, declining to drive up to the front door. Instead, we parked next to the mountain of pallets, 4 feet from the dark blue battered truck. Neither of us wanted to park in front. The side door was probably the loading door we would be using, possibly even the back door. That and Carrie really didn't want her car photographed in front of anything that might have surveillance on the front door. Didn't matter the side door might have surveillance, though we didn't see any cameras in either spot... just no front door for her. Her car, her idiosyncrasies. I just didn't like parking in front as it advertised a bit too much of who was where.

I pushed my hair back with a hand trying to get it looking not as fly away as Carrie's. Being jaw length, while traveling in her car, had its advantages.

"Nice dye job by the way." Carrie said, pocketing her keys while slinging her cutesy little purse over her shoulders. Leather I like, but baby blue leather with flowers, I rolled my eyes at that thing. Could she get any cutesier?

"Thanks."

"I thought the dark blue was better but the brown works well. Makes your hips look smaller." She giggled.

I glared at her as I got out of her car. "It's auburn, bitch, and the blue was waaay too distinctive, too memorable." I made a face; I had liked the blue better too. I had gotten better tips for not looking like so many other blond sorority bimbos waiting tables, the blue had definitely been great for tips. "And when you can get into anything other than a 2x mom jean, come talk to me about my size 10 hips!"

Carrie giggled again. Some days I won the bitch game, some days she did. So far, she was three up on me today, but the night was young. I grinned back at her. Game on!

We walked around to the front of the building and went up the warped wooden steps. Carrie's flowered flip-flops made minimal noise clopping around, my dark Keds, less so. There was an old fashioned bell over the door that made a huge clanging sound as we came in.

"Oh my God! We've stepped back into the 1960s!" Carrie was in awe. Her head swinging back and forth to cover the old west style minimalist décor. The room was obviously old with faded to grey wood walls and floor. The floor was made of wood slats, which were tongue and groove, if I could judge anything, and not cheap fake wood floor paneling. Lots of wear and tear, from the scuff marks and ingrained dirt, but in good repair still. The four foot high wood front desk, held an old metal register, the type with huge brass keys that took 3 men to carry. The one jarring, out-of-place item was the coke machine next to another door to the left of the front door. The hum was slight, but noticeable in the quiet. The smell of fertilizer was a bit overpowering, blocking the other scents as too faint to smell.

"Where are the deer antlers? Can't have retro cowboy without deer antlers!" Carry said mockingly.

"I don't believe in killing for clothing or decoration. Can I help you?" Came a voice to our left, as we were marveling over the antique decor. We both jumped, though Carrie was the only one to squeal in surprise. The overall impression was long hair, mud splattered wife beater and blue jeans. The old hippy was wiping his hands on a rag, peering through small oval glasses. We both blinked. This was not quite what either of us had expected.

"Umm… Sorrrrry." Carry stuttered.

Carrie stood on her tiptoes a couple of times nervously. Her impressive cleavage would have given her black eyes if not well restrained. "Make the floor bounce why don'tcha?" I said sideways to Carrie.

"Ohhh, bitch!" She punched my shoulder with a girly hit, nervousness causing her to be sillier than usual. Buying from new dealers was not Carrie's strong suit. After she knew them a bit, they were the best of friends, in soooo many ways.

"Ladies?" The man pulled out a slightly cleaner cloth to rub over his glasses. Without his glasses, I had to downgrade his age by about 15 years.

Carrie bumped my shoulder again. "Err...we're here to buy some plants for our dorm room." I said crossing my arms over my less impressive chest. "Something good." I was using the phrase Tony had given to me.

"What type of plants are you looking for? Low water maintenance or easy to grow? Something that'll survive beer being thrown over it regularly?" There was a hint of a grin. He put the eye cleaning rag in his pocket, holding the glasses out at arm's length to view the lenses.

"Something good... that goes with beer." I said.

"And nachos, or cereal." Carrie added. I glared at her. "Munchies." she amended. Again we were going by the code phrase, if out of order and by more than one person. A ball gag was something I really wish I had now for her mouth though.

"Plants don't usually eat nachos or cereal though we have a good selection of garden plants that are edible. Better for nachos, not so much for cereal. The strawberry plants might be what you're looking for." There was a more pronounced grin as he put his glasses back on. He was having fun at our expense and enjoying making us squirm. The man's shoulders were starting to be more relaxed as he kept talking.

Carrie and I exchanged glances. Were we really in the right place?

We looked back at the hippy again. He was frowning as he looked out the window. "Why don't you girls go into the greenhouse and start looking for some plants you might like. I'll be with you in a moment to help you with your selection for beer and smoking."

I blinked. That was what Tony said was the right counter phrase. All very cloak and dagger. I had laughed at the time, not so much now though. "Umm... ok. We'll look for something sturdy then."

"Try the cactuses." He motioned us to the door behind him and moved to behind the counter. I thought I heard a slight click as the door closed behind us.

Giggling like the collegiate girls we were, all cloak and dagger tough, we walked into a greenhouse the size of a football field. Ok, maybe not that long but damn did it make me feel small! The room was in a deep green twilight from the roof panels and the dying sunlight outside. The sound of the cowbell over the front door banging made us both jump

"More customers for beer and smokes!" Carrie whispered. After a nervous laugh at our own jumpiness, we kept going forward exploring. I glanced upwards to see huge light fixtures hanging from the rafted roof between the glass panes that were over the sprinklers still dripping. Again, Carrie and I exchanged looks. There was a bunch of regular garden plants here. Not a cannabis plant anywhere in sight.

"You sure this is…"

"Yes! Right place. Right phrase!"

"Then where is the crop?"

"In his back pocket?" I gave her a roll of the eyes. "Do I look like I know where he'd be keeping a cash crop in this freaking warehouse in the first 10 minutes of walking in?"

The almost silence was pervasive. No music, no dogs, nothing I would associate with a pot growing operation. Our voices were getting quieter and quieter to match the surroundings even though there weren't any other people here.

"What keeps this guy from getting robbed regularly?!" she stage whispered.

"Maybe he has a room full of slutty bimbos like you to distract anyone who comes to do bad things?" I asked sweetly.

"Bitch!" she giggled though, as if the thought of clones like her being a security force were one she liked.

If he had any plants or crop to sell us, it was very well hidden so far. The plants, he did have were garden variety or landscaping, laid out in rows of 100 feet long on low wooden tables. The wooden planks between the tables were less muddy then under the tables but the smell was still fertilizer, wet dirt and green plants. I took a deep breath. "I want to be a pot grower when I grow up!"

"So you can be Ms. Old Hippy chick?" Carrie asked.

"If I got to smoke everything as a tester, hell yeah!" We both giggled at that.

We started moving down the rows towards a large upright cactus thingy. Several types of prickly plants and plants that weren't spiky but had thick fleshy leaves and fleshy flowers had no scent laid out on the low tables next to the huge cactus thing. I reached out to one plant that looked weirdly phallic.

"Think we found the cactus." I hissed in pain, hastily pulling back a stabbed finger after trying to pet one of the plants.

"Ya think?" Came Carrie's retort, while I sucked on my bleeding finger.

"City girl here, cum guzzling farm bitch!" I snapped at her from around my finger.

"Ooh! Getting creative there. Almost eloquent in your pain. Hey look!" Carrie whispered to me holding up a short round of cactus with lots of long thick spines in a small square of black plastic. "The most prick you've had in a week!"

"Bitch!" I hissed back grinning as Carrie giggled. "You're the only slut I know who'd go for something that small."

"Ouch!" She giggled. "How about this one?" Another small cactus with a main trunk and two arms branching upwards, like a man being held up at gunpoint. Not so heavily spined but enough so to be painful if touched by bare skin. "One for both holes and your clit." She started giggling even more.

"Nah, too straight." I said with a shrug and a sly look. "I want one with a little more curve in the arms. Something to fill your mouth and both ears!"

Carrie started to snicker so badly, she dropped the plant half an inch from her toes. The plastic pot cracked on the wooden boards and spilling out the dirt and the cactus. She jumped back with a squeal of alarm.

"Carrie!" I hissed, getting on my knees trying to clean up the dirt and plant. "Help me before we're thrown out!" She started hopping from one foot to the other, shaking out the dirt in her flip-flops making the boards bounce and creek. I glared up at her as the boards kept bouncing in time with her hopping making the cactus and pot bounce in separate directions away from me.

"I'll get dirty!" she whined making a face, putting her manicured hands behind her back like a 3 year old hiding a cookie.

"Chica, you're already dirty. This at least washes off!" I hissed up at her, making a growly face. Wrinkled nose and bared teeth, the works. And it worked!

"Bitch!" She laughed but got down on her hands and knees, careful of her sorority style manicured nails, to help with the dirt and plant.

The boards were dry with caked on mud, feeling somewhat pebbly through the jeans on my knees. The dirt was scattered all over, mixing with what was already on the ground. I didn't want the hippy guy to run us off without at least letting us talk. As I was trying to sweep the dirt from the pot into my hands, Carrie was sweeping it over the boards into the damp dirt underneath the tables. For some reason this working not together, set us to giggling harder.

I carefully put the handful of dirt I had back in the broken cactus pot. The cactus was a bit more problematic. The roots were shallow but the top of the damn thing was covered in spines, making the task of trying to get a hold of it almost impossible. I pulled the sleeve of my hoodie down over my hand, to get a very careful hold of the plant. The thorns were noticeable but not painfully so, as it would have been if using my bare hand. I didn't want another throbbing finger or fingers as this plant was small, but it required more than one finger to hold.

I heard a soft pop then another. The sound froze me in place. Carrie was still giggling until she looked at my face. "Oh my god, your face, what?" I slapped my free hand over her mouth; I could feel my eyes growing huge and goose bumps racing up my skin. Friday nights were our crime story, popcorn and cheap wine nights. Carrie knew gunfire this way. I knew it from a few closer encounters that were far more real than TV.

Cocking my head toward the front office, I waited for the next sound. We heard the bell over the door clanging. The sound of gunfire was louder. Not silenced this time.

I slowly removed my hand putting a finger to my lips. Carrie's eyes got huge and she stuffed her palm into her mouth biting down. I could just hear a small whimper starting. I wanted to stuff a hand in my mouth to do the same thing but was still holding the stupid cactus caught in my sleeve. Fucking hate, those damn things!

I thrust my chin at her and to the left. She nodded. She would take the left side and I would take the right. We crawled under the plant tables hoping to hide behind the gallon jugs with plants under there. We should be out of sight to the casual observer looking down the rows. The cactus would not come off my sleeve. I tried to ignore it, getting under cover being paramount.

I crawled and scooched my butt around the containers finding a spot where I could lay on my side so my head was lower than the bucket while nothing stuck into the rows. Carrie had to move a couple of containers to the side. The sound was a soft grinding whisper of plastic on dirt. I prayed it was non-carrying. If we got shot or killed due to her fat ass, I swear I was going to kill her.

The greenhouse door, from the front office, opened with a swoosh. Someone wasn't concerned with being heard, I thought irreverently. The sounds of the front office being ransacked came through the open door. There were several voices heard as drawers were opened and banged around.

"Boss! We found 2 other cars." A soft tenor.

"Nope. Should be only one. All the others left at 5pm." The voice was a low growly baritone. I shivered. "Looks like he may have had more company than we thought." The voice was moving from the front office to the greenhouse. "We'll need to look around anyway."

"Fuck! There was supposed to be only the one guy. How the hell did we end up with twenty thousand?!" This voice had a higher pitched edge than the first tenor, which grated on the ears.

"Stop the damn whining Renniks. And don't shoot unless you need to this time. Might need to ask a few questions." The baritone snapped the sound running down my spine. There was scuffing of shoes on the hardwood then soft shushing as they stepped into the greenhouse.

Three people at least, with guns. Carrie's eyes were huge. Mine were getting larger as well. I chewed my lower lip for a second, tasting blood as a dry spot cracked and split. We were pretty well hidden from casual sight and it sounded like these guys were going to be moving further into the warehouse complex. I motioned for Carrie to wait for my signal.

Carefully I raised my head just over the lip of the plastic pots. Three men. No telling whose voice matched with whose. One man was short, I'm talking my height short. Five foot five and that was generous with his platform shoes on. Couldn't tell what type of gun it was, but the John Wayne wannabe actually had a gold finish on it. Looking to be Mary Sue with a big gun, I thought disdainfully, or a rat terrier in a suit. Either way I bet he was compensating for a small dick.

The other guy had dirty dishwater blond hair, flying across his face. Tall, not pudgy, so the padding had to be muscle. *Carrie'd blow him in a sec*, floated across my mind, almost making me giggle. Hell, I'd do him in a heartbeat with the jeans hinting at a really nice tight ass. This one carried a Glock which looked to be a part of his hand as his fingers were. I marked him as dangerous… doable but dangerous.

The man that followed behind made the rat terrier and the long hair model look like pussies on a playground. Tall like 10 feet - ok my mind was gibbering at this point but really tall - he had to duck through the doorway tall. White hair. Not silver but old man white on a young man's face. A face that had character, as Nonni used to say. Enough character, I thought, to shoot a man casually while drinking a cold one. Casual in the killing like Ramon. High cheekbones and craggy lines. His hooded eyes didn't seem to miss anything, sweeping back and forth over the greenhouse. I slumped back down slowly. Fast movements attracted more attention, Rojo always said.

Footsteps came closer. A soft whisper on the dirty floor

boards, from one pair and a clicking of heels following closely. I froze in place counting. Two heading towards the side door and one back into the front room. They passed at the head of the plant row we were at and opened the side door. When the two who had passed didn't find anyone, they would do a closer sweep. Our options were getting worse. Now or never it was.

I looked to Carrie. She could count as well. With a quirk of a brow and a finger motion, we were in synch to run. Carrie eased her car keys from her purse and put them in her hands. The engine key held in her fingers ready. I loosened the cactus from my hoodie so I held the *bastardo* in hand with my fingernails, ignoring the pointy spines, the closest thing I had to a weapon. Looked like I was running interference so she could get the car started. She motioned to the back of the greenhouse we were in. I shook my head and mimed a lock motion. She made a face at me. We didn't know if the door by the car was locked or not, but the odds of it not being locked and not alarmed were not in our favor. Out the front it was.

I held up 3 fingers. 1…2…3! We scrambled out from under the plant tables and were dashing to the front. I made it to the door leading to the front office first and yanked it open.

I don't know who was more surprised; me or the scary dude with white hair. He yanked back in surprise, taking a half step back. I threw the cactus in my hand as hard as I could at his face. I didn't see the blur of his fist slamming into the side of my head, he was that fast. The cactus however connected to his face. There was a snarl of pain as his hands went to his face trying to pull the hooking spines from his face.

My vision was swimming and I was on the ground, one knee screaming at having taken the brunt of the fall.

Another guy came around the front desk trying to grab Carrie who was right on my heels till I hit the wall of scary dude. He only managed to grab her purse as she freaked out and threw a fist in his face with her shoulder and hip behind it. The strap snapped at the chain connection, sending Carrie rebounding into the doorframe and blondie into tall scary and now bleeding like a stuck pig.

Carrie didn't waste a second. Her hand was on my arm as

she pulled me up, by sheer fear, aiming for the door to the outside.

"Run!! Run! Run!!!" Carrie was screaming loud enough in a high-pitched panicking voice as she pulled me with her.

"Fuck fuck fuck!!!!" Was about all I could say under the circumstances, getting my feet under me and trying to run. Everything else was ringing in my ears as white noise.

I was running, staggering fast to be honest, to the car. Carrie shoved me towards the passenger side as she sprinted to the driver's side. I yanked the door open and dropped into the vinyl seat trying to fumble for the seat belt before she started to drive. Carrie got her POS started. I never got the seat belt to lock as I could barely register anything as my eyes were swimming in tears from the fist to the head punch. Carrie floored the car in reverse sending me into the dashboard. I saw stars again before the car's motion threw me into the door then into the seat as she spun and took off down the freeway we had come up not that long ago.

I heard gunshots and twisted in the seat in a knee jerk reaction to the sound. The sawed-off John Wayne was flying out of the front office, his coat and tie flying in the wind. He tried to shoot from the hip, but the sun setting into his squinting eyes kept him from making a connection with the car.

"That's right you bastards! You can shoot us, but we still got away from you first!" I screamed at him. I think he heard it or maybe just me working both hands up and down, flipping him a double bird. He looked shocked, then really pissed off behind his knock off ray-bans. His hands were shaking, sending his shots even wilder.

The tall white haired guy came out. With blood on his face looking as if he were crying blood, he raised a fucking hand cannon with one hand steadying with the other hand and took careful aim.

My eyes got HUGE. "Carrie DUCK!" I screamed throwing myself into the front seat well. My ass hit the floor hard but not as hard as my head hitting the dashboard, making me bite my tongue. I really hate the taste of blood.

Carrie threw herself sideways into the seat where my ass

had just been, while her hands stayed on the steering wheel. The shots were hitting is an almost continuous line. The window shattered into millions of tiny cutting shards. Poor Little Blue started to buck and thump from all the shots taken. Carrie was screaming while driving by braille on the road. I was just clenching the bottom of the seat with my knees under my chin and Carrie's head on my shins and feet. Nothing I could do to help Carrie or myself now.

Then silence. I pulled myself up cautiously to look out the nonexistent back window. Carrie hunched in her seat to not present too much of a blond headed target. The men were barely dots in the background. Either we out-distanced their guns or he ran out of bullets. Either way we were safe for the moment. Fucker, I thought, thinking of the white haired craggy faced man, rubbing my bruised backside, hope those damn cactus spines take out your eyes!

The bleeding man watched the escaping VW in annoyance. He reached for the quick load magazine on the right side of his holster.

"Fucking dick sucking bastards!" the small man screamed over and over again, dry firing the oversized gun in his hand.

"Renniks." Comanche said calmly. The short man continued to scream and swear jumping up and down. Comanche moved into his personal space. "Renniks." Comanche's voice boomed into Renniks ear.

"What?!" screamed Renniks, startled, turning towards the much taller man.

"Shut up." The deep voice rumbled through the air in a menacing tone that needed no profanity to make Renniks swallow hard.

"Yes boss." Renniks looked down meekly, but his lips still pulled back in a primal snarl of rage at the two girls who got away.

Comanche looked down at him for a moment before turning towards the other two. Renniks waited until Comanche had turned away before redirecting his anger towards the group's leader. He glared surreptitiously and shot the finger while fumbling to re-holster his gun. He only thought the words he wanted to say, having learned the hard way and a couple of black eyes how good Comanche's hearing really was.

"Nick, take Renniks and pick up the two girls." Comanche said to the longhaired blond.

"Girls?!" Renniks squeaked in outrage. "You got jumped by girls?" He couldn't hide the derision in his voice for shit.

Comanche looked over his shoulder with bleeding eyes, growling at Nick. "Girls who outsmarted you, gave Cubby a black eye and shoved a cactus in my face."

"Alive or dead boss?" the blonde-haired guy asked, looking Comanche in the eyes, re-holstering his gun smoothly. Unlike Renniks, he had no need to see where the holster was. He could re-holster by touch alone. The gun, an extension of his body, not just a tool.

"Alive. We need to know how much of the warehouse they saw or if they have any information."

"I have their purses if that helps?" Cubby, the heavyset, dirty blonde-haired person spoke up from the warehouse doorway, hesitantly.

"Driver's license?" Comanche asked, diverting his gaze to the weakest link of his team.

"I…" Cubby fumbled with a small blue leather purse, unzipping the top flap to search the interior cautiously.

"Girls don't store used tampons in their purse." Renniks said derisively to Cubby with lips pulled back into a sneer.

Cubby flipped him a left-handed bird while pulling out the requested identification. "Got it!"

"Good. Find out what you can and the likely spots they might go to ground to." Comanche nodded his approval.

Comanche headed toward the truck, Nick following him.

"Hoss."

Comanche merely looked over his shoulder, as he pulled open the back door of the quad cab, waiting for Nick to finish.

"Their car was really fucking shot up. They aren't making it far."

"And?" Comanche pulled out a large leather rucksack, reaching inside for the square plastic medical kit.

"Renniks will beat the crap out of either or both of them. Possibly killing 'em if he gets anywhere close."

"What are you saying, Nick?"

"He's got the temper of Mike Tyson on speed. We're not going to get shit if he kills them." Nick said with a sideways look. The look he got when his brains were engaged for more than just taking orders or herding Renniks.

Comanche gave an amused grin then winced as the smile crinkled his face, pushing the cactus quills a little deeper. Nick could see the muscles bunch in Comanche's jaw as the man bit back any verbal acknowledgment of the pain.

Comanche reached for the tweezers and some Neosporin, flipping the passenger side mirror down. He raised the tweezers to pull the first quills. "I suggest you let Renniks know how much we need the girls alive and… cooperative." He gave Nick a heavy look.

Nick swallowed heavily. "How much latitude?"

"I want them alive. Both of them." Comanche held Nick's gaze for a moment more before going back to pulling out quills. Only the flare of nostrils gave away how much pain and irritation he was feeling.

"Will do Hoss." Nick stepped away from the car, turning to speak with Renniks. He pulled out a pair of fingerless gloves from his back pockets. Words didn't always sink in with Renniks. Sometimes a little incentive helped when applied with the proper persuasive fist.

Chapter Two
And a Strawberry Milkshake

We made it about five miles. The bullets that had gone through the radio and into the engine finally did their work killing Little Blue.

"Fuck, fuck. Fuck!" Carrie could only repeat that over and over as she steered LB over to the side of the road. She was almost in tears.

"Not now, dear, I have a headache." I retorted, staring at the barren industrial landscape of old buildings and dry ground.

"Blue! They killed Blue!" Her hands were starting to shake on the steering wheel. The adrenaline was starting to wear off.

"We witnessed a shooting, were attacked, shot at and, yes, your poor Little Blue has died. Long live LB in our memory! I'm betting hippie dude didn't make it out." I snapped off the seat belt, and reached under the seat for my small black purse. It was big enough to hold my driver's license, two packs of cigarettes and, if I was lucky, a wad of cash that could choke a cat on a good night. Last night had not been that night for cash; but, there was still one pack of unopened cigarettes in there and, man, did I really, really need a drag right now!

"Fuck!" Carrie turned the key in the ignition. "Come on baby! Come on for momma." Little Blue wasn't even making a rumble or a burp. Definitely no purrs coming from her.

My arm was under the seat to the elbow. "God damn it!" The windows had been down and I was stupid. "Fuck!" I hadn't expected murdering assholes to search the car. I had gotten lazy and, at this rate, soon to be dead. "Carrie, please tell me you still have your purse?"

Carrie patted her pockets. The cheap silver and gold rings she wore flashed in the dying light. "Yes cell, no purse. Slow and fat guy got it."

"The one who got your knuckle sandwich?"

She started to laugh at that. "I hope I broke his nose and he chokes to death on the blood!"

"I told you the self-defense classes would come in handy." I quirked an eyebrow at her, which made her laugh harder. "'Cause you know not every guy is going to stop and let you give him a blow job every time you need to distract 'em."

"Bitch!" Now she was really laughing. I started to giggle at her as we both were picturing what might have happened if she had offered the blond a bj instead. Yeah right.

"Call Mark." I said finally, when I could breathe from all the giggling and laughing. I opened the door to get out.

"Why? You hate Mark. And where are you going?"

"Not me, us. Where are we going? Those guys who shot us…" I hesitated for a heartbeat. Carrie sometimes needed help connecting the dots on the seamy side of life. "He has a working car. Our car is now dead on the side of the road. We kinda need to not be here." I nodded to the buildings about 50 yards further down the highway. The sparse desert had given way to an industrial center then to a small dinner, fast food joints, and some crappy hotels. "We're going to not be here, but somewhere over there. Mark, the fucker, is going to come and pick us up."

"You hate Mark, though." She repeated.

"Yeah, but he likes you, and your open door blow job policy. And we really need a dependable ride at the moment."

It was her turn to be outraged, but not much came out through her giggles. Carrie was smart, but she was a bit flaky in some areas and a real slut in others.

When she finally caught her breath, she asked me "All your other friends got broken legs?"

"Other friends?" My lips twitched as I tilted my head with a sideways grin in her direction. "Nah, they are either too flaky or trying to score drugs. Like us. Neither of which translates into a ride outta here."

Carrie reluctantly got out of Little Blue. She pulled out her pink cell phone and started to flip through her contacts. I had to tug on her elbow to get her to start walking in the direction we needed, away from the shot up car. The damn thing stuck out like a sore thumb. We did not want to be advertising ourselves next to it. Our shoes made crunching noises on the gravel. The only good thing we had going for us was that it was still summer, not freezing. That and there weren't any clouds, so no rain either.

Ten yards from the car and Carrie was still searching through her phone. "My god woman, how many Marks do you know?"

"Well there is Mark Stasnny, good in bed but bad breath. Or Mark Jacob, niiiice dick but doesn't know how to use it for anything but peeing and sticking into something wet."

"I can see how he's a good friend of yours then." I snarked with a sideways glance.

She punched me on the shoulder, but still had her eyes on the phone so the punch was slow and not more than a tap.

"There's Mark Jeremy, little dick but really good in tutoring for calculus in exchange for…"

"Stop!" I rolled my eyes. "I really do not want to know the Mark litany. Wait." I stopped in my tracks to look at her." If you have so many Marks, how did you know the one I was talking about?"

It was Carrie's turn to laugh at me. She kept going, not waiting for me to catch up this time. "You're not what they call a people person. You don't know that many Marks just lots of marks. There is only one Mark you would call for help." Carrie shot me a sly grin looking up from her screen.

It sucked worse as she giggled at me while I spluttered. "Yeah, he's a whiny, spineless bitch, but, seriously, I only wanted him for casual sex."

"True. If he hadn't slept with Tiffany, you'd have kept him around longer."

"Yeah, I didn't mind him getting the occasional blow job or fuck from you, but still, I should have stolen his truck." I said glumly, sticking my hands deeper in the hoodie. Cheaters sucked ass. Mark had been fun, but I didn't like cheaters. They ran in the same circles as liars and thieves. I really shouldn't have taken a stupid man as a casual lover.

"You think he'll come out all this way for us?" Carrie sounded worried for the first time at my back up plan.

"Not us, you... and maybe me." I said chewing on a thumbnail thoughtfully. God I wanted a cigarette. The thought of Mark just made me horny and cranky.

"Nah. You wouldn't do well behind bars for grand theft auto. Let's see there is Mark Credesco who..." Carrie started again.

"Lalalalala." I sang stuffing my fingers in my ears. "Don't want to hear about you fucking all the Marks! Besides, I wouldn't have crossed state lines! Would only have been theft." Mmmm... that was a warm thought. Bastard loved that ride almost more than his own dick. His truck was definitely the better of the two things.

"If you had been caught," Carrie muttered snarkily. I rolled my eyes.

"Pfft. Thirty seconds with a screwdriver, a pair of wire cutters and I'd have been gone. No one the wiser. Javier has a great chop shop." I had a big smile at that thought. Casual lover, but still a bitter taste on the tongue.

"Mmmm... Javier." Carrie was reminiscing, or would be shortly.

"Mark. Call!"

"Woof!" Carrie went back to searching through her cell phone.

"Oh, and have him bring enough money to cover our dinners at the diner." I gave a satisfied grin. I knew Carrie would be seeing him afterward for a blowjob reward so I didn't feel too bad about making him pay, again.

Chapter Three
Nickelback to the Rescue

We made our way to the back of the 1950's retro diner. Bright white lights shining down on gleaming chrome counter edging and dull linoleum. The windows were covered in cheap white slat shades, miraculously dust free, and the small booths sported red vinyl seats with the occasional rip, under tabletops rubbed so much there were bald spots showing. The counter faced a long line of windows, wrapping around in an L shape. There was even a glass pie box with whole pies and pieces of pies on white, not chipped, china.

Mostly booths, at the windows, with chairs at the counter for the old men who needed the waitresses to be close enough to hear their complaints and comments on their tired dried up lives. I took the paranoid seat facing the front door, waiting for Mark and praying the white haired guy wouldn't be coming through the door. Carrie and I could play it cool, but we were more than a little bit spooked.

The thought of the scary guy coming through the front door kept running through my mind like a bad rerun of Scream.

"Yeah, yeah, I know, but I'll make it worth your while if you come out and get us." Carrie was using her sultry voice, the one that purred sex. Mark was probably hard and grabbing his keys. I just shook my head again in amusement. Carrie could make men, and some women, melt with that voice; and she delivered on what her voice promised.

"What'll it be girls?" The past middle age waitress asked. Her wrinkles were well pancaked in tan spackle, but the skin under her chin said yellow. A sick yellow at that. Her light colored eyes floated back and forth between Carrie and me.

"Water, for me, and a coffee." I said

"A strawberry milkshake please." Carrie chirped.

"Anything else?" She asked with a bored, but barely perceivable, condescending air. I had thought I was good at being a snarky bitch while waiting tables but I had much to learn from this woman.

"A menu?" Carrie asked

"Hungry already? You'll be getting plenty of protein from Mark soon enough." I snarked.

"Bitch!" This set Carrie off giggling, yet again, but she bent down over her phone to sext Mark so he didn't think about the other passenger. Anything that would get him here faster, I was good with.

"I'll be back with a menu in a moment for you ladies." The waitress sauntered off with barely a look back.

"What'll you bet it'll be 30 minutes before we get water." I sighed. My leg was jiggling up and down in nervous energy.

Carrie didn't even bother raising her head to look at me. "Not taking that bet. Suckers only."

"Then it's a good bet for you." I smirked.

Carrie flipped me off, then went back to the phone. My hands started to shake. I kept thinking of the shots through the back window of the car, glass splintering around me, the tires squealing. Close, very close. Haven't been that close since... I could hear screaming curses... different memory.

"Be right back!" I got up quickly, heading to the bathroom. I didn't wait for Carrie to acknowledge the abandonment.

The hallway was behind our booth, not very well lit, but had his and her bathrooms, just past the open kitchen doorway. Thank god no unisex toilets. I hated those things. I wanted to pee with others who sat down to pee, not be stared at by some guy faking on taking a shit so he could walk by me while I sat with my pants around my ankles. Fuckers.

The door opened on only moderately creaky hinges. Two stalls that smelled heavily of Lysol with a whiff of urine, were against the left sidewall. A blank wall, with only one hand air dryer attached, on the right. The wall was white plaster painted in a light patina of grime. I turned to the cracking sink, turning the faucet to cold to throw water on my face. The mirrors were intact, just a little warped along the edges. I looked up from trying to erase memories and saw three small windows above the two stalls. Using a sleeve to dry off, I leaned hard to the left, trying to reach for the edge of the first window. I could barely touch it. I stepped on the radiator that was under the second and third window, between the sink and the stalls. The windows were rusted shut. Even if they had opened, Carrie's bubble butt would not have made it out. Not even sure, my not starved ass would make it through those rectangular windows. Damn. No back way out through this room.

"Probably coated with eons of grease and dead flies, anyway." I muttered, irritated. "Fuckers!" I smacked the thin particle stall partition. "Too cheap to put in decent sized windows for a person to escape through." Yeah, nothing like being thwarted by cheapskate owners.

I looked up at the ceiling. Solid, not paneled, except for a small rusting metal vent. I chewed my bottom lip. I wasn't even sure Carrie could have walked on the wires holding up a panel ceiling, without falling on her butt.

Stepping out of the restroom, to my right, was a door with an exit sign overhead. I didn't see an alarm sign if the door was opened. I glanced left to make sure the hallway was empty, then moved to the door. I pushed it open cautiously. I could smell the air, heavy and sweet with flowers, grease, rotting trash and asphalt, but heard no alarm and no monitor. A second way out. Yippee. There were a few cars out back, behind the trash bin. I smiled. Even better. Hotwire one of those puppies and we were gone. Time to get Carrie, and get the hell out of dodge.

Taking another deep breath, I pulled the door shut.

"Hey! No sneaking out without paying!" A heavy hand slammed down on my shoulder spinning me around. My arms flailed as I came off balance.

"What?" I snapped. Shit! I hadn't been expecting this as I got my feet back underneath me.

The towering jowly manager stepped into my personal space, leaning close and backing me into the now closed exit door. His nametag proclaimed him a fully-grown adult who went by the name Timmy. "I said, you little bitch, NO SKIPPING OUT ON THE TAB!" He yowled at me. Bastard had to be 6"4 if an inch. Luckily not all muscle, not even close.

"Glad you clarified your concern you fat fuck." I snapped.

The verbal attack took him back for just a second, causing him to take a half step away in surprise, loosening the hand on my shoulder.

"Look you little cunt…" Timmy snarled again.

"Keep your paws off me or I swear I'll scream rape." I glared up at him.

He sneered. "You probably give blowjobs for nickels in the bathrooms. You can start with me right here." Timmy started to reach for me again, more toward my boobs then to my shoulders.

I swept with my right arm, under his incoming, grabby hands, stepping left, and then shoving with the left arm as hard as I could into the fat of his arm and his back fat rolls. This pushed him forward into the exit door.

I turned and didn't quite run back towards the main dining room. I could hear a thud and yowl of pain, followed by profanity. Definitely time to leave!

"Carrie! We need to get…" I skidded to a stop rounding the corner. Carrie had gotten her strawberry shake and something extra. Short and well-dressed was sitting next to Carrie, taking a long slow sip out of her straw. She was leaning as far away from him as possible, not quite shaking. She looked at me with not quite scared eyes. Rat Face in a suit, looked up at me with small mean eyes and smiled, motioning to the seat across from him with a manicured hand. He pulled the straw out of the shake and licked it from top to bottom, with what was supposed to be a seductive tongue move. This guy gave creepy a whole new vibe.

I had half a second to throw a glance to my side of the booth, hoping Carrie got the message. Before I could open my mouth to ask if he got that move from Creepy 101 or gay porn Danny does Dallas, to make him lose his cool and come at me, a huge beefy hand landed on my right shoulder again. A projectile! Right on time too! I grabbed Timmy's thumb and hand and stepped forward while twisting my hip. The follow through was perfect. The manager went into rat face while Carrie managed to scramble over the table to my side and then out of the booth. The loud yell from the shorter guy draws attention to our side of the dinner, not to mention the manager's loud expulsion of air and dinner.

"Carrie! This way!" I grabbed Carrie's arm before she can head out the front door and dragged her back down the hallway towards the exit door.

"What? Why not the front door?" She panted, but followed me down the hallway.

"Rat Face probably has friends waiting for us out front! Gotta go another way!" I yelled back to her.

"Fuck! How did they find us?"

I straight-armed the door bar, slamming it open, not bothering to answer the obvious. The door didn't automatically close; the wide open tunnel funneled loud cursing from behind us, spurring us to go faster.

We ran, stumbling over loose gravel behind the dinner and cut left onto the road sharply. I glanced left and saw headlights flip on, right into my eyes. Headlights. Bright and high like from a really big truck. I hear an engine go from purring to a snarling rumble. I swear I could see scary black eyes dripping bloody tears from behind the headlights. It was my turn to stand with the deer in the headlights look. A chill swept up my spine leaving me in goose bumps from head to toe.

Carrie grabbed my hand and pulled me across the street into oncoming traffic as tires squeal 30 feet away from us. Cars honk horns angrily as we cut across the lanes of traffic. Two cars swerved to the right of us, then we were into the oncoming traffic side. The rumbling truck brushed past, missing us by inches, so close that one oncoming car swerved onto the sidewalk just missing a fire hydrant. Truckzilla's tires squeal doing a 90 degree turn into an alley. The brake lights glowed like nightmarish eyes, as the truck backed into the street and traffic. They were going to make another pass at us.

"Stop! Stop!!" Carrie screamed at the top of her lungs in the oncoming lane of traffic. Another truck came towards us, neither as loud nor as impressive as the scary other truck, it screeched to a stop almost on top of us. Carrie squealed in surprise raising her hands in front of her as if that would stop a one-ton truck from squishing her flat.

I tugged Carrie's arm towards the other side of the road

when the truck's passenger door opens up.

"What the fuck are you into this time?!" A very angry male voice yells at us over the horns behind him from the piling up traffic.

"Go go gogoogogogogo.!" The word blended into one long wail of fear and adrenaline as Carrie dove into the passenger side with me on her heels. The door barely closed in time for Mark to start pulling out. I shot a look out the window to where the other truck had been. It wasn't there anymore. I was betting that whoever was driving wasn't going to give up on us quite so easily.

"That was so fucking awesome! You threw him into that suit guy!" Carrie adrenaline shock started to wear off.

"Fuck! Fuck!" My hands start shaking. I really need a clove cigarette. My hands are shaking so hard I fumble the lighter and then the last pack of cigarettes the hoodie's front pocket.

"Don't fucking smoke in my truck Autumn!" Mark snarled.

"Go to hell, Mark!"

"Damn it, Autumn! Which fucking frat house did you piss off this time?"

"None!" The cigarette dangled from my lips unlit. I was drawing air through it just to have the taste to calm me down.

"Bullshit!" Mark was yelling over the stereo, which was impressive. Nickleback was always played as loud as the human ears could stand, rattling windows and metal two cars over. "You don't get almost run over for nothing!"

Carrie reached to turn the cd player down.

"We saw a fucking shooting, and they know who we are!" I screamed back at him, clenching my lighter so hard the edge was cutting into skin.

"What?!"

"We saw a shooting. At the pot greenhouse, we were going to buy at today. We saw all four of the guys who were involved." Carrie was a bit calmer than I was dealing with Mark.

"And they have our purses." I added bitterly.

"What?!" Carrie almost started to cry. "Fuck!" She whimpered. The full implication started to soak in. Her hands began to shake. She reached for one of my cigarettes. I handed the pack to her without taking my eyes from Mark.

"So fucking explain to me why… No. Don't bother. I don't want to know." Mark beat his thumbs on the steering wheel, but he wouldn't look at me. I stared at his hands for a moment. He had great hands. Long fingers, perfect for making difficult bridges on his bass, and wide palms perfect for holding sensitive body parts. Damn those hands. I took another drag on my non-lit cigarette. Not the same, but it helped.

"They, whoever the murdering bastards are, guessed where the car would die. Hell all they had to do was follow the road into town and look for that POS car dead on the side of the road." I began to fidget with the cigarette between my fingers.

"Poor Blue!" Carrie sniffled.

"Poor Blue!? Fuck that piece of shit. Poor us! They know where we live. We can't go home!"

"What about Blackie?" Carrie was pouting at this point.

"We can't go back, Carrie. Blackie the fish will be just fine." I snapped. Carrie just gave me a pitiful look. It was like kicking a puppy. "Fine! Maybe James can feed him, but we," I motioned to her and I "Can't go back any time soon."

"If this is some ploy to get back together, I'm not buying it Autumn. You are NOT staying with me." Mark gritted this out through clenched teeth as his hands gripped the wheel tightly. He had such beautiful hands, for an ass.

"I wouldn't come back to you or fuck you with a three inch cactus, Mark!" I snarled back. "We need a knight in shining armor. Too bad we got a joker instead." Cuttingly cruel.

"Look you cunt…"

"I'm not the one who cheated; fucking some stupid blond co-ed!"

"I'm not out nailing other guy's girlfriends either, Autumn!"

"You lying mother fucker. You brought home Chris's girlfriend to the house. Drunk horny and looking to nail someone." He turned his head to say a few words in his defense when the truck swerved under the tight grip he was keeping. Carrie squealed in alarm, as the lamppost from the street got very close very quickly.

"Shit!" Mark swerved back into the main part of the road with a squeal of tires.

"Fine. Once! But you were the one who kept fucking her long after that night."

"Well she was better in bed then you could ever hope to be." I put in every ounce of contempt I could in that statement. Wouldn't want him to miss the insult.

Mark slammed on the breaks. "That's it! Get the fuck out of my truck!" Cars honked behind us. Mark and I glared around Carrie's ample bosom. The anger was palpable in that very small truck cab. Hell, the city probably wouldn't have held the outrage in.

The cars driving around and flipping Mark off didn't seem to faze him or break his death glare at me. Carrie got us moving again.

"Mark. Please. Just to the police station. For me. Please." Carrie laid a hand on his arm with her melting blue eyes. Mark looked down at her hand. He didn't shake the hand off, and he did take a deep breath.

"Fine. For you, Carrie." His voice was less angry but still the words snapped out like gunfire.

I opened my mouth to add something even more cutting about him always ready for the next blowjob when Carrie's hand slapped over my mouth. I glared, and she pressed harder. Bitch! I thought loudly. Carrie just smiled and winked at me. Good thing she was my best friend or I'd have bitten her two favorite fingers off.

Chapter Four
A Nice Jail Cell for Two Please

Mark dropped us off 4 blocks later. He gave us a three-finger fuck you salute while I figured he just merited a one finger behind the back as I walked away.

"Stop it. It's done and he's gone, Autumn." Carrie said smiling.

"Yeah, do me a favor on his next blow job and bite his dick off will you?" Bitter? Me?! Never.

"Pfft, not even for you, my favorite slut, am I giving up blowing that dick."

"Bitch." I said with real affection. We both started to laugh. Carrie liked her fun and she knew how to get people to trust and like her. Definitely one smart cookie who could play dumb slut like no other.

We walked into the station and hit chaos. It took the desk Sergeant 20 minutes to get to us after clearing out 3 drunks, one stabber and two prostitutes. Carrie was chatting up the girls to pass the time till the police could get to us. She picked up a couple of useful tips on lube while giving the two a few different positioning options. They were impressed and Carrie was amused. I just chewed on my nails. They weren't allowing smoking in the station and I was in full nicotine withdrawal. Fuck, no, I wasn't going outside to smoke. I'm sure Ratface in the suit wasn't going to be nearly as nice next time we "talked". Moreover, I sure as shit did NOT want to meet tall, red and scary, while he was bleeding tears.

Finally, the harried desk Sergeant called us up. He was on the slightly paunchy side, with really great hair. Somewhere a Pomeranian was bald so this man could have fake hair. Carrie and I looked at each other, but didn't say anything. She was trying to hold in her laughter, but her shoulder and boobs were having mini earthquakes holding it in. That weave did not belong on that body.

"Ok girls, what can I do for you two?" His voice was bored, but professional. Probably thought we were just two chicks there to bail out their bad boy druggy boyfriend. I almost felt sympathy for him, but my night had pretty much burned that out at the moment.

I cleared my throat, as Mt Saint Carrie was about to explode with held in mirth and, therefore, was not up for talking. A true first.

"We saw a murder." I started. "Well not exactly saw, but heard it; then we were chased."

"And my car shot up." Carrie inserted.

"Then almost run over."

"Well we were almost abducted then run over."

"I'd have said attacked."

"Ok, I'll grant you attacked before the abducting/running over, but that would mean we were attacked running out of the green house…"

"Well, hiding then the shooting then the attacking."

"And my car."

"Yes, we can't forget that POS car of yours."

"Hey that was my favorite car!"

"That was your only car that could give you good vibrations before you actually arrived… or did it help you arrive?"

"Bitch!"

The Sergeant kept moving his head back and forth as we both tried to tell what had happened without a lot of cohesion or coherency. He was in serious danger of whiplash at this rate.

"Wait! Wait!" The cop held up his hand. "Slow down. One at a time."

Carrie started. She was good at getting a really unbelievable story to sound very real. In this case, real scary, and making us look like innocent bystanders. I threw in the occasional bit of detailing. Guns and cars descriptions while she gave the blow-by-blow action. The sergeant fluctuated between incredulous and amused, then finally settled on thoughtfully alarmed as we got the whole story out mostly coherently.

He scratched his well-broken nose with a rough knuckled hand. "Ok ladies, here's what we're going to do. I want you two to sit down in those very uncomfortable chairs for a moment or two more while I take this information to someone else." He gestured with a jerk of his round chin towards the blue plastic chairs we had just come from.

Carrie and I looked at each other. If he sent us away, we'd be dead by sunrise. These guys weren't playing around. Carrie was starting to realize exactly how scary this was going to be. She'd graduated from small time pot dealer paying her college tuition to finding that the big boys played for keeps.

"Sir," I started.

He glanced at me with one of those looks that could have quelled stone. I'd seen scarier men tonight so I wasn't even slightly phased.

"We're really not making this up. If you send us back out..."

"We'll be dead!" Carrie interjected breathlessly, her blue eyes going very wide. She wasn't even trying to hide her fear now.

The Desk Sergeant took pity on her soft blond helplessness without sparing a glance at my goth self. I mentally rolled my eyes, but kept a calm façade.

He ran his tongue over his teeth, rubbing the left eyetooth. "You gals have a very… tall tale…."

"But it's true!" Carrie interjected putting her hands on his tall desk leaning forward, as if by sheer intensity she could will him to believe her. Her boobs threatened to spill out of her pink shirt and the black lacy bra underneath and onto the poor Sergeant's desk.

He chuckled. "Let me finish."

"Sorry." Carrie mumbled looking sheepish. She leaned back, putting the girls on leash but she did take a deep breath. This made the sergeant clear his throat before being able to speak again.

"We get some good stories most nights. Some true, some false, and some so strange the person obviously needs medication. Now you two, come in with a story that has some interesting bits that ring true and a few that I'd like to ask you a bit closer on. But that's not my job. I get to boot this one up a few levels." He looked us both in the eyes "Understand?"

"Yes sir." We replied in unison.

"Good. Now, go sit down and I'll be with you in a bit."

We went back to our seats in the main lobby area. I really wanted a cigarette, but the no smoking signs were too numerous and large to really claim ignorance if I lit one up. Carrie started to chew a nail after curling her legs up underneath her. A girl that large shouldn't be that flexible, I thought with a grin. But she was very popular for her…flexibility.

I started to fade fast. In the course of three hours my life flashed before my eyes five times, it seemed like. I wondered why, and where, these other guys had come from. I mean, yeah, the pot guy probably had money stashed somewhere, but the complex was HUGE. How the hell are they going to find anything in that place if the guy who knew where the cash was, was dead. Didn't make sense. They had been too well dressed to be a shoot first and steal 'em dead type of group. Julio would have done that, but he had been a POS punk; looking for the fast cash or score, not thinking more than his next fuck or snort. I shook my head trying to clear it. Julio was long dead. Shot on the corner of 6th and Callahan.

The lobby wasn't cold, nor was it hot. It just smelled like humanity before shower time. That too was starting to fade. My hoodie was warm and my eyes were closing. Carrie was chatting up the tall, wigged and heavily made up drag queen, whose Adams apple was the size of my fist. The discussion seemed to center on a fight that broke out with two others over the ownership of a pair of custom-made five inch red and white leather boots. I was losing track of who was claiming ownership and who had permission to wear the boots. As amusing as the story was, and the cat calls back and forth with very creative name-calling, I was falling asleep.

I blinked several times, before losing the fight with heavy lids. Carrie seemed to be awake and lively. She'd at least keep me from getting rolled. I know I fell asleep as the office noise just blurred into soothing white noise. The police station melted away. I saw a busy street in the projects I grew up in. There was this thick furred yellow dog sitting on the sidewalk in front of Ramon's house. I frowned. We never had any dogs like that. Ramon and Julio liked pitbulls and rotties. Anything else was what they liked to call bait or dog food, like kittens and cats. They paid street kids to catch and bring over the strays. The dog on the sidewalk tilted its head with a huge dog grin and winked at me. I ignored the dog, even a winking dog, to walk into the old shabby house. This didn't feel like one of my nightmares, something else was going on. The halls were wide and covered in industrial carpet, which was fucking odd, like the dog. Rojo's house had wood floors except in the bedrooms. Those had nasty old blue piled carpet from the '60s.

"Hey chica!" Juan was in a large glass and metal doorway, wearing his baggy faded jeans and a comfortable Tejano band T-shirt. I grinned and bounded over to him, giving him a long hug. "Hey esse! You got something for me today?" I could feel the grin on my face pulling my cheeks tight.

"I got something good for you girl! I got a new vault, just for you." He returned the hug.

"Pfft. Ten says I'll have it opened in 2 minutes." I said linking my fingers together and pushing out in a stretch. Yep, I was ready for any vault he had for me. An old game. One I was really good at.

"20 says you can't get it open in 20 minutes." He had that twinkle in his eyes that had me almost worried. Almost.

The vaults were lined up in what felt like a small room, but the vaults stretched so far I couldn't see the end of the line. "We open all these and I'll never have to do another job for Rojo again."

"You could even kill him yourself this time." Came a voice. I flushed looking around guiltily. Juan hadn't spoken. He didn't even seem to have heard. The only other living thing with us was the yellow mutt from outside.

I shook my head, clearing it mentally to concentrate. The vaults were gorgeous but they started to bleed every time I turned the tumbler and felt the slightest of clicks through my fingers. The vault opened with a moan so painful, I could feel it vibrate into my bones. I startled awake. Fucking odd. I rubbed my hands up and down to warm up my chilled arms.

Carrie and the drag queen were gossiping about makeup tips and blowjobs. The drag queen seemed to be pro lipstick on the dick while Carrie preferred lip-gloss, leaving a less visible traces.

My lips twitched. She liked commando blowjobs, in, suck and gone. Only she and the person being blown, knowing. Well unless she was really trying to be a bitch then she'd break out the bright pink lip stick that was hellacious to get off. The guy, or girl, was really screwed trying to explain to their S.O. why they had someone else's lipstick on their fun party parts.

I was about to interject a snide comment when my eyes landed on someone I knew. Hairband guy from the greenhouse. We'd been followed. Again. "Fuck." I whispered.

"Autumn do you want to try Billie to pick us up?" Carrie asked when the drag queen turned away. I shook my head concentrating on hairband dude. He was casually chatting up one of the clerks in the front area while looking around. A few feet from us. I swallowed hard. He was looking at Carrie and I when the girl kept getting distracted by incoming others. He noticed my stare. A slow smile that seemed more predatory then sexy spread across his lips. He looked to my right with a slight frown. He turned back to the clerk, with that slight smile, saying something that made her giggle. Turning his back to us, he sauntered out the front door. An incongruent thought about his butt nicely framed in the not too tight jeans he wore, cut through my fear and sleep fogged brain.

"I think I want a nice safe jail cell."

"What?!" Carrie hadn't seen hairband guy.

"Hairband guy was here!" I hissed at her. Her eyes got very wide. She went still then relaxed.

"He still here?" Her voice dropped and she had plastered the "fun time girl" smile on her face. She leaned in close as if we were sharing a secret.

"No. He just left." I started to chew on a nail.

"Wheeeee." Her shoulders relaxed a couple of inches. "So, can't leave out the front door."

"I'm betting the cops don't have a back door we can access either."

"Want me to see if I can get us the secret pass code out?" Carrie batted her long eyelashes at me, with a twinkle that usually ended with us embroiled in something. I was about to say something snide about needing knee pads when a voice interrupted.

"Ladies." The desk Sergeant spoke from just in front of us. We both jumped, startled. Carrie gave a squeal of surprise, which startled the Sergeant into taking a half step back. I snickered at her.

"Bitch!" she mouthed at me. I gave her my most wicked of grins.

"Uhmmm." The Sergeant cleared his throat. "We have a couple of people who'd like to talk with you two young ladies, but in a quieter room. Please follow me." He gestured with his hand emphasizing with a tilt of his chin towards the back area. We got up with only one or two snide comments from the drag show chorus to follow him to a safer location.

The room we were ushered into had 2 chairs, one couch and a table. The fabric was old, and worn, smelling of stale cigarettes and old coffee. At this point, we didn't care. We weren't being booted out the front door where boy band butt and the bleeding eyed giant were, and I was going to get to take care of my nicotine habit. A win for the night.

"Make yourselves comfortable. It'll be a few before anyone can actually get to you two, but we do want to ask a few questions." The Sergeant nodded and shut the door firmly behind him. I counted to 15 before going to test the doorknob.

I shook my head to Carrie.

"Locked." She said thoughtfully.

"Your knees are saved for the moment." I said with forced amusement to Carrie with a flat face. She was worried enough to not rise to the bait. She signed bug under chin with a question. I shrugged. I'd never been held in a non-interrogation room before. This was as much a first for me as for her.

"Got any spare cigs?"

"Maaaaybe."

"I'll trade taking the chairs for the couch if you supply me with one or two."

"I can go for that!"

"I'd hope so. You were snoring like a truck driver out front."

"Bitch please, you've never stayed with one trucker long enough to find out if they snored or not before moving to the next one." I reached into my hoodie pocket for the cigarettes. "Fuck!"

"What? You ok?" Carrie looked up from arranging the chairs just so, blowing back stray wisps of hair.

"Down to the last four." I sighed.

"So we party down with two each and get more in the morning."

"With what cash? Scary dudes have both our purses which include cash and my back up cigarettes. And Mark sure as fuck isn't going to come back to supply me with more."

"Hmmm, Cory would probably pick up a couple of packs if I called and asked him to, as well as driving us to his flat. The one with the pool and the gorgeous two roommates."

"Cory is as gay as they get." I pulled out two cigarettes for her and two for me.

"But his roommates aren't." Carrie had that sly grin again.

"They sample the wares?" I settled on the couch waiting for the punch line of this story, pulling the lighter out of thin air.

"That is soo cool when you do that." She came over to get a light for her first one.

"Nah. Well Thomas did the wild thing with me."

"Uh huh."

"Hey! I helped him with his accounting homework! I thought a good dicking would be just the thing to say thank you. He was most, accommodating." She took a long slow suck on the cigarette as if demonstrating how good the thank you was. I rolled my eyes with a shake of my head.

"Wait. He's in grad school and you were helping him with his accounting homework?"

Carrie shrugged. "It's not that hard. He was making it far more difficult than the questions asked for."

"What did he end up with for a grade?"

Carrie took another drag and winked. "An A and his prof said who ever had tutored him he should be paying double. Hence the tag team of him and Travis. What can I say, numbers and dick really turn me on!"

I busted out laughing. I couldn't help it. "You go girl!"

"Well, Tommy, what do you have for me tonight?" Detective Drombal asked, his fingers fidgeting with a pen. He was on his third cup of coffee for the night and ready to take off the tie. He had his notes from the field where he had returned from the first death of the night. The report would take a few hours to write up but the night was still young, something exciting could happen.

"You just get back from the stiff at the diner right? Silver Bullet diner?" The Sergeant asked.

Drombal looked up. "Yeah. Was odd. Some dust up about a girl, or two girls, and an argument between the manager and the pimp from what the witnesses say."

"Think I got your girls in a holding room."

"Yeah?"

"Yep! I also think your night is about to become a hell of a lot more interesting."

Jose raised an eyebrow, but he was cautious. "How so? Whenever you have that look… yeah, that look like the cat got both the canary and the cream, means you're holding a pair of aces."

"The girls came in with this story about being at the warehouse, ya know the one you've had DeSantos trying to get into for surveillance and getting fuck all. Well they tell a tale of a dead body, men with guns and being rescued from the Silver Bullet by one of their ex-boyfriends after being followed by one of the same guys who were at the warehouse."

"You believe them?"

"The blond of the two couldn't lie to save her life. The brunette has street eyes." He said with a wave of the hand towards the side door.

Jose leaned forward. "College age? Blond, heavy set with huge tits and blue eyes? Brunet, curvy and wearing a long sleeved jacket even though it's 85 outside?"

"Either you've seen the video of who just walked in or you're developing some serious ESP shit. Describes the two to a T."

Detective Jose Drombal dug around his desk for a moment to find a file. He pulled out a file with hand written notes and several photos. "These two?"

Then Jose pulled out a more recent picture. The girls in the photo were doing collegiate things, such as drinking coffee, poring over books, smoking cigarettes, chatting with others. Tommy took a closer look. "Yep! Well the blue haired girl has brown hair now. Ah yes… That's them."

"So why a file on these two?"

"These two are the highest volume pushers on campus that we know of."

"Then why not bring 'em in?"

Jose made a frustrated growling noise. "Can't pin them with anything. We have compromised witnesses and search warrants that have come up empty. It's like these two can make pot appear or disappear on command."

"Got them in a nice locked room for at least a couple of hours now." Tommy said with a wink. "Both of 'em to scared to step foot out of the police station. Dude, you're the one holding a pair of queens now."

Jose leaned back and gave Tommy a predatory smile.

"Hmmm… maybe some good cop bad cop?"

Tommy shook his head. "Don't know about that. Blondie I'm betting can play dumb with the best of 'em. I'm betting she got pretty far on those tits alone! Man could smother happily in them. The brunette, she's going to be a hard one to crack, though. Whatever got them in here, you're going to have to be either nicer or scarier than them."

Jose waved him off. "Leave that one to me. I am going to break those two and make 'em sing." He stood up cracking his knuckles in anticipation.

"Hey, Jose!" A sleek woman in dark slacks and a v-neck

purple blouse came up to his desk with another file in hand. "Glad I caught you!"

"What's up Trish? I have an interrogation or two to handle."

"That diner murder tonight. We got a lucky hit on the glass fingerprints."

"Nice. Who's the dead john?"

"Don't have a hit on the dead guy, but have a federal case from the other guy. A hit man, Dan "Goldfinger" Richel." Triggered a federal hit."

"Ugh, fucking Feds."

"Looks like he's been a person of interest for a few years, but couldn't be nailed with anything, then dropped off the radar till now."

"Good luck Jose! You're going to need it."

"Fuck you Tommy." Tommy just waved him a one-finger salute whistling a jaunty tune as he headed back to his desk among the freaks and geeks.

"Damn! I have two that I really need to interview."

"Two?"

"Yeah, the two girls who are selling on campus. One of 'em that screwed you over royally in court? The ones who never carry but always sell? They involved in this?"

"According to Tommy they say they are."

"Can't touch them." Trish's smile was viciously hard edged, showing teeth.

"What?!"

"Read it and weep." Trish gave him a hard edged smile that could cut steel. "Got three feds on their way here in about 30. They want all information including leads and witnesses. So, no pissing in their pool with questioning the witnesses."

"You really do hate me."

"Only since you took my three best cases." Trish gave him a finger wave as she walked away with a satisfied swing to her hips. Jose watched those hips with a real twinge of regret and interest.

"Bitch. Should have stayed away from that one too." Jose muttered under his breath. What could he say? Crazy in the head and really crazy fucking in bed. He scanned the email.

Fuck. He might be able to sit in on interviews, but he wasn't going to get anywhere on his own cases as long as the feds were here. Hmm, but afterwards. There was always an after. "Well Jose, let's just make those federal asses feel right at home." Nothing like playing nice to get the goods later."

"Jeremy! Grab your bags. We've got a couple of hits." Said Agent Daniel Lozano right behind where his tall Asian partner sat.

Jeremy jumped slightly, shooting his partner a glare. Daniel smirked while Jeremy exuded the injured air of someone long put upon.

"Where to, Daniel?" Jeremy's hands made a few more keystrokes on his laptop. His hands made automatic adjustments for two missing fingers and two joints shorter than the other long digits.

"Outside of Val Verde." Daniel started to do a sweep of the room for personal detritus.

Jeremy looked at him blankly for a second, then turned back to his computer, typing in the name on Google maps.

"Outside of LA." Daniel said helpfully, grabbing a bag and a hanging suit bag from the closet. He was a whirlwind of motion getting things moved from dresser to rolling bag.

Jeremy observed the map for a second before saying "I'll be done here in a moment if you could wait."

"Talking to your girlfriend again?" Daniel grinned, folding his pants and shirts to precise measurements, fitting his clothes in an organized Tetris fashion.

"Finishing up being dumped. Thank you." Jeremy said glumly. His mouth down turned, with sad eyes. He looked at the screen, before turning away once again toward Daniel.

Daniel stopped his frenetic motions, looking up with wide eyes. "Oh, man! I'm so sorry."

"It's not like I didn't see it coming." Jeremy sighed. His fingers moving over the keyboard, without his need to actually see the letters or stopping his conversation.

Daniel looked at the folded shirt in one hand and a rolled up belt in the other. "Errr…would you like me to leave while you finish up?"

"You're almost done. You can fill me in while you pack. She and I can finish this conversation after you leave." Jeremy did blank the screen though. Personal conversations being personal.

"And you don't even get your own room to rant and rave in either." Daniel toned down his voice slightly.

"The internet and this job are fickle." Jeremy intoned but he motioned to Daniel to continue. "You said we have two hits?"

Daniel blinked for a second. His mind on his own divorce before being pulled back to the original conversation. "Right! Darts' fingerprints in a morgue and Renniks' fingerprints outside of Val Verde. There are also two witnesses."

"Great! Are we going to be sympathetic or hard nosed?"

"I don't know." This time Daniel did stop to look at his partner closely. "This may hit home for you today."

Jeremy frowned. "Can't see how two witnesses would hit home for anything."

"One of the witnesses is from Rojo's old gang. Autumn Roberts."

Jeremy's face went from expressively mobile to burnished stone. He rubbed his injured hand with the missing fingers. "She do the killing of Darts?"

"No. She's one of the witnesses."

"And she went to the police?!" Jeremy's eyes were wide with shock.

"Seems there is something else going on. Why we're being called in."

"This oughta be a good day."

"Night." Daniel corrected. "Crime scene isn't that old and I want to catch both Roberts and the other girl while they are still disoriented." He disappeared into the bathroom for toiletries.

"A very good idea." Jeremy tapped a long index finger to his chin for a moment. "Do we have someone to help guide us?"

"Yep! Agent Branin."

"He was the original investigator for Comanche Jack's case wasn't he?" Jeremy raised his voice slightly to be heard.

Daniel was nodding stepping out of the bathroom, zipping his black shower kit closed. "Until he got too close that is. He should be a good source. Been at this site for a month or two. Not a lot of work with the cops there though."

"We can still work with this." Jeremy wanted to get the evidence on Comanche Jack's gang. Too many bodies piling up wherever he went.

"Ok, I'm done. How long do you think you'll need?" Daniel pulled his bag's handle up with a jerk to lock it in place for rolling. The suit bag he threw over his shoulder.

"Not more than another five minutes. We were already past the yelling and crying as it were." Jeremy glanced at his computer, his expression unreadable.

"I'll get us a taxi to the airport so you'll have about 15 minutes to say goodbye and get packed. See you in a few." Daniel opened the door and headed briskly to the lobby.

Jeremy touched his computer screen. There was a chat going, but not with his girlfriend. They had broken up three nights before. Mostly due to him not being home, but she also wanted someone more... conventional than a gorgeous, but absent, FBI boyfriend.

The spreadsheet though was more troubling to Jeremy then the breakup had been three nights ago. Jeremy tapped his fingers thoughtfully.

"Someone is lying." Was all he said, before saving his work then heading to his own room to pack. His thumb rubbed where the scar tissue formed over one of the fingers. The finger itched, sometimes sharply like ants trying to bite their way out. Sometimes Jeremy just rubbed the scar tissue to remind him of his own mortality.

The feds walked into the glass walled interview room, in an almost smooth formation. The lead FBI was also the shortest. Next was the tallest, with recently cropped hair in standard issue haircut, the skin where the hair had been shorn paler than his neckline. He went left and started to close the blinds on the windows. The third guy with curly reddish brown hair went right closing those window blinds.

"Good evening gentlemen!" Jose said with an almost unforced cheerfulness. "I have coffee for you. I am..."

"Good evening, Detective Drombal." The short one interrupted. Jose blinked with a slight twitch. "Detective Gleery gave us a heads up you were waiting here and anxious to get started. Seems we both have a mutual interest in this case."

"I'll be sure to thank Detective Gleery personally for all of her help." Jose managed to not clench his teeth. He even managed a smile. By the short fed's look, Jose could tell he wasn't fooling anyone. Jose gave a mental shrug, fuck 'em, he thought.

As if on cue, Detective Trish Gleery walked in with a few files and a laptop, along with the obligatory pens and notepads, and a smile that looked sweetly innocent. Compared to Jose, butter wouldn't melt in her mouth.

She handed the files to Jose along with the pens and notepads, the gleam in her eyes said she knew he couldn't kick her out or be a snarly bastard without looking like a douche in front of the FBI. He gave her an unkind look with a harder edge to his smile, and a forced "Thank you!" He didn't growl... much.

She set up on one end of the rectangular table, closer to Jose, but not next to. No buddy-buddy help there.

"So gentlemen, how can our office be of help to you?"

"We need to see your files on Carrie Reith."

"Carrie Reith? Umm.... sure, agent?" Jose let his voice trail off suggestively.

The curly haired FBI agent laughed. The shorter one turned to give a quick glance. The curly haired guy just smiled, non-repentant. "You're right. Where are my manners? I totally forgot them as the cases are coming to a head." He said with an easy charming smile. "I am Agent Lozano. The one to my right is Agent Branin, and the tallest one is Agent Fier."

"Fier?"

"Family name." the Asian agent said with a straight face.

"Ok then." Jose said with only a minor twitch to the head.

"This is the file I have on Carrie Reith. I don't have much of a file on her companion Autumn Roberts."

"We have a file on Autumn, but we didn't have anything on Carrie. She's under our radar locally."

"And Autumn isn't."

"Not even close." Came Lozano's tight lipped response.

Lozano pulled out one of his files. Not huge but not a two pager either. Both men exchanged files with an air of passing loaded guns.

Jose started reading Autumn's file, half way through he whistled. "Son of a bitch! No wonder I couldn't find anything."

"She play you?" Fier looked up from reading over Lozano's shoulder. He was rubbing his hand. Jose did a double take. The hand was missing a couple of fingers.

"Fuck yeah. Thought I had her in a good pigeon hold. She's been leading cops on goose chases for years it seems." He snarled at the file. His blood pressure going up a few notches.

"She learned in a hard school." Lozano said mildly. He was tapping a finger over a section of Carrie's file. "It says here you had sexual relations with Reith? Enough evidence that a judge sided with her in a trial deposition that you were harassing her."

Jose's face contorted with rage. He was slow to smooth it out before he could speak. "Yeah I tapped that ass. I was drunk at a bar and saw an easy pity fuck. I didn't know at the time she was moving pot to all the hot spots and dealers."

"You spent the night with her." It really wasn't posed as a question.

Trish glanced at him sideways with a raised eyebrow. Jose glared back. He had managed to keep the details quiet but hadn't been specific on details. Cops get sued for harassment one way or another all the time.

"Umm… yeah. More like a long weekend."

"You smoke with her?"

"Pot?! Fuck no; we do take piss tests here."

"You pass out around her?"

"No!" Jose was getting indignant. "I'm not on trial for feeling up the wrong bitch to fuck."

"No, but we think your phone may be compromised. Reith's classes seem to show a strong interest in, not only in business accounting, but computer science and coding."

"So?"

"We think that when she and Roberts hooked up, they started working in tangent on how to keep the law from being an issue by setting you up with Reith then cloning your phone as a start."

It only took a second for the implications to sink in. Jose blanched. "My calls! My texts!"

"If there was any connection to your computer, your work email, etc. as well." Said Fier, glancing up from the files.

Lozano nodded. "They would have been able to keep tabs on your conversations, work and personal, as well as any location your phone was at."

Jose started cursing in Spanish. Gutter Cuban Spanish.

Fier laughed.

Jose glared at him. Agent Fier held up his hands in a placating gesture. "Hey, I'm always looking at ways to expand my languages!"

"Oh, I'm sure he can teach you a few new phrases." Detective Gleery said dryly.

"When did you start trying to strong arm Roberts into informing on Reith?"

"About a week after they moved in. I wasn't getting anywhere with finding pot on Reith, but I knew she had a new roommate."

"That was how long ago?"

"Two years ago."

"And nothing?" Lozano sounded skeptical as he looked between the file in his hand and Jose.

"We got close a few times. Roberts was always happy to feed me information. We found the pot, but not her fingerprints, in at least three frat raids. We had two people who thought it was her, but they recanted." Jose pulled back his lips. He'd been played hard.

"Why did they recant?" Asked Branin.

"I don't know." Jose snarled.

"Was that about the time Roberts started to be one of her friends?" asked Fier leaning forward intently, his dark eyes intent on Branin's face.

Jose stopped mid interjection to look up at the wall and then at his phone, concentrating. "Son of a bitch."

"Jeremy?"

Agent Fier looked down at Lozano. "Roberts probably learned from Ruiz how to intimidate without leaving any visible scarring. Or maybe something that isn't visible with regular clothing. Toes and balls were Santo's specialty." Fier said taciturnly. At Lozano's questioning look, he continued "Santo was Ruiz's go to boy for silencing the friendly way."

"Balls?!" Drombal said in surprise.

"Friendly? That's what you call friendly?" Jose asked skeptically.

"Autumn's sister hooked up with a Monte Rojo gang leader." Branin commented not looking up from the files. "Subtle wasn't their strong suit." he said, looking up through heavy brows, but still managing to convey the feeling he was looking down at the police across from him. "Autumn was pretty young at the time. The leader died roughly 9 years after taking in Lisa Roberts. Enough time for a six year old to learn a few tricks."

Jose chewed the inside of a cheek. Tommy's words came back to him. "What would make Autumn willingly come into a police station knowing we have files on her?"

"What indeed." Said Lozano. "Looks like we need to ask a few questions."

Chapter Five
Can't Make Him Disappear

We had been asleep for roughly two hours, according to the black and white clock on the wall, when four men walked in. One was a plainclothes officer in casual clothes. The other three were in suits and ties, with very shiny black shoes. One of these things did not match the others; I thought, irreverently, trying to clear the fog from my brain.

Carrie sat up and brushed her hair back, already starting to be perky. Me, I could barely focus on the incoming men while struggling to sit up. Bleary eyed, I brushed hair from my face while reaching for cigarettes. "Fuck!" Gone. Damn it.

"Good morning!" Carrie chirped from her chair. Even with slightly tousled hair, she still had to look 10x better than me.

"Hello, ladies," the policeman said. His voice was both cheerful and oozing happy. I recognized his voice. The face came into focus with a blink or two. Carrie gave Detective Drombal a happy good morning smile, with a particular gleam in her eye. She had had a lot of fun keeping him occupied that weekend. He didn't do more than narrow his eyes at her in a sideways glance, before glaring at me with a fixed smile that was anything but pleasant. The other men might explain why he wasn't happy to see me, I was betting. "Officer Drombal, what a pleasure." I drawled, giving him a dismissive wave of the hand. His lips drew back in a snarl. Carrie and I exchanged a look. Yep, that game was up.

"Want a few tacos for breakfast Ms. Roberts." He said with tight eyes and sharp smile.

My smile was more predatory. "Nah. I prefer eggs benedict and some coffee. With a couple of cigarettes." A breakfast favorite of his.

Drombal had his mouth open to snap something else when

the short suit interrupted. "Thank you, Officer Drombal." A clear dismissal.

"Gentlemen. I'll leave you to it." Drombal wasn't happy, but not disappointed either. He had a self-satisfied smile, when he nodded to Carrie and I, letting himself out of the room. He was going to be trouble, I thought with a blank face.

The three moved into the room, facing us, but still managing to cover all of the room's lines of sight. Professional, but definitely government with those suits and haircuts.

"What time is it?" I asked. Trying for polite, but terse was the best I could muster while struggling to sit up on the butt eating couch.

"Still early. Only 2 am." The short one said with an easy smile. He walked forward to offer me a hand.

For some reason the smile pissed me off. No one should be that happy at two, fucking, am, after I'd been shot at, hit and chased. I stood up, coming into his personal space almost close enough to kiss him. This didn't even phase him. There was a hint of a raised eyebrow as I glared up at him. The guy had balls. He didn't flinch from me in his space, just raised an eyebrow and quirked his lips. He topped me by three inches, putting him closer to 5'9. He was a little short for my taste, but clean-shaven, with absolutely gorgeous wavy chestnut hair.

He turned to Carrie to offer her a hand, but one of the other two had already done so. The Asian guy. Now he was tall. Easily 6'2 and built like a linebacker with pants that showed off his nice ass. Holy hell! This guy could star in my X rated film any day.

"I think I'm in love." Carrie sighed, taking his hand with a melting smile. The Asian guy gave her a polite smile, but there was a twinkle in his eyes. She had that effect on everyone when she was being flirty.

"Tall doesn't equate well hung." I muttered, glancing at Carrie, trying not to stare.

"It can't be the safe house of FBI short guys!" Carrie fluttered her eyes while trying to whisper coyly from the side of her mouth. There were a few lip twitches to that one.

"Don't answer that." said the Asian guy.

"Oh! I'm sorry! I didn't mean to hurt you further." Carrie exclaimed. She had changed her grip in his. As if to hold his instead of him holding hers. His hand was missing two fingers. Index and pinky. Not the normal loss pattern.

He stiffened slightly. "Nope, that's an old old injury. Long since healed." His posture belied the flippant answer. Something or someone had done a number on him. I tilted my head slightly to get a better look. The scars at the end of the fingers weren't old, rather mid-way between dark brown and pink and healing. Maybe two years old.

"That is so good to know. I wouldn't want to hurt you." Carrie fluttered some more

"And, yes, we are FBI." Said the guy with the ruddy complexion, tersely. His hands were relaxed at his side, flex slightly. I'd have rolled my eyes, but the third guy was raising my creep-o-meter to scream. He stood somewhere between the other two in height, with sandy curly hair and a ruddy complexion. It wasn't that his eyes were narrowed in a face that had been made to laugh, they were just dead. I'd seen eyes like that before. Ramon had had eyes like that. Julio liked to hurt things, so his eyes always lit up when he was causing pain. But Ramon, Ramon never cared one way or the other if someone was bleeding or dying.

"Can you tell us who you are and about the murders you saw earlier this evening?" Asked the first guy, collecting our attention once again.

"Murders?" I asked blankly. "Plural? We were at one murder. Just the guy at the greenhouse. This hippy dude." Carrie and I looked at each other for a moment. The short FBI guy studied my face for a moment with narrowed eyes. Not bad dead eyes. Eyes that considered nuances as if judging the worth of words like a chess master before a move of his pieces. I curled my lip slightly, I didn't like feeling like a chess piece being considered for sacrifice.

"What about the manager from the diner?" was all he asked. He was trying to keep a straight face at my annoyance, and mostly succeeded, too. Then it clicked, the bastard was pissing me off on purpose!

"What about him? Last I saw of him, he was in Ratface's lap, swearing a blue streak in a booth while Carrie and I were running out the door."

"Still alive?"

"Well yeah. Kinda hard to swear if you're dead." I crossed my arms over my chest taking a deep breath.

"How did he end up in… Ratface, was it, lap?"

"I threw him there.

"Threw him?"

"I went to the bathroom, coming out he was in the hall and trying to grab me. I ducked him going to the main room where Ratface was waiting. He was sitting and holding Carrie hostage like. Manager guy grabbed me by the arm so I threw him into Ratface. We ran out the door."

"Why do you call him Ratface?" Asked the red-faced man.

"We didn't actually get a chance to get proper introductions, ya know." I snapped, blowing air into my falling bangs. I sat back down putting my work boots up on the table.

For some reason, propping my feet seemed to irritate the short one, so he changed tactics. "Right. Introductions." The short guy looked at his two companions. "My name is Daniel Lozano. The tall fellow is Jeremy Fier." Jeremy gave a warm smile to us that even extended into his dark brown almond eyes. Swoon! I could tell Carrie was all but slobbering herself ready to lick anything if given a chance. "And then, Karl Branin." Karl gave a narrowed eyed, half of a not smile. More like a sneer on his ruddy face.

"Charmed." My voice conveyed my sincere uninterested in a bored tone.

"Autumn!" Carrie gasped. "Don't mind her please! She needs the two 'eens to be human in the morning."

"'eens?" Jeremy asked with a blink of the eyes.

"Caffeine and nicotine."

One of them had to clear their throat not to laugh aloud while I glared at Carrie. "Well we can fix the caffeine portion at least."

"I'll get us something to keep us going, why don't I." Karl said cryptically and left abruptly.

"You would be Autumn..." Daniel's voice trailed off suggestively, waiting for me to finish. I smiled, settling back further into the couch. He pursed his lips but there was definite humor there. We both knew we were playing head games. So far, he was up, but the night was young. I grinned.

Agent Lozano turned to Carrie. "And you might be?" He asked with a smile. This guy knew how to work the honey charm to get what he needed.

"Carrie, Carrie Reith." She smiled in a way that lit her whole face up. She had turned up the charm as well. I had to give Carrie that she knew where and when charm would help smooth things over for her when straight up brains couldn't. Charm and I were going to be two ships passing in the night at this point I think.

Lozano turned back to me, "So, back to the manager. How did he end up in Ratface's lap?"

Carrie got up from her chair to sit next to me on the couch. Lozano took one chair with a nod of thanks to Carrie, while Fier took the other chair.

Agent Branin showed back up with two coffees, cream and sugar. "What, no donuts?" I muttered, as I eyed the cups put in the middle of the table. Carrie elbowed me hard in the ribs.

"Cops ate them all." Said Branin.

I was dying for caffeine, but wasn't touching 'em. Carrie started to reach, but stopped with a sigh when she saw I wasn't going to take one.

"Not to your liking?" Agent Fier asked, motioning towards the coffee.

"I'd rather you take a sip of them first." I said. Fier looked at Lozano, gave a slight shrug.

"Ummm… sure." Fier opened the lids took a sip of each one. The liquid was noticeably lower than when opened. I took my boots off the table to reach for one. Carrie took the other.

"What was that about?" Lozano asked as I dumped 5 of the 8 sugars into my coffee. Carrie took the other three. She took all of the creamers thankfully. A truly good friend!

"Open container rule for parties." I said.

"Open container rule?"

"Guys'll spike a girl's non-locking lid, then wait till the drug kicks in, then fuck her while she's unconscious. If she's lucky, it'll be in a back room, if not it'll be the floor show with videos running." Agent Branin nodded with half closed eyes. I couldn't tell if he was agreeing or remembering. The guy was seriously creepy.

"Personal experience?" Sexy Asian guy asked something akin to pity in his voice.

"Not mine, but a couple of girls and one guy I saw at several parties." I said with a shrug. "One of the girls committed suicide. The other two transferred out."

"I don't think the FBI is in the habit of drugging people we are talking to." Lozano said quietly.

"Maybe." The coffee was actually decent. The sugar made the coffee just the way I liked. Sweet as love and black as death. Carrie was sighing happily while openly admiring the agents. Glad someone was having a good time, I thought acidly. At least the coffee didn't suck tonight.

"Manager." Prompted Lozano.

I shrugged. "I threw him into the well-dressed short guy who showed up, but he was alive and swearing when we ran out of the dinner."

"Threw?" Asked Karl.

"He kept trying to grab my arm and shoulder, so when I saw the suit guy with Carrie, and the manager tried to grab me again, I did an over the hip throw to distract Ratface. Carrie went over the table and we ran out the door. Last I saw or heard of the fat man, he was swearing pretty voraciously."

The FBI guys glanced at each other.

"Start from the beginning, please?" Asked Daniel, but it really wasn't a request.

We finished our recital about the same time we finished the coffee. I set my cup down and leaned forward towards Agent Lozano. "So isn't it rather odd for the FBI to take an interest in a murder?" I asked. "Shouldn't ya'll be out catching terrorists or hijackers?"

"Yes and no. Terrorist and hijackers are for the CIA to look into. A common murder we don't get involved in. When a murder is committed by a group of men we consider dangerous/vicious or proficient in creating bodies we take an interest."

"Bodies plural?" Carrie squeaked.

Karl looked at us both. "You're very lucky. The white haired guy is known in some circles as "Comanche" or "Comanche Jack"." I frowned while Karl continued, "And to date is wanted for the rape and murder of 16 women and the deaths of 2 men." He stopped for a second, doing a mental recalculation. "Well with this one, 3 men."

I blinked, but kept still. Not still enough as Daniel looked at me sharply.

"Would you girls mind going back to the scene with us? We want to get a bit better idea what happened and what you saw."

"Really?! It's 2 am." For a party girl, Carrie wasn't much for staying up past 2 and it was a good 30 minute drive from the cop shop.

"Fresh in your mind." Fier said in a smooth baritone voice and a pleasant smile. Carrie was melting again. I could see her knees weakening and ready to spread. Smart as a whip but damn the girl loved her some dick.

"What do you mean by a second body?" I asked, not really wanting to know, but hating to feel clueless.

"The manager was shot at point blank range. Probably by your suit guy. Though we need to clear you both by swabbing for gunpowder residue." Said Karl.

"What? Why would we need clearing?" Carrie looked at him with wide startled eyes.

"There was an altercation. This is just a process of elimination. No harm no foul to you girls." Lozano said in a straightforward manner.

"Will this hurt?" her voice dropped to not quite a whisper.

"He wants you to bend over, spread wide and say ahhh." I said with a straight face.

"Fuck you!" The exclamation was accompanied with a finger gesture.

"I win!" I tucked in a shoulder, pumping my fist.

The FBI looked on in various states of confusion or

amusement. Just another night for us, minus the whole body count thing.

The hand swabbing was painless but somewhat chilling as the alcohol dried. I did mouth ahhhh at Carrie while she was getting her hands wiped down. There was hand fumbling while she tried to flip me off and failed. I just smiled widely. That was almost as good as orange juice out the nose on her.

Once the swabbing was done, the two of us were escorted from the room to the back of the station to where the cars were kept. Agent Fier kept up with Carrie, while Agent Lozano and Branin walked with me. Carrie, being her usual self, was only slightly drooling over Fier while talking about fantasy football games. There was a lively discussion between the two on this season's starting lineup, which was a couple of months away. She could read one of those games and have a draft up that would take in the top 4 spots on the Yahoo leagues.

I couldn't ever keep up who did what or why this one guy in tight pants was grabbing another guy in tight pants. Sexy butts, but that was all I got from the game. Carrie kept trying to explain the logistics, but it was lost on me. She considered this one of her failings in life. I usually considered it an annoyance, and would go back to studying.

Branin interjected the occasional comment as he stayed at my back while we walked. Lozano walked next to me, close enough to almost hold hands, while Branin was almost on my heels. I really hated someone at my back, but creepy Karl the Klingon was getting on my nerves more than anyone else had. The way that Lozano kept constant eye contact on where I was or doing while we walked, wasn't making me feel any more secure. I was starting to feel like the only thing missing were handcuffs.

The walk was short, with only a slight detour to see Detective Drombal. I noted the lay of the room and security. Carrie was probably looking at the computer monitors and trying to assess the security. We each had our little hobbies to keep us busy.

Lozano touched my elbow. "If you could wait here with Ms. Reich for a moment please." He made eye contact with Fier, who nodded but kept up his conversation with Carrie. I only kept half an ear on the football league conversation, preferring to watch the main floorshow. Drombal looked up from his files, saw us and smiled. A wide, with lots of teeth showing, smile. A quick glance at Carrie showed we were both thinking the same thing. We were definitely going to have issues when the FBI guys left. I chewed the inside of my cheek thinking.

Lozano and Branin went to Drombal's desk with a purpose. Drombal handed off a couple of files and some car keys. There were a few terse comments, but either hands or backs kept me from trying to read lips. I wasn't great at it, but I could usually pick out a few words. My arms itched. I rubbed the hoodie sleeves over them, like I would to warm up. I really wanted to find out what was in those files.

After a moment or three, Fier was called over to the others with a tilt of the head from Lozano. All four of them showed interest in the files Drombal had in hand, as well as something on a tablet.

Carrie nudged me from the side and whispered. "I smell smoke." She was giving me the smile of ditziness that hid a lot of what she was really thinking.

I took the hint and changed my 'I'm thinking of how to dispose of a body face' to 'I have a calculus test tomorrow and I haven't studied' worried look. No longer was I looking like I had a hole that needed a body to fill it.

"Better?" I mouthed from the side.

"Much!" She gave the giggle as if she had told the best punch line to a joke.

The agents' faces returned to their neutral expressions that gave no hint to what was going on. I wondered if that was trained or natural. I probably would have to wait to find out if I ever got a chance to train as an agent. I made a face.

"Ok, we are ready to go." Said Lozano, handing Fier one of the key sets. "Carrie, I believe you said you drove to the warehouse this evening."

"I can remember how to get there." She said with a smile.

"Agent Branin will accompany you with agent Fier driving. While Ms. Roberts and I follow."

"What, we can't all fit into one car?"

"And deny Agent Fier the pleasure of Ms. Reith." Lozano said deadpan, but was a slight sly grin. Fier blushed a very interesting shade of reddish bronze. Branin just humphed with a "Wasting time" comment.

"Then by all means, let's take two vehicles." And away we went into the cooling night.

Chapter Six
Long Drive and a Short Chat

The white Mercury was nice. Leather seats and working a/c. I could get used to this type of car, I thought, snuggling down into the soft plush leather seat.

"Comfortable?" Asked Lozano, amused at my almost purring while I adjusted the seat.

"Mmm, very. Just need a cigarette, something meaty and life is good. But since those aren't forthcoming, I'll have to settle for acceptable." I said with a sly grin of my own.

Lozano clipped his seatbelt together over the seat then sat down on top of the strapping.

"Some safety role model you are." I was both envious and appalled. I had read the statistics on accidents and seat belts. You weren't catching me without one unless I had no other choice.

"As an officer of the law, I may have to exit the car quickly. Those seconds I save by not wearing my belt can mean the difference between catching or losing a killer, or saving a life.

"How do I get your job?"

He pulled out of the parking lot, turning right on the main thoroughfare. Fier looked to be about two cars ahead of us. His car was a light blue Lincoln.

"Stay out of prison and go to school." Was all he replied, concentrating on the traffic.

"So far so good on that front."

He glanced at me with a tilt of the head and an unbelieving look.

"What? I haven't gone to jail once… let alone prison."

"Buying pot can get you put in prison."

"We were buying plants for our apartment. It IS a greenhouse." I said with mock primness.

His lips twitched. "How about we cut the bullshit, and you answer the questions without hedging or lying."

"Only if it goes into writing nothing I say will be used against me or Carrie." I countered hotly.

"How about we drop the pot buying issue and I ask questions on other things for the next 25 minutes."

I stopped and studied his face. He was confident, relaxed. Right now, we were clean. Wrong place at the wrong time collegiate seniors. My eyes narrowed.

"I'll play your game." I dropped the breathless voice for my normal tone, and a long hard stare at him. "What do you have up your sleeve Agent Lozano?"

Lozano had that smile again. He was going to be annoying I thought. "When we were in the holding room, what made you flinch when Karl said bodies?"

I looked at him with a frown. "Flinch?"

"Twitch?" he countered

"He's lying". I turned away to look out into the pristine night sky not even bothering to sugar coat the answer. I leaned a cheek against the cool glass. I did not want to go back to the greenhouse. Not any more that is.

"Is that the psych major or the criminal justice major?"

I turned back; I could feel my face blanking. "I never mentioned my majors."

"Nope. I made sure to collect all files on you. Both of you for this meeting."

"Curiosity?" I ran a hand through my hair. I was really jonesing for a cigarette at the moment.

"Prepared. Comanche is a bad guy. We need to know what we're walking into, including the witnesses involved."

"Innocent bystanders." I corrected.

"From your files, neither of you are that innocent. So, again, why the twitch and why do you think he's lying?"

I chewed a lip listening to the humming of the tires on the road. Lozano shot a glance at me, only tapping a finger on the steering wheel to show his intense interest. Man had patience; I had to give him that.

"Men have certain tell signs when they lie. Karl, he's good.

Good at lying I mean. He almost believes what he's saying. It's the almost that gives him away though." I said, my thoughts weren't on Karl though. "Some of his statement may be true, but some part or parts of what he said he knows are lies and he gives those parts away."

I searched through my hoodie's front pockets again, hoping vainly for a cigarette. Fuck. Nothing. I must have sighed.

"No smoking in the car even if you could find one." Lozano said.

I glared at him, making him chuckle. He was made of sterner stuff then Mark even if he was being a goody two shoes. I adjusted back into the seat in a huff.

"Where did you learn the men lie tricks?"

"They open their mouth." I snapped.

"Seriously."

"Seriously. Honest men are short and sweet, and to the point, mostly. Long-winded or convoluted descriptions or answers are usually lies. Look for those and add eye movement or hand gestures."

"Bitter much?"

I looked at him long and hard. What came out of my mouth was not what I had been thinking first. "I watched my mother get beaten and used by multiple rotating boyfriends while my sister and I tried to evade getting petted or fucked by the pervy ones. Then I watched my sister get hooked on drugs, knocked up and knocked around, always believing the rat bastard of a boyfriend's lies, till he had her hooking for drugs, taking anything he gave her or her tricks gave her. She OD'ed while 8 months pregnant. His child, he made her wear condoms with the other johns, but she was carrying his child and he fucked up her life then killed her. So, yeah… a little bitter here."

"You got out."

"I got out with a streetwise education that dovetails nicely with my double major."

"You have 387 credits."

"What can I say, I'm an overachiever and your files are more than just the standard who, what, when, and where."

"Just being prepared. If I'm not mistaken, this is also your last semester."

"Yep. What's your degree in?"

"You tell me." I could tell he was laughing at me. Fine. I could do this. I focused on him. A talent I learned in a hard school. Size up a person, connecting with them and getting into their heads.

"You're an idealist." I started. "You believe in truth, honesty and the pursuit of happiness even though you see the darkness. You reach for the good. You got a degree, but not a useful one. English or history I'm guessing. You went into being a beat cop... no academy, then FBI. You did something well enough or special enough to be noticed. Hence, you're a field agent. Your degree is superficial to what you do, but important to who you are." I gave him a hard-edged smile. "How close?"

He didn't say anything for a moment. "Your guess was only partially right. I was in the military first, and then went for an accounting degree. I got a job auditing at first. I found money trails in place that had been overlooked or hidden very well. I was given a break for field work."

"You prefer dead bodies to money?"

"I prefer living people who are safe to dead bodies. By the time the money trail was obvious the body count had usually started."

"True, but that's not what you were really after, though, was it."

Lozano gave that slight smile again. "What part of his statement was a lie?"

"Back to this again are we?"

"Can you answer the question?"

"His eyes cut left when he mentions Comanche and bodies. His hands twitch too." I made a small motion with my own hands trying to mimic what I'd seen. "He's either discarding or pushing away what he says because he knows it's not real."

"The bodies are very real."

"I'm sure they are...they just weren't made by Comanche."

"The DNA evidence..."

"Anything Karl has touched is going to be tainted. He's a liar." I said flatly. "If he's held it in his hands or had access to it, then something is wrong."

Lozano didn't say anything for a few minutes. I replayed what had bothered me in the police station over and over again. Picking apart which pieces, Brennin had twitched at.

"I appreciate you answering the questions."

"You just don't think I'm right." I was more amused than offended.

"I think you're biased against authority and men." He measured out each word carefully.

I rolled my eyes.

"Looks like you're saved from any further questions. The greenhouse is ahead. A couple more miles." Lozano was offering an olive branch.

"Good, I was starting to need a pillow." I wasn't going to be mollified.

Lozano laughed. First time I'd heard it, low, rich and real. "Dreams are good, unless the pillow was for other things." A sly look.

Laughing, I rolled my eyes. Yeah, yeah, yeah. "How long have you been chasing the white haired guy?"

"5 years." Any warming up that had been happening just went back to chilly.

"19 bodies in 5 years? Rather large body count and you guys not close to him until now."

"We started making the connection 5 years ago. The spree has been going on for a bit."

"So nothing hard on the guy or just can't catch him?"

The sideways glance I got could have melted stone. I smirked slightly.

"You pulled wings off of flies didn't you?"

"Nope. Why do that when torturing your fellow man or woman made for more fun?"

Lozano's hands gripped the wheel as if they were strangling someone instead of squeezing hard plastic. "He disappears like smoke when we get close." He growled in frustration, answering the question.

I drummed my fingers on the armrest. "Can't trace him or his posse?" I gestured quotation marks for the "posse" part.

Again the glare. Sheesh, ask a few irritating questions and get scorching looks. Still working on the "Fuck you" from him but again the night was young. I hid a grin.

"No."

"No what? No him to trace or no posse working with him… cause we distinctly saw more than one scary hombre in there."

"No, we can't track him or the two he has with him."

"Two?" I frowned. "He had three."

This got me another look this time; more of a questioning frown. "Tell me about the ones you saw."

"Ratface."

"Got him." My turn to glare at being interrupted. Lozano chuckled and gave me a not subtle in your face smile with teeth. I blinked and sat back in the seat. Bastard was playing "Fuck you". Ok then, I know how this was played. Game on!

"Rat face," I continued "short with an over compensating gun that took both hands to hold."

Lozano nodded.

"Boy band butt guy." That got me a look but not an interruption. "Long blond hair, tight butt, and a very practical sized gun. Probably a Glock or Ruger."

"You get a close look?"

"Pfft…if I had been close, I'd have been able to tell you make, model, and year. All I got was a glimpse." I only snarled a little in irritation. I hated not knowing what someone was shooting especially AT me! Was bad for the health.

"Any other distinguishing features other than a butt that made you and Carrie hot?"

"Off hand, no. Though the police station may have a decent enough picture of him."

"What?!" Lozano twisted so hard to look at me that the car swerved a little off the road. His phone began to ring as he over corrected then corrected again putting the tires firmly back on pavement instead of the trucker's ruts.

He tapped his ear bud, cupping a hand around it to hear better while resting his elbow on the window ledge. "What? Yeah, fine. New information. Get Drombal to review the video from the front of the police station for a guy with long hair, blond, nice ass possibly carrying a canceled a medium sized pistol." He listened to the air for a moment, the hand on the steering wheel clenching and unclenching enough so the knuckles were changing colors. Lozano nodded to the voice from the other car. "Sounds good. Hold on, let me ask about the third one. That could be Marcus." He turned to me. "Was the other guy about 6'4, broad and black?"

I blinked at him. "Umm…. no. I'd say 5'11 if that and fat. Dirty blond, very white." I thought for a sec. "He clutched his lap top like a teddy bear and not much of a beard." The pale face that floated in front of my memory's eye was definitely that of a gaming geek I'd see on the weekends at the coffee shop holding LAN parties or playing by themselves. Unique in their slovenly appearance, lack of hygiene or grooming, and always with their square headed girlfriends at the ready.

"You sure?"

"White is very distinctive from black. So, yeah… I'm sure the fourth guy is not black or built like a quarterback."

"Did you get that?" Lozano turned from me. "She did? So we need to find out what happened to Marcus." Again, the nodding. "He could be incoming as back up or dead or somewhere else." Lozano rolled his eyes but his voice never changed. "We'll need to make sure one way or the other." Another pause "We'll compare notes in a few then." He clicked off.

"The boys grilling Carrie?" I asked sweetly.

"They are going to verify what you saw and what she saw are the same." He said coolly.

"You know if Fier offers to give her 15 minutes of Asian bliss, she'll give him all she's got and then some." I said fluttering my eyes at him.

Lozano stared for a sec, letting the car drift to the right, then overcorrected to the left again, processing my comment.

"Are you two good friends? Because if I had a friend like you'd, I'd be tempted to just leave you somewhere really bad." He wasn't joking.

I had to think for a moment. "Yeah, we're good friends. And I've bailed her out of a couple really bad situations. So I doubt she'd ditch me for saying what she's thinking, even if it offends your prudish sensibilities." He took the flat stare I gave him at face value not asking for more details.

"I see you're not offering to go to bat for a night with Fier."

I snorted. "I doubt Fier would last a night without a brain aneurysm, and he's not my type."

"You have a type?"

"Yeah… quiet and stupid. Find 'em Fuck 'em, maybe feed 'em, but definitely forget 'em. No questions, no muss, no fuss. "

"This goes for the girls too?"

"Pretty much. Equal opportunity for sex. No strings though."

"Why so?" He actually seemed curious.

I shrugged. "Too many complications." Mark had been a definite complication and irritation. I had broken my rule with him. My teeth were grinding together thinking on him again. I took a deep breath, consoling myself with thinking of nasty things to do to his truck when we got home safe. Bastard.

"Easier to leave?"

I gave him a slight bitter smile. I decided to change the topic.

"So what is this Injun dude doing here? Last I looked women were in the city unless he likes random rapes with dicks."

"Nope, he likes areas rich in targets and ya'll fit his profile; although, your friend Carrie, may be outside of his parameters."

"Too cutesy or too slutty?"

"Heavy." That stopped me. I had to think on this for a second. Carrie could stand to lose about 40 lbs, but still, she wasn't barrel shape or quadrupled chinned. She wasn't a model, but she wasn't the type you threw out of bed either.

"That's pretty sexist!" I said, with real heat.

Lozano shrugged. "What can I say, all of his victims have been young, collegiate and definitely within normal standards."

I shrugged it. Not my kink. "So again why is this guy in the middle of nowhere killing?"

"We're not sure."

"Oh, that's reassuring." Heavy on the sarcasm.

Lozano gave me just a slight glancing glare before rolling his eyes. "This is why we're going to the warehouse with the two of you at gods awful in the morning."

"Do you think he really killed all of these people?"

"The evidence is pretty strong." Was the neutral reply.

I tilted my head observing him. "But you have your doubts." It wasn't a question.

"There are…" a slight pause. "…a few loose threads."

"Like?" I pounced eagerly.

"Ongoing investigation." He said primly, with a slightly egging smile.

"And all information is sacred." I harrumphed.

"Something like that."

Fuck you, I thought, slumping into my seat. Point to him.

Chapter Seven
Run!

The green house was dark when we pulled up. Not that I had been expecting any lights or anything to be on, it wasn't Wal-Mart, but this place was seriously creepy in the dark. I hugged my arms close.

Carrie was giggling and chatting up the men when they got out of their car. Always the flirt. I grinned. She could probably tell me their grandparents' names, ss numbers and how many credit cards with limits at this point of everyone involved. God bless her for being mostly normal, very smart and only a mildly neurotic nympho.

"Cars?" Lozano asked, as Karl got within conversational range.

"Nothing on the way in, and nothing to either side." Said Jeremy. Carrie passed me two of her bummed cigarettes. She motioned a hand to Karl.

"Damn Klingon." I muttered, pulling my lighter out of the air, then tossing it to Carrie. Only Carrie heard the Klingon comment, but heads still turned.

All three of the FBI agents had stopped to stare at us.

"What?" she asked, lighting hers then tossing the lighter back to me, which I made disappear into my hoodie with a slight of hand.

"What?" I asked taking a drag and frowning at them. My frown turned into a warm smile as the first rush of nicotine hit. "Ahhhh… yes!" The night was looking better already.

"The lighter. Did you just pull that out of the air?" asked Jeremy.

"You mean like this?" I pulled the lighter from thin air again, then made it disappear. Carrie giggled while she took another drag.

"Yeah, like that." Said Karl, but he wasn't amused like Jeremy seemed to be. I gave him a flat look with a smile.

Carrie bumped into me. Manners… right manners. I turned my attention back to the clove flavored smoke and the agents, smiling.

"Neat trick." Said Lozano. He had raised an eyebrow, not really surprised it seemed, just taking notes.

"It's good for parties and cops." I said with a bright perky co-ed smile and a flip of the hair. Lozano pursed his lips but didn't say anything more.

Fier snorted. Lozano quelled him with a glance. Easy to tell who was in charge of that trio. The three went back to their discussion.

"What we have here ladies and gentlemen is the classic old school horror movie makeup." My voice dropped as far as I could into a false baritone register. "The classic smart heroine and her amusing sidekick."

"Don't worry dear; I'll give you a shot at the men as my adorable sidekick." Giggled Carrie.

"As long as I get to pick the dildos I get to use on them, too!" I said with a mock glare while taking another drag.

"Deal!" Carrie gave me a girlie punch on the shoulder. "Can't have you getting too horny and turning the horror flick into a porn."

"Then we have our escorts!" A firm nod on my part.

"The strong leading man, Daniel."

"He would look good in gold and black spandex."

"Would prefer more of an ass though. His is a little flat."

"Hmm… not that flat." A motion with the cigarette. "There are butt inserts to correct that. Nah. Real is better. Maybe a butt implant." I mused, considering the object of our mutual discussion.

"Mmmm…. yes, please!"

"Down tiger! Back, beast, back." I mimed the snapping of a whip. This set Carrie to giggling even harder. "Oh yeah. Then we have our loyal, but expendable, sex security in red, Jeremy."

"Dies off screen. Very tragic." She made a sad face and took another drag, trying to pull her hair out of her face at the same time. Nothing and no one got burnt, but it was close.

"Of course. Can't frighten the young children too much."

"Scars them for life."

"To true!"

"Possibly a good on screen PFB who bravely dies while protecting the heroines escape?"

"Plausible." Another drag, I blew an almost perfect circle. "Then we have the evil plant, the human looking Karl the Klingon."

"You really don't like him." Carrie made a moue of sadness. "He's nice. Gave me cigs for us both!"

"You thought Tiffany was nice when she gave you cigs too." I flashed an evil smile at her.

"She was for about five minutes. Then I blew her boyfriend in the closet when she got too bitchy." She said with her high-class look, nose in the air looking down (well up) at me.

"That was every other day that Tiffers got bitchy."

"Yep! And the boyfriend was very happy every other day too!"

"Slut."

"And proud of it." Carrie gave a snap of the fingers as she jutted out her shin and waggled her head side to side. I really couldn't keep from laughing at her for that one. This just made Carrie start laughing, which triggered us both to laughing harder. Scared we might be, but, damn, we were going to try to die laughing!

"You girls want to join us?" Came Karl the Klingon's voice a few yards ahead of us. Seemed the agents had started to move and now needed our warm bodies to proceed through the scary building. Yay us!

Carrie and I glanced at him then each other, and started laughing all over again. We linked arms and followed. I stored the second cig in my front hoodie pocket for a later stress treat. Foresight was my specialty.

The police had come and gone, leaving little police pellets and tape behind. I had to stop a second. Déjà vu sucked like a bitch. I hadn't had to cross police tape in *seven*, I thought for a sec counting backwards, *no, eight years. Sucked then and it sucks now.* This time though I didn't know the victim or the victims.

The FBI didn't have guns out, but they were being cautious. Jeremy was on point, with Karl and Lozano following. Lozano motioned for us to stay behind and be quiet. The police tape killed the laughter that Carrie and I had had going. Now I just chewed my lips and wished I had a gun or a car. Nice big car with lots of road. I really didn't want to be here.

"Lights?" I asked, hating how my voice had gone to high and breathless, instead of controlled. The coke machine was casting enough light it made the dark seem deeper, thicker and the shadows more real.

"Coming up now." Said Daniel.

"Not scared are ya?" Karl asked with a malicious edge to his voice. Seems I wasn't the only one to have a real dislike going. Always good to know who were the real players in the "Fuck you" game were.

"Not with you here big boy." I snapped without thinking, batting my eyes at him in mock hero worship. His eyes narrowed and the muscles in his jaws kept bunching. Fier gave a snort of amusement while Carrie just giggled. Karl glared at them both.

Lozano ignored the exchange and gave the lights a flip. The lighting started low then hummed bringing the room into white neon glaring detail. Carrie and I both sucked in our breath hard. The blood splatter of the hippie dude was to the right of the cash register, sprayed on the walls like a badly done red spray paint. Just thicker and a lot more of it then in a spray can.

I swallowed hard. Carrie clutched my arm as we stared.

"We never saw the body on our way out." I said my voice soft in the quiet wood room. Carrie stuffed a hand in her mouth, biting down to keep from crying out. The man hadn't deserved to die like this. Ten minutes, had given me a fair read of the man. The blood splatter showed that he had been behind the counter coming out to talk to whoever had come in after us. The amount of blood on the wall said arterial. The pool of blood on the ground said he had bled out.

"Why was he shot? You can't ask a dead guy questions." I

stared at the blood pool talking more to myself.

"Thought you said you saw the murder?" Lozano asked.

"We were in the greenhouse, when we heard a gun go off twice." I tore my eyes from the drying blood pool to look up at the FBI agent.

"Show us?"

Nodding, I turned towards the greenhouse door. I had to tug on Carrie's arm with cold hands. She turned to me with huge eyes and stopped biting her knuckles. Reality was sinking in, and this wasn't a reality she could handle.

"Come on chica. Nothing more you can do here. You've got lots of security to keep the bad from happening." My voice was soft as I tugged her to follow again. She blinked and shook her head as if shaking off water or a bad dream.

She was definitely shaken to the core, but I had confidence she'd bounce. Those boobs were good for at least a 5-point landing all on their own. Carrie must have seen something on my face with the last thought. She stuck out her tongue and made a face.

"You're going to freeze your face like that and never get another bj date again." I said.

"Pfft, better than your natural face any day." She snapped.

"Aaaaand she's back, ladies and gentlemen!" Carrie mimed a swipe at my arm with a punch, missing by a mile. I smirked.

"Ladies… if you don't mind. The night is late." Came Lozano's dry voice from behind us. We turned and blushed like naughty children with our hands in a cookie jar. Lozano held the door to the greenhouse area open for us. Carrie and I looked at each other, the belly of the beast awaited.

The greenhouse was just as quiet as it had been previously. For some reason the lights on did not make the greenhouse feel smaller or safer. Instead the overhead lights illuminated all the nooks and crannies with stark clarity, making it feel ten times bigger. The lights showed rows and rows of plants, pallets lined the walls as well as huge barrels, all very convenient places to hide the bodies or men with guns. Nope, not paranoid at all, why do you ask?

Carrie was so nervous she kept stepping on my shoes as she

walked down the center aisle, bumping into me every few steps. The third time in six steps, I had to turn and glare at her. She gave me such huge eyes, I felt like I had just kicked a puppy. Karl seemed to take pity and offered her his arm. She just looked at him so gratefully; I could see her thinking of the "proper" way to thank him later. I rolled my eyes with a slight shake of my head.

"Where did you say you hid?" Lozano asked. His voice was loud enough in the quiet hush that I jumped back from where he stood by two feet. He had the courtesy not to laugh, but one of the two behind weren't so restrained. I didn't dignify either with a look, just contained my glares to Lozano.

"Please." He held out a hand, palm up motioning to the warehouse. I kept my head up and walked past him towards the cactus.

The boards were muddy, but less so then when we had first crawled for cover under the plants. I motioned to Lozano where we hid. Something wasn't right and I kept looking around for what was off.

Carrie sighed with a little pout. "Why can't they have grown the good stuff instead of house plants?" The FBI looked at her. She blushed. "Not that I would ever, ever! In a million years touch pot." She said hastily, her eyes going very large and innocent.

"Your slip is showing Mother Theresa." I said blandly.

"Shut up!" She hissed, but was unable to maintain any sort of composure before giggling halfway through.

I frowned. Déjà vu hit. I walked to where Carrie had been hiding.

"See something?" Asked Lozano from my elbow. I jumped 3 feet in the air, coming down with a cocked fist.

"Dude, I'm going to hit you and NOT regret anything if you don't start fucking putting a bell around your neck." I snapped. My voice was breathless, but growling instead of a giggle like Carrie's.

Lozano gave me a bland smile, but he did take half a step back.

"If it makes you feel any better, he does that to me all the time, too." Said Fier.

"Glad it's not just us." I muttered.

"See something?" Lozano repeated.

"Yeah, more like not something." I sniffed. Lozano waited poised.

"Carrie do you smell anything?" I asked. I wanted to confirm what I was thinking.

Carrie sniffed a couple of times with a tilt of her head. "No. It's not as stinky as it was when we walked in."

"Is this relevant?" Karl asked, obviously irritated at our slow moving crawl through the warehouse.

"Fertilizer." I said. I walked to the space between the plant rows.

"Fertilizer? We're standing here waiting for information on a murder and you're talking about fertilizer?!" Karl did icy sarcasm very well.

"Brennin." Lozano's voice was sharp. Karl subsided, though his face looked like he was sucking on lemons.

"Yeah." I was distracted. "There were, like, three pallets worth of bagged fertilizer here." I made a motion to the mud. "Made the place smell..." I had to find the right word. "Interestingly."

"The place reeked of it." Chimed in Carrie.

The ground was muddy, where several large square things had sat, but muddy around the dry spots. There were tire tracks dug into the mud heading through the large double metal swing doors heading deeper into the complex. Carrie and I both traced the tracks through the doors and looked at each other. White girl went even whiter and I know I didn't want to go through those doors either.

"What time do the sprinklers come on?" Fier asked. The others looked at him. "Sprinklers make the dirt floor wet enough to take on an impression, but they haven't come back on to erase either the tire tracks or get the dry areas wet again," he stated patiently.

"Right. So someone else was here, either between the killings or after the police." Lozano looked back to Carrie and me. "Was there enough time for one of the men you saw to move pallets from here to wherever then find you at the diner."

Again the glance. "Umm…" I started.

"What she's trying to say is that she's never driven a pallet jack, except in bed so the three minute window doesn't really apply." Carrie said.

"Bitch!" My turn to hiss at her. But we were grinning. Anything to stall going deeper into the warehouse.

"Seriously. For five minutes, be fucking serious, you two." Snapped Lozano.

Oops. Someone had just reached their party fun time limit on the two of us.

"I don't know, Agent Lozano." I said meekly. "There was a 15 minute window from sitting down to rat face showing up at the diner." I shrugged. "I, we have no idea if this is enough time to move things around."

"Jeremy?" Lozano turned to the tall agent, who seemed to be lost in thought.

"No."

"No?"

"No, that's not enough time to find a pallet jack and move 3,900 pound pallets from here to wherever unless the person was intimately familiar with the layout and the equipment."

"So someone else is party crashing?" Carrie squeaked.

"It looks like we may have another player or players here." Brennin said. His voice steady in the gloom.

"Fucking marvelous. We should have a bouncy house and balloons now." I said with a snort. "Seems this has become a block party!"

"You're not helping, Autumn."

"No? Fuck you. This isn't my job and I don't want to be in this place when Comanche comes back or door fucking #2 opens up for either Jason or Freddy Krueger." I was rubbing my hands over my arms again, but this time I didn't even try to hide my fear. "This place is fucking creepy and going downhill quickly."

Lozano narrowed his eyes, but nodded. We were now liabilities and no longer viable assets. Fine by me. Kept me out of the fucking fun house kill zone.

"Right. Jeremy you're with me. We need to find the timer on when the sprinklers went off for a time window. Karl, you're with the girls." He motioned for Karl to stay in the greenhouse area with us. He jerked a hand towards Jeremy to lead through the door heading out of the greenhouse into the unknown.

We were going to split up. I did bite my tongue though Carrie and I traded glances again. Horror movie 101… never split up. The good news, Carrie and I weren't going to have to go any further. The bad news was having Karl as babysitter. This wasn't my idea of a good time either. Time for another cigarette.

The cigarette smoke rolled off the tongue, so warm and spicy… almost chocolaty. No, what, me addicted? Never. Now I was thirsty, though.

"So, umm… any chance we have any change for the coke machine?" I asked.

Karl ignored me to plant one ass cheek on the plant table. His foot was jiggling with impatience. Seems he didn't like babysitting either. Carrie went through her pockets but they were as empty of cash as mine.

"Mind if we get one from the front room, Agent Brennin?" I asked in my sweetest voice. Carrie shot me a worried look. I gave her one of my "nothing to see here smiles" which only reassured her slightly.

"Whatever." Came Karl's curt reply.

"Want one Carrie?" I asked.

"Nah!" Came her reply in a kittenish voice. I could tell she was going to try and bum another cigarette from Karl, and possibly a blow job if she could. Yep, definitely time for me to vanish for ten. I was five feet from the door and could hear Carrie's giggling carry across the greenhouse. The girl was a smooth operator. I made a bet that in 3 minutes she'd be wishing she had knee pads for those dirty floor boards though.

"Seriously woman! Can you NOT go without semen for 3 hours?" I sighed. I shook my head. She liked the notches on her head board. If she made this one I'd spot her the next ten points. A blowjob in a greenhouse, with murderers on the loose, and with an FBI agent. That was going to be hard to top by anyone.

I rubbed my arms again as I went. Turning the knob to walking into the front room, "It's not splitting up! It's not splitting up!" I said with emphasis, trying to keep the hairs on the back of my neck from standing up.

"If you say it enough you might believe it." A deep voice said softly to my right and behind me. A hand came across my mouth so fast I never had a chance to yell, pulling me against what felt like a warm wall. Half my face seemed to be covered by a really, really big hand. I twitched in response and felt another hand push the muzzle of a gun under my chin.

My head jerked towards the voice. I saw two guns and three men standing to my right. Ratface, longhair and the geek. My leg twitched for an instep stomp. "Kick me and I will be very angry." A very deep and low voice behind me said into my ear. The almost rumble vibrated along my jawbone. The only one in the gang I couldn't see, but I could figure out who was behind me. Now I was scared.

I nodded carefully. I breathed out and slowed my breath, my whole body covered in chills. This was only going to get worse for me. Waiting for my chance, any chance, no matter what was going to be better than killed and dumped. These guys didn't play nice. They played for keeps in a high stakes, winner takes all game. And pawns got killed off regularly. Another slow breath. Had to keep the hamster wheel from spinning out of control in my brain.

The gun was removed from my chin, but the hand stayed over my mouth. The arm moved, but, since he didn't back up, I assumed the gun went into either a side holster or the back of the belt. When his right hand was free, he grabbed my right wrist, pulling my arm behind my back. Not painful yet, but the promise was there. The left hand was still planted very firmly over my mouth.

I was the picture of meek. Looking at three men in front of me through lowered lashes. Ratface looked both angry and smug. There was a fresh and shiny bruise across his left cheek that bled into the shiner. I did not smile or smirk, but dropped my eyes for a moment. I really hoped that bruise hurt him.

Longhair looked on with a blank face, but the geek looked sick and scared. Looked like geek boy was getting more than he bargained for with his new buddies.

"Raise your left hand to tell me the answers I want to know. Do you understand?" The voice was a deep growly whisper, but no less scary for the softness. I nodded once, raising my left hand to shoulder height.

"How many in the other room?"

I held up 2 fingers.

How many guns?"

One finger and not the middle one, though I really wanted to. Scared, yes. Dumb, no.

"How many agents?" One finger.

I could feel the wall take a deep breath. I could swear he was centering himself. He then gestured to Ratface and Longhair. Longhair had a small round thing he started to screw into the barrel of his gun. A silencer. Fish in a barrel for them from this range.

Carrie! They were going to shoot Carrie! I panicked. I stomped on Comanche's right foot as hard as I could while biting down hard trying to draw blood. Comanche let go for one second, swearing. That was all I needed.

"Carrie!! Run!" I screamed with every bit of fear and anger I had. That was all I got out before being thrown against the front wooden counter so hard I saw stars where the old man's blood splatter was.

I slid down to the floor, unable to gather my wits or my breath. The pounding in my head was getting louder, though the sound might have been connected to the really large boots I saw by my head. I did hear yelling from the greenhouse but no shots.

"Run Carrie!" I whispered. Then nothing.

Chapter Eight
What is Behind the Door

There was a dog sitting on my chest. A very large dog with yellow fur and very sharp canines. I knew this because his face was 3 inches from mine, with a huge grin, seemingly very pleased with his new best buddy, me. His tail was wagging and brushing against my legs. At least I hoped that was his tail thumping against my lower legs and nothing else. Ewwww. Nasty mutt.

The dorm room couch wasn't comfortable to start with, but even more so with a huge ass mutt sitting on me was my first thought. I flayed my arms to either side. One arm tried to get a grip on the back of the couch, while trying to yank the mutt of my chest with my other hand.

I couldn't even get my back an inch off the couch the damn thing was so heavy and it was too damn big for me to just pull off with my other free hand. I glared at it. I could almost swear the mutt was laughing at me with its doggie grin and large yellow brown eyes.

"Really? Who, the hell, let the damn fucking *perro* into the apartment? We'll get fleas!" Hated fleas. Little bastards were a bitch to get rid of. My arms and legs started itching at the thought.

"Great, now you're giving me fleas, too." I sighed, slumping back onto the lumpy yellow plaid couch glaring up into the grinning dog's face. Soooo happy to see me. Just wait, I thought. You're going to the pound as soon as I get your heavy ass off of me.

"You might want to wake up, Niña." The dog's lips and jaw moved. And he could talk. Very surreal. I touched his mouth. It was a dog's mouth. I touched my head. No pain or swelling.

"You can talk." I said dumbly, stating the obvious. "I must

be asleep."

The dog stood up over me, looking down. "No, not asleep" he agreed, leaning down, "but you may want to WAKE UP!" His jaws snapped within centimeters of my nose.

The dream shattered around me. I sat up with my heart pounding in my chest and my head pounding in time. "Fucking spiked frat party keg stands." I groaned. No, wait. That is not what happened tonight. Memories rushed in, making me shake; clutching my arms close to my body.

I couldn't see anything. I touched my face to make sure there was no blindfold. No blindfold, but there was a tender spot and wet. I sniffed my fingers, smelling copper and chemicals. Blood. Great. Well, Comanche did say he'd be pissed if I kicked him. "And I did bite the son of a bitch, too." I felt my lip curl in satisfaction. Hope the bite got infected! Headline reads: Gangrene by college student takes down notorious serial killer. My outrage almost turned to giggles. I was starting to lose it. "Get a grip girl and get the fuck out of where ever this is." My voice was stern but my head was still loopy.

There was a faint chemical smell. With my luck, it was highly carcinogenic and my skin was going to melt off any moment. It didn't smell like the fertilizer in the main room but I wasn't going to pull a lighter out just to get roasted because I couldn't see. Sigh, time to go exploring in the dark.

The floor wasn't bone dry, but covered in something damp and gritty over metal. "Owww! Mother fucker!" I swore hard. Fuck my legs hurt like a bitch, like the shins and knees had been worked over with a bat. So did my right hip. Damn. Comanche really must have kicked the shit out of me after I passed out. What a sore loser. "Hope you get shot in the guts you pissant piece of shit!" I snarled. My voice echoed through whatever it was I was in; telling me the space wasn't large. Like a living room, but wasn't so cramped I could touch the ceiling or walls from where I stood.

Keeping a hand over my head I stood slowly, I did not want to bump my head against a low ceiling. Adding more bruising to my already sore head, due to self-inflicted stupidity, was going to suck. The floor curved upwards on both sides of where I was so I followed the curve to the wall, standing slowly. Every step was treacherous. Whatever was on the floor was not just damp but slick as well. Greaaat.

Too much room for a metal barrel, I thought, but what, the hell, is this place! I tapped on the wall. "Fuck!" I sucked on my knuckles. "Way to go fucktard." I mumbled through the knuckles. I reached out more cautiously this time to the wall. Smooth. Glass smooth metal. With curved sides. "He dropped me in a milk truck? *Bastardo*!" Ok so maybe not a milk truck, with the chemical smell, but I was betting it was one of those round metal tanker type trucks.

The headache was getting worse. Not sure if it was from the bruising already done or the addition of chemicals, but, at this rate, I'd be having a full blown migraine in five minutes. Once that happened, life was going to really be miserable. Well, more miserable than being beaten up and thrown in a tanker of some sort. Oh yeah…my life was great at this moment.

Sarcasm is your friend.

Ok, the tanker had to have a ladder. Somewhere. I clung to this thought. If there wasn't a ladder, I was going to lose it badly and very soon. Reaching out my arms as wide as they would go, one in front and the other to the side, I stepped slowly away from the wall I was leaning on. It didn't take long to find the ladder, just 6 steps and a jammed middle finger.

"Not going to be using that finger for a while now am I?" God this was sucking. I climbed slowly, not sure how tall the tanker was from the inside, but I didn't want to smack my head any more than it already had been. My feet kept slipping on the rungs, so even the few steps to get to the hatch took longer than necessary.

The hatch was round and raised on a short column, with an inner pull bar that went from side to side. With the slippery crap on my soles and lack of leverage on the bar, I couldn't get the damn thing to budge.

I slipped five times and fell three. I kept climbing up to try again and again. I tasted bile and my skin got hot. "Turn, damn you! TURN!" The hatch was still firmly closed and panic was setting in.

I started to pound on the lid hoping someone, anyone, could hear me. My hands were bruising and I could feel the skin split as I hit metal protrusions but I didn't care. I was screaming through tears until I was horse.

I had watched too many horror movies of being buried alive. This thing was bigger by a coffin but a coffin it was and I was trying to claw my way out.

"No! NO NO NONONONO!" I screamed over and over. I felt the lid give way under my hands. I pushed harder. The lid opened and the light streaming in was blinding. That didn't keep me from trying to scrabble my way up and out on slippery soles. A shadow fell across my face. A moving form. I violently shook my head trying to clear the blur of tears and light. I needed to see, yet couldn't let go of the railing or I'd fall back down. One hand was on the rim of the lid tube while my other hand was still on the ladder. I noticed distantly that both hands were missing swatches of skin and bloodied.

The shadow formed into a man. Tall, white hair, high cheekbones and a face that had recently been punctured by thorns. Comanche. I swallowed hard.

He reached down offering a hand.

I looked at the hand, then his face. "Why?" My voice a hoarse croak.

This startled him I think. He blinked, giving me an odd look. "You want to stay in there?" He sounded surprised. His voice was deep enough to vibrate bone. Proximity didn't seem to be an issue for the voice vibrating thing. Neat party trick.

"Why help me out when you put me in here?" I clarified hoarse voice somewhere between a scream and a sob.

"I didn't drop you in there." His spine stiffened in umbrage. He met my eyes, not looking away or denying the fact I had been thrown in. Truth. There was concern in those eyes. A rare enough emotion, and usually only from Carrie; so rare I almost missed it.

I hesitated a second, swallowing, but took his proffered hand. He pulled me up in one smooth move. My knee twinged sending me stumbling against him. Solid muscle through the white shirt. Enough strength to break a person in two without breaking a sweat, I thought. I stepped back waiting. Weary. His eyes narrowed.

"Turn."

"I would prefer to be hit or shot from the front." My voice was steadier, but no less hoarse. I looked him dead in the eye, a challenge. I wasn't going to be executed without a fight or at least some self-pride. Begging never worked on bad guys, just got them off harder when you did.

His lips moved and I could swear he was biting the inside of his cheek. There was a glint of laughter in his looks that made me stiffen. His voice was steady and bland though, "Good thing I'm not going to shoot you then isn't it. We are however getting down from here and moving somewhere else."

My response was cut short as his Bluetooth went off and he held a finger up for quiet. His eyes, however did not leave mine. No chance of running.

He touched the little black earbud with his left hand. I could hear a soft whisper but nothing definitive. His side conversation was intriguing though.

"Tie them." Was the first curt response

"No, he can't shoot them." The sigh was slight, but his voice took on a definite edge of irritation. With narrowed eyes and a gesture of his chin, he motioned for me to turn. I decided time was still on my side. I might find Carrie and get the hell out of here if I cooperated a few minutes more.

"Do NOT leave Marcus alone with them."

"No. Cubby is not an acceptable babysitter for him."

I raised my hands and turned. We were inside the actual warehouse portion of the greenhouse. This section was huge. I could have run track and field in here dodging tankers, statues and a few other weirdness before hitting the door to the next section. I was in no shape for a foot race. I mentally crossed that path out.

There was a side door 20 feet away, though. I looked sideways through my hair without turning my head, stealing visual cues without giving myself away.

"Good." Silence then the hissing sound of air blown through teeth in irritation.

"Henchmen not working out as planned?" I said in a meek voice. He put a hand on my shoulder guiding me, firmly towards the downward railing.

"What can I say, all the smart henchmen were already hired."

I stumbled, looking over my shoulder, past his hand. Seriously? Sarcasm with a half-smile. His face turned serious as soon as he saw me look. Ah well. Can't let the prisoner see you laugh.

"So you have the Wal-Mart of henchmen? This does not bode well." I turned and walked towards the railing to get down.

"Yeah, things do tend to get messier when you have to scrape the bottom of the linoleum floor." This time I actually got a chuckle.

I noticed there were about 15 other tankers in this huge area. Four others had their lids open. This made me pause for a sec. He really hadn't dropped me in one of these damn things.

I swung down the railing steps, ready. I could make the side door when Comanche hit the railings to come down. I knew I was faster than some old guy. I touched ground turning to run when the thump next to me caused me to start then reassess my last thought. Old guys didn't jump 15 feet down from tankers, spring back up standing and look like they were ready to do that again. Was this guy anything but scary?

I took a deep breath. I couldn't make the door with Comanche standing. Then, he shouldn't be standing... I nodded to myself. Let's make this happen.

He motioned with his chin towards the back door. I turned dutifully meek, with my head down. Carrie would have laughed her ass off. But then again she'd seen me do meek right before a sucker punch. I felt his hand on my shoulder again, guiding me towards the far back door and his Wal-mart of henchmen. I didn't think I moved. I grabbed his hand and stepped back into him. Even as he was reacting, I rolled him over my hip throwing him down as hard as the rotation and gravity would allow, and, with a pivot, I ran towards the door like Rojo's dogs were on my heels.

Comanche landed with a thud, but managed to tuck into a

roll with a not so silent snarl. I heard his footsteps, running almost within reaching distance as I grabbed the doorknob and pushed, slamming my body into the door and screaming. The door swung open and I slammed it shut, fumbling for the lock. I looked up through the window expecting to see a very angry, very large bad guy behind me. Nothing.

"Autumn!" A voice shouted behind me. I screamed again, jumping high with a turn, punching towards the voice. I missed punching Jeremy in the chest by an inch. Anyone shorter or closer I'd have gotten them in the chin. Daniel grabbed my wrist and swung me towards him.

"Where's Karl?!" Daniel yelled. I was hyperventilating and shaking. Daniel grabbed my shoulder, his gun in his other hand still, shaking me. "Where is Karl? Where is Carrie?"

"Comanche." I gasped out, pointing to the door I had just come through.

"What do you mean Comanche? Where is Karl?" Daniel was getting seriously pissed at me.

"I don't fucking know!" I yelled back, breaking his shoulder grip. "I don't know!" I yelled back. "I'm trying to tell you I don't fucking know!"

"Where is Karl?" Daniel's voice upped a notch trying to out shout me. "What happened?"

"I went to get a drink, while Carrie was trying to cajole your fucking Klingon into letting her give him a blow job. Bad guys were in the lobby area. I got knocked out and woke up in a tanker!" It might have been the wild-eyed crazy look I had going, or it may have been my hands bleeding all over his. Perhaps it was my voice, which could now dub for a bad monster movie, that made Daniel reassess the new information that Comanche really was closer than he thought.

He let go of my hands and pulled his gun to shoulder height, nodding to Jeremy. They were doing the FBI mind reading thing again.

"Stay behind Jeremy." Daniel snapped as he glided towards the door, I had just come through. I squeaked and moved behind Jeremy, but not so close I couldn't run if the scary man popped up again. Daniel nodded the count to Jeremy. They went in on three. Daniel twisted the metal knob, pulling it open quickly and stepping through in a single smooth motion, moving like quicksilver on a tilted board, clearing visually left then right. Jeremy moved in behind Daniel, both covering all the views to confirm it was just us.

Jeremy motioned me forward with a tilt of his head, his eyes still scanning back and forth with his gun at the ready. I crept forward. I didn't care if they thought I was a coward, Comanche scared the piss out of me!

I was soo not being left behind or splitting up again if I could help it. I tried to be Jeremy's shadow without actually stepping on his shoes. I could just see him turning and shooting me if I bumped into him following too closely. Ok, maybe not shooting me, but I wasn't going to push him or Daniel on that one.

Another thought went round and round in my head. Why hadn't the scariest bad dude to date followed me through those doors? Had he seen something? As in Jeremy and Daniel? Why hadn't he shot me when I ran? Or shot the two FBI agents and me when I did run through the door. I didn't know and those questions were usually easier to answer; as in dead bodies told no tales. The hamster wheel brain ramped up.

The second time in the tanker room was no more charming then the first. I just got a longer, better look. The room was freaking huge for a garage. Easily twice the size of the green house, and filled front to back with tankers. If I didn't know it was a green house with a reputation for pot, I'd have said it was a storage facility for trucks. Some of the trucks had hazard signs, some didn't. But they were all tankers.

Even with the rubbernecking going on, I heard gravel crunching. I stopped with a tilt to get a better audio. The sound was familiar, but not from Comanche. His steps, even when running after me, had been almost silent. This sound was… the same as Daniel and Jeremy's. Flat bottomed dress shoes on gravel, walking as if searching. Only one other person would have the same sound, probably with curly hair. I gave a silent snarl. Now I wished for a gun of my own.

I started looking closer instead of just being scared behind

Jeremy. I thought I saw a shadow move up high, over the tankers, but couldn't be sure. No use speaking up if I didn't see anything, so I didn't say anything this time, just bit my lip.

"Nothing." Jeremy stage whispered

"Could be three or four ways out of here." Said Daniel, just as softly. "And probably just as many hiding places under or around things."

"Not seeing anything under the tankers."

"Just means we haven't found or seen something. Doesn't mean someone's not there."

The agents were a couple feet in front of me, while I was listening and not looking. "Tell me everything." They turned to me. I was still focusing on the footsteps and not their conversation. There was no yelling or gunshots.

"Autumn!" Daniel hissed at me. I started, wide eyed back at him. Daniel didn't put his gun up but he lowered it to his side, facing me. Jeremy glanced at me; inscrutable, turning his back to Daniel, watching if anything came up on us from behind.

"Ye-es"? My voice was still raggedly breathless and not my own. I hated it at that moment. I swallowed and tried again.

"Yes?" not nonchalant, but not quivering in fear either.

Daniel closed the few steps that separated us, taking my hands with a gentle touch, turning them over to look at the damage I had done trying to pound my way out of the tanker. He had warm hands, I thought distantly. Not crushingly strong, but not dainty either. My hands hurt, but they weren't as badly damaged as I thought.

"Tell us what happened when we left you." His voice was gentle, though no less demanding, and his eyes were still roaming the area around us, but that didn't soften the intensity from the need to know. He was trying for reassurance. I felt scared. I wasn't going to say terrified yet, but that was option number two.

I nodded, pulling my hands from his and into my hoody, and then rubbed my sleeved hands over my arms, flakes of blood sticking to the hoodie. "I was thirsty and wanted a drink from the coke machine..." I started. Five minutes later and a slight alteration of saving myself from the tanker then being jumped on the way to the door, caught the agents up with everything.

Jeremy did give me a quick smile before turning back to scanning. "Takes guts to try and outrun Comanche." Jeremy said, with a quick glance at his wrist, "It's been 45 minutes since we split up."

I gaped at him. "Carrie." I whispered and swallowed hard. 45 minutes was long enough to do enough horrible things and dispose of a body.

Daniel's eyes were still narrowed. He knew I wasn't telling all the truth and I really didn't give a fuck. "And Karl." he said.

"And Karl." I tried really hard to keep the dislike from my voice. Think I was about as successful as Carrie from going for the biggest dick in a frat room.

Daniel tried another tactic. "So you really have no idea how you got here?"

I opened my mouth, then closed it. "No."

"No?"

"I could guess but I don't have any evidence and I'm already pissing you off." I snapped, glaring.

Daniel glared right back. So much for the nice FBI agent routine. Daniel took a deep breath and took a step back. He and Jeremy exchanged another of those partner looks.

"We need to find the others." Jeremy said blandly. Daniel nodded. I almost rolled my eyes. Really? I thought to myself with all the sarcasm I wasn't going to say. Carrie would have been proud. Tact, I was actually getting good at tact with authority.

Chapter Nine
That's Going to Bruise

We back tracked through unfamiliar areas of the warehouse. Unfamiliar to me, but the agents seemed to know where we were going. Jeremy was in front and Daniel brought up the rear. They put me in the middle, which was just fine with me. Jeremy was good scenery to look at. I was dying to ask questions. Like where they hell had they been for 45 minutes. Yet, Every time I tried though, even in a whisper, I was hushed. I glowered quietly and kept moving.

We made it back to the front greenhouse plant room, through the side door everyone seemed to disappear through, without seeing anyone, good guy or bad. At this point I was starting to chew on my nails. Nothing good ever happened from splitting up like this.

Jeremy started heading to the front entry room when Daniel hissed for him to stop. Daniel ducked down, looking through the containers, then straightened with a hiss. "Carrie!" He jumped up and ran to the end of the row cutting over two others, before turning down one. I followed close on his heels.

Where we had been sitting, she laid crumpled on the ground. I cried out, "No!" Pushing Daniel to the side, sliding to my knees next to her head. Blond hair splayed around her face but no blood on the ground. I reached a shaky hand to move the hair from her face. Daniel moved up next to me bending down to put two fingers to her neck.

"Alive." He said looking up. I went limp with relief and closed my eyes, feeling hot prickles behind my lids. Damn if I was going to cry in front of either one of them. I swallowed hard, blinking hard a couple of times. No tears no foul.

"Back up." Daniel tried to shoo me away from her head.

"Fuck you!" I looked up with a snarl.

"Easy, girl. Let him check how much damage she took." Jeremy's voice was right behind us. He was still guarding our backs.

I pulled my arms back and crawled backwards on my knees a couple of steps. I bit my palm to keep quiet. Daniel's hands were gentle as he felt over her head. He frowned, massaging one spot.

"How bad is she?" Jeremy asked.

"Got a lump back here but not feeling any bones grinding."

"Concussion?"

"Could be. I'll need to check her eyes."

Daniel motioned me forward. "Need you to put her head in your lap while I check to see how her eyes dilate." I scooched forward again, sitting on my heels. Daniel lifted Carrie's head to my lap. I moved her hair out of her face again. My hands notably less shaky. Jeremy handed Daniel a pin light attached to his keychain. I looked up at him quizzically.

"My cats like to chase the light dot." Jeremy actually blushed for a sec. I had to giggle.

"Good to know you have pets like normal folks." I said smiling.

"Nothing normal about you two." Said Daniel as he opened Carrie's eye lids shining the light first in her left eye then her right.

The second light woke Carrie up with a start. She started flailing ineffectually for a second.

"Easy, easy! It's just us, Carrie." I said soothingly, grabbing for one of her flailing hands, holding tight.

"Autumn?" Her voice was a bit shaky.

"Right here."

"What's going on?" She asked fuzzily, moving to sit up and not succeeding.

Daniel didn't try to keep her down. We helped her sit up.

"No concussion." Daniel said, handing the key ring back to Jeremy.

"Autumn?" She was starting to get upset.

"Easy girl. You got slapped by the world's biggest cock and fainted." I said, putting a hand on her arm.

She giggled and clutched her head. "Damn, and I didn't' get to even suck it!"

"Give it time. The head'll suck soon enough."

Daniel just gave me a disgusted look. "Well, you two are back to normal."

"We still need to find Karl." Jeremy said.

"Yeah, he's not even wearing a red shirt." Mumbled Carrie.

"A what?" asked Daniel frowning down at her.

"An away team security red shirt." She clarified for him, which just made him frown harder. I started to giggle, but stuffed a sleeve in my mouth before I could draw too much attention.

"A Star Trek reference." Said Jeremy deadpan. Daniel glared at him, which didn't seem to faze Jeremy in the least.

"Carrie, what happened to you?" Daniel looked down at the sitting girl, glaring but trying hard not to. His evening was not going well.

"I… I was sitting, talking with Karl, when I heard Autumn yell for me to run." She made a vague gesture with her hand, trying to turn, looking more wobbly then helpful.

"What else?"

"I felt a really hard hit smack me on the back of my head."

"Then?"

"Nothing."

"Nothing else? As in nothing else happened or?"

"I was out cold." She shook her head, then clutched at it. "Oww!"

"Yep! Sucking has begun." I said.

"Bitch!" Carrie giggled.

Jeremy and Daniel exchanged glances.

"Looks like you two have a problem." I said. I did not gloat. I did not!

Daniel's look said otherwise. Damn! "How do you figure that?"

"Carrie and Karl had their backs to the front room, watching the door you had exited. Comanche was in the front room."

"One could have snuck up from behind."

"No. All four were in the room with me when I yelled. "I

stuck out my chin, challenging.

"You realize you're accusing an FBI agent of knocking out a witness."

"He may have done it as the easiest way to keep her out of harm's way." Jeremy said, glancing over his shoulder while helping Carrie up from the muddied floor boards. She staggered up slowly; I slipped a hand around her waist, letting her put a hand around my shoulder to steady her.

"Knocking her out with bad guys coming in?" I said incredulously.

"No bad guys now." Daniel angrily gestured. "And no bullet holes in her either!"

"No Karl, though." Jeremy interjected again, earning Daniel's glare.

"Leading them away?"

"Or he doubled back to take out one of your witnesses and just needed time to get the other one." I snapped. I could feel my chin starting to jut out just waiting for the punches to start swinging.

"Enough." Daniel's voice could cut steel. He traded looks with Jeremy. Jeremy looked away first.

I bit my tongue for 30 seconds. A real record for me. "You don't trust him either." It wasn't really a question.

"We need to find Karl. Daniel said ignoring me. "You two," He stabbed a finger at Carrie and I, "Stay here."

"No." I said.

"Autumn." The voice was a warning, his face set in stone.

"We split up last time. This time will get us killed." I was shaking. I knew if we were left alone we would be dead. "We'll follow you if we have to. We are not being left behind." Nothing was making me back down.

Daniel rolled his eyes, but did not argue my flawed logic.

"Fine. Follow behind and don't speak."

"Can I whistle?"

"No."

"Can I hum?" Daniel glared at me while Carrie giggled and Jeremy hid a guffaw. They had caught the movie reference. Daniel didn't and knew he was missing something. I was beginning to warm up to Daniel. A sort of a love hate thing.

Our merry little band of misfits started moving forward. I really wanted to sing the "Ohee oh" song from the Wizard of Oz, so merely hummed a few bars. Carrie started to giggle loudly and Jeremy's shoulders started to shake. I did stop once we moved out of the front safe growing room. No sense in pushing my luck with Daniel or Comanche.

We went slowly into the second, then the third greenhouse. The third greenhouse was front to back cannabis. The scent was warm, heavy and heavenly.

"Oh!" Carrie inhaled deeply. Her chest rising to new, and more impressive, heights. "Can we stop for five minutes?" Her eyes were shiny and large with appreciation for the growth in front of us.

"No. And you can't smoke any either." Jeremy said gently. Daniel was ignoring us both at this point.

"But, but…"

"It's going to be burned in the next 24 hours as it is." Jeremy said with a glint to his eyes.

Carrie sighed sadly. "All that lovely green being wasted." You would have thought someone was going to euthanize her puppy she sounded so sad.

"I'm sure you two will be able to score somewhere else." Came Daniel's acid response.

"Not like this." She giggled. "Swimming in pot."

"Carrie. Shut up!" I snapped. Her injury was making her brain and mouth disconnect. But Carrie took the hint and closed her mouth, but she continued to inhale heavily.

We kept moving through the cannabis forest. The skin on my neck was crawling. Daniel and Jeremy felt the same as they got very quiet and very focused on the tall plants around us. A whistle sounded to our left an odd, almost violent set of notes.

Daniel repeated the whistle, then Jeremy. The bushes rustled then parted on the left hand side. Karl stepped out with his left hand up, but a gun out in his right.

Karl looked at the group then rushed to hug Carrie. "Hey, girl! I am sooo sorry for smacking the back of your head." he sounded contrite and worried.

"That was you? Owww!" Carrie whined putting up a hand to her bruised head.

"Yeah, figured they would rather follow the FBI then hurt the downed girl."

Daniel shot me a look. I held eye contact, then cut my eyes left then back. He glared.

"I found something." Karl said. Going from contrite to smug in a heartbeat, motioning towards the back wall area.

"We'll follow your lead." Daniel said.

"Bag of gold and a six pack of Bock?" I muttered. Again, the glare from Daniel. Ugh, whatever dude. Carrie and I hung back a few steps as the others started moving through the greenhouse with faster steps.

"I don't think you're going to get into his pants that way." whispered Carrie.

"That's a relief."

"Just sayin'."

"Shouldn't you be blowing some one?" I snapped.

"Head hurts too much."

"That's a first!"

"Yeah. I need to smoke a joint or three."

"We're in the right spot."

"Wrong crowd though." Came her mournful reply.

"True dat!" I agreed.

Chapter Ten
Going for a Swim

The office Karl led us to, was up two flights of industrial concrete stairs; a square box with an overview of several rooms. The room was long with walls that did not connect to the ceiling very well, drafty and dusty. There were several cork boards on the back wall and a huge wooden desk that looked like a third-hand 1940s refugee from the Salvation Army. Probably weighed a ton, too, I thought. That was not a Wal-Mart $50 particleboard piece of shit. Dark, heavy, solid wood, but no longer sleek or elegant. The desk had seen years of use and abuse, like a Harley old lady.

The window in the middle looked over the tanker room I had been locked in. I didn't stay long gazing at the open or closed tanker lids. My hands throbbed harder. I turned away with clenched fists, which wasn't helping the pain.

The window to the left looked out over a variety of heavy equipment machines and cement pillars and statuary. I frowned. The statues and pillars would have done well in the cover of a plant store but I hadn't remembered seeing any in the main two rooms.

Some of the statues and pillars had been broken. At this height I could see that some of the concrete floor had been as well. I couldn't tell what had done the damage but there was a lot of mess around the middle section. Looked like the destruction was working its way outward from the center area.

The far right window overlooked the main room of pot and two other rooms of pot in different growth stages. There was a smaller room with a pool at the edge of a younger pot forest. The shallow end held a variety of water lilies and other varieties of water garden plants. The deeper end was too murky to see the bottom. Carrie whimpered at the sight.

"No you can't run naked through the cannabis forest." I muttered to her.

"But, but, no one would know!" Her emphatic reply distracted the FBI guys from their huddle as they looked up and over.

"You're scaring the children." I lowered my voice to just above a whisper

"Pfft. I doubt they haven't seen everything I have."

"And the only three who haven't." I said waggling my eyebrows at her suggestively.

"Bitch!" she giggled in mock outrage, trying to throw a punch at my shoulder that went wide, even for one of her normal punches. We both laughed at that.

"Damn, can't even hit the broad side of a barn!" She tried to poke me in the stomach.

"Maybe if you offered to suck the paint off the barn, you'd have better luck." I leaned away from her incoming poke, only to have to catch her as she over balanced and started to fall.

"Think I need to sit down." She said clutching her head. Her voice was slightly breathy and worried.

"Probably the best idea yet today!" I refused to be worried, but I was very careful, steadying her.

"We should have come out yesterday." Carrie said mournfully.

"I think you were on a date, and I had a final yesterday."

"Oh, yeah… bring facts into this why don't you." The tone was only mockingly aggrieved.

"One of us has to have priorities." I smiled, flashing teeth at her.

"It was a good date!" Carrie said emphatically. As I half walked, half carried her to the couch under the far right window.

"See a window with a great view."

I helped Carrie to sit down on the faded couch.

"No!" Carrie's voice snapped reality back into focus fast.

"What?" I asked bending over concerned to help her up again if needed.

"It's going to infect me!"

"What?"

"The couch! The 1950's plaid… ewwww!"

I shook my head in disgust. Carrie pouted that she hadn't gotten a bitch out of me lately, but she settled down on the refugee half cloth and half hard plastic plaid couch with a giggle and an, "Owww!"

She gave a happy sigh though once her ass was on the damn thing and she turned to gaze out the window. The pot forest did indeed look very inviting. Too bad we wouldn't be able to so much as touch any of it. I was pretty sure Daniel would have us strip searched when this was over just to make sure no buds had migrated to pockets or such. Damn that man.

I looked at the back wall where all three FBI men were at and talking animatedly. There was hand waving and pointing, but no voices were raised. Karl had his hands up in a placating gesture. Daniel had his back to me, his shoulders moving, but his hand gestures blocked by those nice shoulders. I had a very nice view of the backside. I gave a slight sigh. Even under the suit coat, you could see where the slacks cupped his ass, showing tight and firm. The kind you wanted to sink nails into. My mind wandered into dangerous territory for a moment, before I rolled my eyes at myself, bringing reality back in stark relief. Too bad, too, he had such a nice cherry cheeked ass.

Another section of the wall was covered in news articles covering missing persons, unsolved bank heists, and a map with pins stuck in a large random seeming array of locations. I ambled over to the wall with the articles out of curiosity.

Jeremy came up behind me. His footsteps clear on the faded cheap linoleum. "Looks like the Jimmy Hoffa hiding house of crime." I said dryly, after reading a few of the articles.

Jeremy was speed-reading over my shoulder through several of the articles, frowning. "These cover a large span of time."

"How much time? How many people?" Daniel asked. I jumped slightly. Fucker could walk softly when he wanted to. His eyes cut left and twinkled when I glared at him. I bit back a smile, but, damn, that had been sort of funny, even if it was at my expense.

"Looks like 19 different missing persons over 3 years."

Jeremy continued thoughtfully.

"Any connection to Comanche?" I turned my head slightly to look at Jeremy ignoring Daniel.

"All three of the male victims, but only two of the women."

"So how many total?"

"Five out of ten."

"So possibly another five to be found here connected to… him." Daniel ran a speculative gaze at the board. Ramon had that look, but connected to soccer teams when he laid down a bet. Bodies had just made him smile.

"Or more." Karl said from the side, joining in the conversation.

"Not into dead bodies." I said firmly. There was only a slight waiver in my voice. Bodies were messy and caused complications. That and I kept seeing my sister lying on the floor. Foaming and bleeding. I took a deep breath and blanked my thoughts for a moment.

"We'll try to save you from seeing anything too harsh." Karl said dryly, walking to look out the middle window.

"Why thank you kind sir." My sarcasm was contained and only slightly acidic. It did make it easier to not think on bad memories when that asshole spoke, though.

Daniel walked over to Karl, who was looking at the rooms below us containing the half-destroyed statues.

"Let's get to looking." Daniel said. Karl nodded once. They divided the room up between the two of them while Jeremy kept reading news articles. The large wooden desk had five drawers down each side. Daniel took one side, Karl the other. I started to yawn. There was no coffee. Not sure if I'd have trusted anything in this dilapidated reject from a gas station office. The only thing missing was the smell of diesel and motor oil. I made a face, sticking out my tongue in memory of those smells. I shook my head, trying to clear the old memories.

I turned to Carrie. She was slumped against the armrest with her eyes closed. Girl never snored, but sometimes drooled. I grinned. She wasn't at the drooling phase, yet. Good thing she was a friend or I'd have been drawing a penis on her face. Another yawn crept out, cracking my jaw. I settled on the other end of the couch, closing my eyes for just a moment. I wasn't going to sleep, just resting my eyes, listening to the agents rummage through the office debris.

I dozed off and dreamed of the large yellow dog watching me from the ceiling, upside down, where the broken overhead light was.

"Why is there a big ass mutt on the ceiling?" I asked turning to Carrie next to me. There was no Carrie. I looked around. There was no one else in the room either.

"Oh, this is a dream again."

"Some dreams are more important than others." The dog said.

"Are you the same one who told me to wake up in the tanker?"

"Yes, yes I am. I'm glad you remember me. You may call me Coyote instead of mutt."

"You are rather hard to forget." I said, frowning, looking around the room. The mutt, err… Coyote was still on the ceiling standing upside down. "The others must still be in the room, and not in the dream kind."

Coyote stood, stretched, then circled the light before sitting down again in the same spot. I watched in confusion.

"No. They left you sleeping. Presumably safe."

"It's not?"

"Depends on who you ask." Coyote smiled. The teeth gleamed white, wet and sharp. Very disturbing.

"I should wake up." I was feeling very uneasy.

Coyote stood and circled the light once again before sitting down. I tilted my head at him. "You should go for a swim." He started glowing so brightly it was like staring into the noonday sun.

I threw an arm over my eyes to keep from being blinded in the dream; jerking myself awake in reality by throwing my real arm over my eyes.

I woke with a start, disoriented. I shook my head and looked at the ceiling. No yellow dogs there. "I fucking swear no more late night parties with the FBI. Their parties suck." I jerked my neck left then right, trying to crack out the kink in it, then sat up while rolling my shoulders.

Carrie was still out like a light, curled up on her side. Her mouth was open slightly. She never snored, but I'm sure she'd be drooling. I grinned evilly. Damn if I didn't have anything to take that girl's picture with for some serious blackmailing. She'd bite her favorite dicks to keep that from hitting the net.

There was a noise behind me. I frowned turning toward the window, listening. Nothing. Then more noise closer. Faintly I could hear yelling. I stood up trying to see what was going on. Maybe Daniel was finally kicking the Klingon's ass.

"Eh, not going to get that lucky today. Err… night." I muttered, searching vainly for a cigarette. "Oh!" I looked up and over at the pot field. A whole ripe, untouched and untainted field of pot. Part of the field was waving in the breeze. Why go with tobacco when I can pick something. "Time to take the edge off." Oh yeah. I could see this now… Then I frowned. There was no breeze inside the greenhouse. Why was the pot moving like there was? What the fuck!

The pot came right to the edge of the pond. I saw someone in a black suit toss a body into the pond, white shirt and dark pants. Then dive back into the pot field, the plants thrashing gave the location heading back towards the far side of the field. I couldn't id the person being thrown or the person doing the throwing. Either way someone was having a worse day than me. The body in the pond was still moving. More jerks then actual movements though. "Like their spasming…"

I hesitated for only a second. I hit the door to the office with an open hand. The door had been ajar and opened with a loud thud when hitting the hallway wall. I flew down the twisting stairs, throwing open the bottom door. The pot was still there and still over my head. I looked up at the overhead office to try and orient myself. Having an idea of where I was in relation to the pond set me to running again.

I got to the pond just in time to see the body was still twitching, but sinking fast. Fuck no, I wasn't going to jump in! I couldn't see the bottom and there were no pool side numbers marking how deep. I liked my neck in one piece. I slithered over the side into the waist deep cold murky water. The bottom was treacherous for walking on with squishy mud and the odd shaped rocks under foot as I tried to walk/run through to the body.

There were only bubbles showing where the body was now. I tried to reach with just my hands and arms with my head still out. I couldn't quite reach. I hesitated for just a second.

"Fuck! You'd better be worth this." I snarled before taking a deep breath and ducking under the surface. My hands grabbed stiff cloth and the vibrations of twitching flesh pulling up to the surface. I turned the body over so the head was face up not face down. I almost dropped him right there and then. Comanche Jack. I swallowed, but gritted my teeth.

"Damn it. If I didn't owe you my life at least once…" I muttered at him. I hauled Comanche up to the shallows while doing a mad scramble on the squishy slippery pool floor.

I kept pulling and tugging, but between his body mass and wet clothes, the best I could do was haul him part of the way out of the shallow end. His lower legs and feet were still in the water while the breathing portion was out. Unfortunately the breathing parts of him weren't. Breathing that is. I growled at him.

"Fucker. You would need mouth to mouth wouldn't you!" I dropped to my knees next to his torso, tilting his head to the side while opening his mouth. I ran a finger inside to make sure there was nothing obstructing the airways. A bit of water came out but no fish and he still wasn't breathing.

"Carrie and her damn CPR class for a chance to blow the instructor." I tilted the head and pinched his nose. I took a deep breath then sealed my lips over his pushing air into his lungs. I shifted positions to straddle his chest, pushing on the diaphragm to simulate breathing. Counting, pinch, breath, push. Three rounds then the ground under me shook, bucked and heaved. Comanche Jack sat up violently enough that our heads butted, causing me to see stars again, stunned. I don't remember being thrown over onto the ground, yet found myself flat on my back with a knee at my throat looking into a very pissed and angry giant Indian warrior.

I lay very still and took shallow breaths while looking up.

The knee was uncomfortable, but not crushing. Yet. Comanche Jack was not focusing clearly. His eyes were dark and wild. There was very little white showing as his eyes tried to focus while swiveling his head all around.

"Hands!" He snarled down at me.

"Can't asshole. Something big and nasty is sitting on my chest crushing my throat." I glared back up at him.

He glared back down at me, but he did shift off of me, standing up and glaring down at me.

"Undo my hands now!" He reiterated.

"Yeah, yeah, yeah!" I sat up, reaching for my keys with the handcuff key on them curtsey of Drombal's spare. "Fuck!"

"What?"

"My keys were in my purse that you fuckers took."

Comanche narrowed his eyes more.

"You can get as pissed as you like, but doesn't change the fact my purse is gone with the spare handcuff keys." I snapped at him, standing up. "Unless you have lock picks, you are screwed. Looks like you're going to have to sweet talk the person who threw you in." I poked him in the chest. My head barely coming to his shoulder. If I hadn't been glaring up a mile high, I'd be glaring right into his nipples. Not exactly on my list of sightseeing tours this trip.

"In my hair."

I blinked. "Come again?" Then giggled. I had to bite my lip to keep from laughing at what I had just said, but, hey, it had been a rough night. Girl's gotta live a little or at least a little longer.

"I said in my hair. I have lock picks. That is if you can really use them." He said, snapped in a challenge.

I looked at him for a long moment clenching my jaw. "An unusual place for 'em." But I made no move to search his hair.

He could see it in my face. I was going to leave him and make a run for it.

"I saved your life." He said quietly. There was a heavy intensity to his look.

"Think I just saved yours as well!" I snapped.

"This is saving my life?" He gestured with his chin at the

pool surrounded by the pot. "Any second someone could come back and shoot me since the drowning didn't work."

I chewed my lip. "Fuck you!" But my voice lacked heat.

Comanche chuckled, knowing he had won the argument.

I glared at him walking around to his back. "If you hadn't saved my life, I'd have left you!"

"Thank you."

"Shut up for a moment." I was not a gracious loser. I tugged on the braid. He didn't move. I tugged harder.

"Ouch! Why are you pulling on my hair?"

"Look tall white and tight butted; I can't reach all of your hair with you standing. So sit!" You would have thought I had asked him to strip for dollar bills or something. My mind went there. Him in a black leather thong, war paint and feathers. That chest, from what I felt, was made for licking.

Damn it! Down girl, down! I was really going to have to get laid when this was done. And not by my favorite vibrator either.

I knelt behind him lifting up his wet braid. The damn thing was down to his waist and as thick as my wrist. I tried to undo the red leather thong tying the braid. The leather was wet and hard to get the knots undone.

"Leather? Really? How cliché." I muttered around the knots tugging with my teeth.

"Stereotypes are there for a reason." Comanche said, with an almost haughty tone. Hard to be haughty when you're trying not to laugh at the girl chewing on your braid.

"Fucker." I muttered stilled chewing. At that he did laugh. A low rumble that made me grin. The thong came off with only a little more tugging and chewing.

"Gah, that's nasty!" I spat then draped the leather tie over Comanche's wet shoulder. "Here, hold this for me will you?" I asked sweetly.

Comanche laughed again with a shake of his head. "I can see you were just a sweetheart growing up, weren't you?"

"Yep! And Prom Queen too." I started to undo his braid. The hair was lushly thick and soft. I had expected rough and coarse.

"Tiara?"

"True dat! All big and pointy, flashing like a disco ball. You know the kind they had for you when you were growing up in the '70's." I was undoing the braid a lower section at a time, winding my fingers through the thick hair looking for the lock picks and trying not to purr. Damn, like fur! I bit the inside of my cheek concentrating.

This time his whole chest began to shake with surprised laughter. It took him a few moments to stop trying to repress the laughing. "Not that old!"

I snorted. I had found the first pick. Small supple. Ahh… the professional's set. Small, very easy to hide, and a bitch to use if your hands were unsteady.

"32 piece kit?" Just to confirm.

"The picks?"

"No, your fashion wear." I rolled my eyes even though it was lost on his back.

"Yes."

"So why are you hiding them in…" I never got to finish that.

"Can you get the cuffs off?" He was starting to get twitchy though we'd only be here a few moments.

"So much for having fun in wet clothes and handcuffs. Some men are always hurrying to get to the finish." I draped his long wet hair over his shoulder to get a better look at the cuffs.

"This is not comfortable." He said turning to glare at me over his shoulder.

"Testy! However, I can see why. Now hold still for a moment." The cuffs had been slammed hard on his wrists and closed tight. The skin was bruised from where the cuffs were cutting into the skin. It hadn't helped when Comanche struggled in them. Probably while trying to get away.

I licked my lips. "This may get more uncomfortable." I said. This was probably going to really fucking hurt. "I need you to bend your elbows and lift your arms up." He complied as much as he could, which was almost good. I scooched under his hands and lifted his arms a little higher to rest his forearms on my knees. He grunted once, but said nothing else. His hands were in my crotch. If only… not! I twitched in suppressed mirth again.

"No free feels." I said trying to add levity into the pain. The most I got was a look over his shoulder with a raised eye brow. I bent over the cuffs concentrating on the right one first. I shut everything else out. Only the lock existed. Fit, lift twist. And click.

Comanche brought his right arm forward, flexing and twisting the wrist. The wrist was far more abraded then the first cursory look had told me. I hissed in sympathetic pain. Comanche just motioned with his chin over his left shoulder.

"Way ahead of you." I lifted the wrist to a better position on my lap. More comfortable for him, and less compromising for me.

The left hand pick slipped. "Fuck!"

"Problem?" The bass rumble was laced with concern.

"Be another sec." I snapped, hunching my shoulders. "Mother fucking…" I hated fumbling. Julio would have cuffed me hard enough across the ear or cheek to have left a bruise. Son of a bitch is dead, I thought through gritted teeth, glaring at the second handcuff. I bared my teeth at the memory.

"Lose a pic."

"No! I am not that fumble fingered."

Comanche grunted a, "Hmmph." I flipped him off with a growl.

"So do you remember who threw you in?" I asked, bending over the second handcuff again. Nothing like asking the awkward questions in an awkward position. Least I wasn't the one handcuffed to the bed post and no key in site. This time.

"No."

"So someone snuck up on you with a step ladder, cuffed you, then threw you in a pond for fun?" I put lots of innocent butter wouldn't melt in my mouth intonation into that question.

Comanche actually turned to look at me with an almost indecipherable look. I did get I was beginning to irritate him though. I grinned back at him. What? Me tug on Superman's cape? Always!

"Tazed."

"That a name?"

Again with the cool steady look.

"Sheesh. That would explain how someone could sneak up on you. Not to mention the twitching and burns on your shirt."

The second cuff clicked off and not a moment too soon. Not that I thought he'd kill me, but men, at least the men I knew, had a tendency to be heavy handed. I butt walked a foot or two before bouncing to my feet. The lock picks slipping smoothly into my hoodie front pocket.

"Took your time." Comanche Jack said, rising smoothly to his feet, alternating hands and wrists to rub circulation back into them.

"And you're welcome!" I turned to leave. I was so outta this place.

"No." A hand closed on my arm. Not hard but I would have to put serious effort into dislodging his grip.

"No?" I turned back, frowning down at the arm.

"Games been changed." His eyes were not on me or my tugging of his hand, but looking into the distance. Someone was not in the here and now.

"Can you get any shorter in your explanations?" I snapped, tugging at the hand. Useless. Like trying to break a vise grip wrapped in velvet to let go. Fucker.

Comanche looked down at me as if seeing me for the first time. The look was, troubled. I went still and meek. That got me a raised eyebrow, but a minimal explanation.

"This was supposed to be an in and out job."

"For the bank heist money?" I asked remembering what Jeremy had said in the office I'd been in.

"No." He shook his head as if answering an internal question for himself then to mine. "No." He repeated. "For information. Not money."

"Dead guy up front says differently."

His face creased in annoyance. "He was dead when we walked in."

"So someone came in after us, but before you, and shot the innocent bystander hippy dude just because?" Lots of disbelief was conveyed.

He was looking upward towards the office. Then nodded to himself. "Time to get moving." This time the vice like grip was a little firmer, politely pulling me along with him to the stairs. I was sure I could protest, but I wasn't going to be able to stop the moving wall any time soon with just words, or, if it were Carrie, blow jobs.

Thinking of Carrie got me worried enough to chew on my inner cheek.

"Bystander, yes. Innocent, no."

"Who?"

"The man up front you mentioned." Comanche Jack looked down almost laughing. Someone wasn't tracking. I flipped him off, giving up the pretense of being meek and mild. This got me a chuckle. At least I was good for amusement. It was when he thought I might be good for other things, I'd start getting worried.

"So you say." I retorted.

"So the seven bodies we found say."

I swallowed. I hadn't seen any bodies yet but the night was wearing on and things were not looking up.

"You're not exactly free of making bodies either."

"And how many have you made, Autumn Roberts?"

"How the fuck do you know my name?!" I stopped dead, glaring up at Comanche Jack. He stopped much like someone indulging the puppy they were leash training when it had to go piddle.

"Your purse."

"I will want that back." I looked up at him with a glare, poking another finger into his back.

"Uh huh. That's high on my list of things to do." He turned to face me. "I notice you don't deny knowing it though." He touched above my eyes lightly. "Or here." He touched my lips. Gentle pressure. Warm. I snapped at his fingers, which he moved faster than the last time.

"I'm shocked." I squealed in outrage trying to hide a shiver. My voice cracking.

"That's a first." Was the dry reply.

"Not everyone is a killer." Like you was implied, but not spoken.

"But you are." Again that half smile full of knowing.

I gave him a flat stare. "Not everyone is an innocent bystander."

"Exactly." He was quiet for a moment before musing allowed. "I do wonder what Daniel's files say on you."

I froze for just a moment. FBI files. Fuck! I hadn't even thought about those. "I liked it better when you didn't talk."

"Most people don't like me speaking the truth." There was a flash of a sharp edged smile. Amused, predatory. Like Coyote's in my dream. I frowned at that, shaking my head.

"Dude let go. I don't give a shit what you're wanted for, but I'm heading back to my friend and waiting." I tugged again with the same results. Nothing.

"No. If someone is willing to kill me then no one is safe."

"Pfft. If you haven't noticed… Everyone wants to kill you hombre."

It was his turn to frown.

"Was told you were the worst of the worst murder and rapist." I really shouldn't have, but I was getting pissed off.

"So you heard. What do you think?" His voice was mildly amused and he did not look pissed at being told what a lousy human being he was.

I opened my mouth then shut it. "Not a killer to me. Several opportunities and definitely someone who has, and is willing to kill, but not a murderer. Or a rapist." I added thoughtfully.

"Why do you say that?"

"Seen killers, murderers and rapists. You have the killer vibe but not the sleazy overly sexual predatory vibe like a rapist when it's just the two of us."

"So what's your definition between a killer and a murderer?" He seemed genuinely curious.

"Murderers kill because they have to. Like being jacked or defending themselves. Killers." I shivered. "Yeah, they just like to kill. Doesn't matter who or why, but they like to kill."

"Fair enough."

I moved towards the door that leads to the upstairs office. Comanche stood like a rock for a moment, not budging though he held my arm loosely. Now or never I thought. I tried for a twist on the right heel to put my left knee in his groin, using his hand on my arm as a fulcrum point. He slapped my leg away with a free hand, stepping into me, making it impossible for me to kick while changing his grip so fast on my arm I never had a chance to move, putting me in a hold with my arm painfully behind my back again.

"Now will you stay put?"

I didn't bother answering as I tried to stomp with a foot hoping it would loosen his grip of steel. His crotch was no longer a viable target and his head was too far for me to head butt.

It was as if that bastard was reading my mind. As my foot came up, his foot lifted and hooked around mine. Locking me on one foot while his knee had come behind my knee bending into mine forcing me onto one knee. This twisted my arm further up behind my back, forcing a gasp of pain.

"Stop." He said, without animosity in my ear. I glared over my shoulder.

Far as I could tell this was not a beginner's hand to hand lesson for him. And I was very much the beginner here. He loosened the arm pin slightly. I sucked in my breath as the pain flowed like water, reversing course along the nerves.

"I need to get back to Carrie. I don't want to leave her alone. If you're not the murdering rapist, someone else here is!"

"No one was with her?"

"No. We both had been knocked around a lot today and the FBI guys let us catch a few z's on the couch upstairs.

"How did you rescue me if you were asleep?"

"Weird dream woke me up." I said with a twist of my lips. Coyote's teeth snapping in my face was not the way I wanted to wake up. A bottle of jack and a playgirl model performing cunnilingus would have been my preference.

Comanche Jack ran a tongue over his lips as if his mouth had gone suddenly dry. "How weird?"

"Fucking talking dog, wait… said his name was Coyote or something, sitting on the ceiling of the office told me to go for a swim." It was as if an electric jolt went through Comanche. He changed his grip again and started dragging me back to the pond.

"What the hell asshole!" I yelled at him, tugging against the vice like grip. "We just came from here!"

He didn't bother responding, if anything he started moving faster towards the pond. Three feet from the murky water there was a blast of sound heat and power behind us. The pool surrounded by the tall waving pot went into stark relief as if a very bright ball of flame came into existence. There were no soft edges as the memory seared into my brain. The ground bucked and heaved, throwing us toward the pond. The last foot we didn't run or even jump into the pond, but more like thrown in like a babe to sink, swim or burn.

The air was slammed out of my lungs on impact. Comanche pulled me down into the deep water wrapping his arms around me to keep me from the surface and the rolling fireball burning overhead. The light illuminated more than just the surface. There were bodies at the bottom of the pond. Bodies with eyes gone and screaming as crayfish crawled through their open mouths and picking through their clothes for the flesh underneath. I jerked hard, slamming into Comanche, my legs bumping into another body that was bobbing next to us two feet from the surface. Her dark hair moved with the eddies of current we were causing, swaying her to and fro mimicking life in the worst possible ways. The open eyes were just starting to cloud over.

I panicked. I tried to claw my way out of Comanche's arms and out of the pool of bodies. Comanche locked his grip tighter around me, wrapping his legs around mine, refusing to let go as the surface still burned. Comanche being far denser than I, caused us to sink closer to the bodies. I poked fingers into his abs. This only caused him to shift grips from around my arms to my fingers, holding, but not breaking, my hands while crossing our arms over my chest, keeping me trapped. I couldn't even slam my head into his nose; he had pulled me tight to lay his head next to mine so that there was no space between us, his hair forming a silver veil around us partially blocking the bodies. Still I struggled, but brick walls were rarely moved by trapped fists. The bodies were closer and the fire still overhead. If I could have sobbed at this point, I would have.

My lungs were burning and my eyes haloing the water and bodies from lack of oxygen. The need to breath began to overwhelm the revulsion of the bodies and still we did not surface. I looked longingly up towards the surface. With the fire burning bright from above and any oxygen left in my lungs being consumed, hallucinations were going to happen. It just wasn't the one I wanted. I'd have died happy with a playgirl model dipped in dark chocolate and a huge schlong waiting for me to come and lick him and do really fun naughty things with. What I saw was that damn yellow mutt laughing at me from over the edge of the poolroom, cocking his head to one side. The light was fading and so was Coyote, the fucker. Couldn't even stay and watch us die.

Comanche's head jerked as if he had been tased again. He unwrapped his legs and gave a powerful kick upwards, moving the water hard enough to cause the body next to us to move almost as if she was dancing. We broke the surface gasping, pulling in the sweet harsh pot smoke flavored air, tinted with just a taste of gasoline. Comanche letting go, pushing me towards the edge; I grabbed the blistering hot tile, uncaringly, as I tried to pull myself out kicking my legs. As I kicked, I could feel something bumping into me. I knew it was the body and she was dead. Nothing I could do for her or to her, but it was still a dead body. I could not get out of that pool fast enough, but I could not get the leverage and started to slip back down into the water.

Comanche had already rolled over the edge of the pool and was standing up. He knelt down in front of me, offering a hand. I almost glared, but I think I looked more panicked as I kicked the body again. I grabbed his hand, clinging to a lifeline out of that damned pool. He pulled me out as if I weighed no more than a wet cat. I staggered up then went to my knees, just sucking in air. I didn't scream or sob but I did start to shake. Fuck this place. I wanted to go home! Hell, I'd have taken a nice jail cell at this point. Anywhere else had to be safer.

Comanche squatted next to me, but gave me just a few seconds to compose myself again before tapping me on the shoulder. He had wrapped a bandana around his face to block the smoke. His eyes glimmered in the half-light. Rather similar to Coyote's I thought which was quickly followed by another thought. With the wet hair and the bandana, I could almost see us in a bad western movie. All he needed was a colt revolver and me in a bonnet and prairie dress fainting in his arms. I started to giggle.

"Now we get your friend Casey." He said ignoring my giggles.

Chapter Eleven
New Friends

"Carrie." I corrected, but nodded in agreement to the gist of the statement, while sucking in more sweet/smoky air. Comanche stood up, reaching down to pull me up by an arm. We started towards the upper office again. The explosion had ripped through part of the pot forest creating a burnt path that cut through in a wide swatch towards where the broken statues and equipment were. Seems the warehouse was mostly metal or concrete and the most damage was to the pot. The office from where we stood, looked undamaged, maybe slightly smudged, but not on fire or dangling precariously from cables.

I must have said something as Comanche responded to that thought.

"Small flash fire. Quick, but only hot enough to burn plants and paper, not enough to damage metal or concrete."

"Oh… umm… good to know." The pot was still burning merrily along, though more like smoldering and smoking which was fine with me. Even though it was getting hard to see, I was pretty giggly and getting happier by the second.

Comanche stopped. I bumped into him with another giggle. Comanche just shook his head turning to pull my hoodie off.

"Hey! No funny business now." I said pulling it down as he tried to pull it up. "Gotta take me out to dinner first!"

That got me a raise eyebrow. "You're stoned and getting worse. Pull the hoodie over your nose to block some of the smoke.

"No. The hoodie does not come off." I was glaring now, even though I really just wanted to giggle.

"Autumn."

"No. Not up for discussion. Hoodie stays down and on. Pants will come off faster than the hoodie." I said with a lascivious smile. Well as lascivious as I could under the circumstances.

This seemed to shock him as he took a step back, raising his hands almost like he was trying to placate a crazy person. Eh, maybe. The hoodie did not come off though!

"Fine, but we still need to get your friend Carrie." He said blandly, holding out a hand.

I tried nodding my assent haughtily, but I probably just looked silly, dripping wet and squelching water from my Keds with every step. Comanche did not laugh, though I could see his eyes crinkle at the corners. Whatever. I smiled and took his hand.

"Thanks BB." I said enjoying the touch now that he wasn't trying to kill Carrie or drown me.

That caused his eyebrows to raise up. " Thanks BB?"

"Well for saving my life. Again."

"You're welcome. What's the BB?" He asked over his shoulder, heading towards the office. Déjà vu.

"Boy Band Butt." I said giggling, which made me sound like Carrie. This just made me giggle even harder.

He missed a step, but didn't look back while pulling me along. "Shouldn't that have another B in there somewhere?"

"Now you're just bringing logic into this argument."

"An oversight of mine, surely, trying to talk sense with a stoner."

"Hey! I am not a stoner!"

"Uh huh."

"I enjoy a good toke like any healthy American girl, or Danish girl." This got my stomach rumbling. "Mmmm… Danishes. Errr… Danishie? Danishesese?"

"Danish. And it's your own choice."

"Thanks! I am soo happy to have your approval." The eye roll was being missed done at his back, but I'm pretty sure he got the gist in my voice.

I started to compose limericks about strong hands and wide backs. As far as I know, I didn't start rhyming out loud since Comanche didn't misstep again.

Luckily, before I could ask his opinion about limerick

number 5, we found the doorway with the stairs leading upwards. The door shimmered. Not from heat but from all the wonderful pot I was inhaling. I took another deep breath, holding for 4 seconds. Lots of smoke, no need to be greedy. I giggled again. I felt Comanche's hand squeeze mine. I stuffed part of my hoodie sleeve from my free hand into my mouth. See I can take a hint! More limericks were needed, I nodded firmly.

Comanche cocked an ear towards the door. I did the smart thing, sucked in a deep lung full and held my breath while he stood listening. He opened the door at the same time I let the smoky air out of my lungs. I dropped Comanche's hand and pushed past him to take the stairs two at a time. This surprised him so much he was a second behind me, but made no move to grab me as we jogged up the stairs.

I burst into the room heading straight for the couch. No Carrie. "I wonder who she's blowing now?" I giggled then stuffed a sleeve in my mouth at the really girly sound that came out.

"She sounds like a really great girl, the way you talk about her." Came Comanche's voice dryly behind me.

"Oh she is. And smart too!"

"Smarter than you?" He sounded genuinely curious. He was looking through the room. Prowling. Long, not lean, very muscular. Nothing seemed to be escaping his attention. Very pretty. I grinned then sighed. Sooo not happening, but nice butt.

"Yep. I mean I'm smart, but she's like a genius material if slightly lazy."

"You keep implying she's a slut." He said looking over his shoulder. His eyes glimmering. A girl could get lost trying to understand what was behind those gorgeously expressive eyes.

"Pfft. Slutty has no bearing on intelligence. No one expects the fat girl to get laid or sell dope to fund their college tuition."

"So you knew the pot was here."

"Duh! I am distribution and contact for buyers and sellers. Carrie is transpiration. That's not right. Transportation and cover. Incorporated even."

"Cover?"

"Yeah, we would go to parties and she would tart it up a bit.

Do the slut thing with me in tow as her wallflower friend. This allowed us to get into all sorts of places for selling pot.

"Weren't you worried about cops or under cover?"

"Why she had me." I said smugly.

"Knew them well did you?" He had made it to the corkboard with the newspaper clippings.

"Well enough we hadn't been caught and were paying our tuition and rent." My brain and mouth were not connected. I couldn't believe I was saying all this. I bit my hand, hard. That cut through the giggles and the pot haze somewhat.

"For how long?"

I bit harder. The pain was somewhat grounding. I shook my head. "No. Too much."

"Too much?" Comanche was giving me his full attention at this point. His eyes sharp like a hunter's. Like Rojo's before a big deal was going down. I swallowed hard, shaking my head. The smoke was working its magic though. Comanche's ears seemed to slightly elongate and start to go fuzzy with his jaw elongating.

"You know you look like Coyote at the moment." I was definitely losing my grip on reality. Comanche's eyes were blinking at this comment, out of a very different shaped head. "Either that or you're turning into a werewolf err… coyote." I was tilting my head to watch the transmogrification.

His laugh was soft, but very sincere. "While I've been called a lot of things, and done a good many to earn them, I am pretty sure that lycanthropy is not one of my talents." He had moved to stand in front of me. I reached out, tugging on the bandana playfully. He stopped my hand and I could see his chest moving in silent laughter. "You would probably enjoy talking to my aunt though."

"That's too bad. You'd be even more interesting then." I was smiling, watching his long hair sway around his waist and halo his head. Very sexy. Pfft. Who was I kidding? A five-dollar vibrator would be sexy and stimulating at this point.

"What?! You mean I'm not interesting now?" He said in mock outrage. His face was back into focus as human. High cheekbones, strong jaws and a generous mouth if a slightly thin upper lip. The scratches from the cactus were giving him an almost movie war paint effect. The dark eyes were definitely laughing at me.

"Heh. Band boyish butt, but so far pretty bland." I said with a slight flick of the hand dismissively. I realized as I said this, it was true. I was very unafraid of him, attracted yes, scared no. Something was not matching up here. I knew he was dangerous. Ok I had been told he was dangerous, but not to me.

He was saved from answering as we heard footsteps on the stairs. Comanche grabbed my hand, pulling me behind him as we moved to the side of the room against the wall next to the door. I knew enough from watching TV shows that he was close enough to get the drop on any one walking in, as long as they weren't clearing the corners like Daniel and Jeremy had done earlier. I didn't pray, but now it has crossed my mind, would be the time to start.

The first through the door was Ratface with a gun drawn, looking surprised and dismayed at the empty room, shouting something over his shoulder to whomever was behind him. He just cleared the door when Comanche grabbed the wrist holding the gun, lifted that arm up and turning Ratface to the door while grabbing his other arm up and behind in an all too familiar painful grip. Ratface squawked like a chicken being throttled, swearing loudly.

Long hair guy ran in wild eyed and gun at the ready, facing down Ratface's gun aimed at his chest. Longhair followed Ratface's gun up his arm to Comanche, who was standing Ratface up on his toes awkwardly with a pinned arm. Longhair relaxed slightly.

"Fucking put me down damn you fucking dumb ass!" Ratface wasn't stopping the yelling, not catching that it was one of his own guys holding him fast like a fly on flypaper.

"Shut up, Renniks." Comanche's voice was a deep gravelly baritone of scary badass in Ratface's ear.

Renniks snapped his jaw shut so fast you could almost hear his teeth chipping from impact. Longhair was slipping his gun into a holster that fit at the back of his waistband. Smooth and economical motion. Like it was part of his body, not just a piece of hardware. Scary. Very scary. I swallowed hard. These guys played rough. My mind flashed back to the dead hippie dude's blood on the floor. Then the bodies in the pool. I swallowed bile. Comanche may or may not have added to those, but some of his team certainly seemed capable.

I bit the inside of my lip. Too much pot. They might have killed, but the woman in the pond had been there for less than two days, maybe three. Still floating and eyes just starting to go milky. These guys had only shown up within the last few hours, same as Carrie and I. So someone else was contributing to the body count. Still wasn't making me feel better about the company I was keeping.

"There are fucking bodies all over the place." Longhair snarled.

"The feds are at the safes..." Renniks started rubbing his shoulder as Comanche released him. His gun was still out, making rubbing his shoulder more awkward.

"Put the gun up Renniks. Now!" Comanche looked down at the much shorter man. Renniks swallowed and stopped rubbing to fumble with his shoulder holster, but he didn't protest Comanche's command.

I tilted my head really looking at the shorter guy. He was just as sleazy now as he was at the diner, though the fresh black eye was new. Covered his eyebrow and an inch or so below the eye. Nicely purpled too.

"Can we get the fuck out of here now, boss?" Longhair asked. He didn't whine like Ratface would have but he definitely had an air of someone slightly freaked out. Someone else who hadn't signed up for a rerun of 'House of 1000 Corpses'.

"Safes can't be fucking opened without the keys! Marcus tried to just crack the locks but the fucking pieces of goddamn shit exploded!" Renniks was getting wound up again.

"Where is Cubby?" Comanche asked ignoring the low level hysteria.

"Following."

"He's not exactly the fastest with that fat ass of his." Ratface sneered with a curl to his lip. Right on cue we heard heavy breathing and a very heavy tread on the stairs.

I caught a glimpse of a furry tail on the ceiling out of the corner of my eye.

"How did Marcus die again?" Comanche asked.

"He fucking exploded!" Comanche looked at Renniks. Renniks toned it down but was still animated with waving hands, luckily no gun this time. "He was going to try the safes without the keys, saying there wasn't a safe he couldn't crack. So he was doing the spin and feel thing he does, writing numbers on the safe. Tried one set of numbers and the safe exploded."

Marcus… oh yeah. Big black guy that Daniel had asked about. Looked like he wasn't a part of the group anymore. More like parts. I stuffed a sleeve in my mouth again.

"And you obviously weren't in the room."

"Fuck no! We'd have been dead." Renniks rolled his eyes, giving Comanche a slightly dismissive look over his shoulder. Ratface really didn't have any common sense when to shut the fuck up, I thought. Comanche may not kill casually, but I bet he had a mean right hook.

"Then where were you when he was doing this?" Comanche asked, looking between Longhair and Renniks. They both fidgeted like kids with their fingers in a birthday cake's icing.

"Cubby found another body on the way into the safe room."

"And."

"I stayed with him while he was throwing his guts." Said Longhair. "It was in bad shape. Had to be at least a week worth of rot."

"Thought I told you to stay with Marcus." Longhair looked away first. Comanche turned to Renniks. "Why weren't you with Cubby?"

"He's a fucking pussy!"

"Say that again you asshole when I get done trashing any credit rating you have or any bank accounts you think are hidden." The heavy, dirty blond nerd had finally shown up. He was looking a hell of a lot more worse for wear than the other two. There was a definite green tint to his skin. One too many dead bodies I imagined.

"Keep your hands outta my money you retarded piece of shit!" Renniks snarled at him reaching for his gun.

"Renniks." Comanche's voice was mild, but the intent to harm was implied.

"Marcus threw me out of the room when he started to spin the dial. Said my breathing was bothering him. We sure as hell aren't going to get into those safes now!" Renniks sulked for a moment. I stared hard, full lower lip pout and everything. Damn this guy was a prima donna! I laughed aloud.

"That's for sure. You guys aren't corn fed Russians to be whacking a safe open." I giggled, thinking of Renniks trying to hammer his way into a two inch safe trying to split a seam.

Renniks jumped almost two feet up when I spoke. Longhair had his gun out and pointed at my head before I had finished the first sentence. Cubby just clutched his backpack harder. I had to give him points for not having left as of yet. I was still trying to leave, but I wasn't leaving without Carrie. This merry band of psychotic misfits didn't seem to be his scene, but he still stuck with them.

"What the fuck is she doing here?!" Renniks was fumbling for his gun and failing as his hands dropped the gun shaking so hard.

"Who is she boss?" Longhair hadn't put the gun away, but he hadn't shot me. Yet. I was so comforted.

"Hostage." Comanche said blandly, motioning for Longhair to put up his gun. Longhair hesitated for a second, but shrugged then put up the gun.

"Really? Cool!" I said, walking to the middle of the room. I looked right under the light where I thought I had seen Coyote.

"Boss?"

"She's stoned on pot smoke. We were down in the middle of it when the safe went off."

"Ahh." Longhair let the statement stand. He didn't seem to need more of an explanation.

"So is this where you tie me up and threaten me with horrible sexual depravation? Deviations? Deviant acts to make me talk." I tossed over my shoulder, tilting my head side to side looking at the dusty square light cover. I took another long deep breaths of smoky air. "Mmmm… If this doesn't qualify as a good toke, I don't know what does."

Comanche ran a hand down his face. His henchmen just looked confused. Well, the other two, Cubby just started laughing.

"You sure boss?" Longhair seemed to be having a conversation with Comanche, but it wasn't what he was actually saying. All in the sub text.

"Yeah. Tell me what you can." Comanche motioned me to sit down on the couch then sat in front of me on the floor, moving like silk, so smooth was the motion. He must do the cross-legged yoga thing regularly I thought. He handed me a comb from a back pocket, and the red leather thong. His crew seemed non pulsed. Hostages weren't that common it seemed. Yay! I was an uncommon commodity. Body? Bystander? Bystander, that was it. Innocent bystander. I started to giggle again.

Comanche was pushing his long hair behind his ears which was definitely having a mind of its own. Moving from behind the ears to cover his face or drape over his shoulder coquettishly when he flipped it back.

I worked my legs in a comfortable position on either side of his chest. What me trying to enjoy the feeling of man between my legs? Never. Though his hair was silky on my fingers as I ran the comb through his hair. The hair closer to his head was different then the hair towards the ends.

"How many bodies Nick?" He looked at Longhair, draping arms over my legs. Comfortably, like we had practiced this for years. I don't think he was really body shy or at least he was comfortable enough with stoned college chicks to relax.

"I've counted around eight so far." Said Longhair. Nick. Wonder if that was short for Nicki? I put the comb down feeling with my fingers what I had guessed at.

"Shot or strangled?"

Comanche caught one hand and put the comb back in hand and positioning my hand lower. I took the hint and combed out the longer sections trying to not tug hard before starting to braid. I couldn't remember how to do a four strand braid so a regular macho three strand braid it was.

Renniks and Nick looked at each other. This seemed to be a new thing for their boss. The whole having a hostage comb his hair before he got down to the dirty business. I could work with this.

Renniks started the body count. "Two in the hall. Shot."

"Three in the corner looked bludgeoned."

The ones in the chairs?" Renniks asked

"Yeah. The next room had the other three."

"Oh yeah. Those poor sods."

I looked up from braiding at that comment. Renniks didn't have any empathy that I'd seen. For him to say that had to be bad, but his voice didn't convey pity. There was something elusive I couldn't quite put a finger on. I looked over at Cubby, still standing in the doorway. He was turning greener. Ahh. Those most have been the ones that had made him lose his dinner.

"All done!" I chirped, finishing tying the leather thong in a bow, flipping the wrist thick braid over his shoulder. Comanche looked at the bow then at me with raised eyebrows.

"In case I have to take it off again, I won't have to chew on it." I chirped with mock girlishness. That just earned me a slight smile and crinkled eyes.

"Thank you."

"Anytime!"

Comanche got up on well-oiled joints and motioned Renniks and Nick over towards the corkboard. They were huddling, talking in soft voices looking at some of the articles.

Damn this was my day… night for déjà vu.

"Hey, Cubby was it?" He had not been invited to the huddle and was standing by the door still clutching his laptop like a teddy bear. I was sure it was probably the only thing in the world that loved him back.

"Yeah?" He was cautious. Not only was I visibly stoned, but female. And us females were tricksy things. I swallowed my giggles.

"Flip on that light switch on the wall next to you, will ya?"

He did. Damn. Still no light. Typical. I still looked up at the fixture. Was that a shadow or was it my imagination. One way to find out.

I pulled a rolling chair over and climbed up, using the back to brace myself until both feet were comfortably balanced on the arms, then stood up slowly. The light cover was frosted glass and old. "Fucker's older than I am." I muttered. Which was probably true.

The shadow was real and not a figment of some damn dog. I reached into the cover, feeling around. A small velveteen pouch was there, three inches in diameter. Square. My fingers just closed on the pouch, making me stand on tiptoe while reaching further in the glass fixture for a better hold. The chair decided to take the opportunity to roll out from underneath me. I squealed for a second and hung on to the light cover. The light cover was only attached to a ceiling tile and ceiling tiles were notorious for not being able to hold a lot of weight, like while hanging up light bulbs or trying to have sex in a swing attached to said ceiling tile... Don't ask. It was a butt bruising learning experience. The light fixture came loose from the ceiling tile and I came down with a thud trying to cover my head with arms and hands. The sound of shattering glass as the cover landed next to me on the ground was obnoxiously loud.

The crash covered the sound of a small jangling pouch in my hand disappearing into a sleeve.

"You ok?" Cubby asked. He helped me up as I rubbed my butt cheek. Yep, ceiling tiles and my butt did not mix. Owwww!

"Probably. My turn to rescue you now." I giggled. He just looked confused, not getting the joke. Sigh. Location jokes while stoned were always hard to explain. So I didn't.

Comanche was looming next to us, with Cubby's hand on my arm as I was tilting dangerously to one side even with his help.

"A hunch with a fuzzy tail that ended with shattered glass and dead bugs." I said, grinning upwards to the looming man and gesturing towards the littered ground.

I got a glare, but not a fuck you.

"Sit!" he growled at Cubby and me, pointing towards the couch.

"Really?" I swear this was getting old.

"Really."

Cubby slunk to the far end and opened up his square-headed girlfriend without another word. This must be something commonly said to him. Sheesh. That boy needed a backbone.

"Woof!" I said, sitting on the other end of the couch. Comanche glared at me as he went back to his huddle, causing me to giggle and leaned over the side of the couch, enjoying the world tilting with me.

Nick didn't keep his voice quiet. "Boss, she's a liability. Not to mention really stoned."

"I hadn't noticed." Comanche was actually pretty good with sarcasm too. Nick opened his mouth, but Comanche cut it short with a clipped sideways hand gesture. They went into their huddle. Their voices lowered as they went over the newspaper clippings. We, Cubby and I, were being thoroughly ignored. I was enjoying the high to really give a shit, though a cigarette would be nice right about now. I licked my lips while searching my pockets in vain.

I heaved a sigh. I was sooo going to have to fix this no cigarette issue when this was over. My mind started going on tangents of flavored pot cigarettes. Clove or lemon flavor? Perhaps a nice herbal. Something that would complement the taste of pot. Spicy.

Chapter Twelve
Dark Hallways

I was pretty lost in the tasty smoke ideas when a flicker of fur to my left caught my eye. I turned and looked with a curious tilt of my head. The door seemed to tilt with me while the walls stayed upright. Coyote sat just outside the door. His tongue lolled out and he had what would have been an abnormally large doggy grin. I had to think for a moment. That smile would have split the head of any regular dog, yet, on Coyote, it just looked natural. Weird mutt.

Coyote gave a quick tilt to his head then turned, walking towards the stairs. He looked over his shoulder flicking an ear at me, slowly wagging his tail. I giggled at him. Why not, I thought. Comanche's crew was still deep in discussion and ignoring those of us in exile on the couch. I got up and walked through the door, following behind Coyote. The pouch fell back into my hand. I dropped it into the front pocket of the hoodie. I counted 8 keys by feel. Maybe. I hoped I could still count, but I was still sure that numbers hadn't changed while I was high.

"I just need to be higher." I said aloud.

"That would not be a good idea." Said Coyote.

"Pfft… what would a mutt know of getting high?"

"Other than it opens you up to being highly suggestible to suggestions?"

"You mean like following a figment of someone else's imagined pantheon that can talk? Don't know what you're talking about." More giggles.

The stairs ended at the other door. Coyote looked at me then at the doorknob. Damn dog needed thumbs. I opened it up. The pot forest was mostly gone. There were a few plants left but those were scorched and drooping.

"No more pot." I said mournfully.

"Probably not your biggest concern at the moment." Came the reply to my left.

"No, I'm being led through hostile Indian territory by a talking dog." The thought of Comanche hostile just made me wonder what really was under his shirt and his pants. Hmm… maybe him and Daniel? Nah. Bad combination. Differing heights let alone different personalities. Sigh. I put that thought in my happy fun girl party file for late night alone time and my favorite vibrator.

"You would rather be sitting back in the office?" Coyote interrupted some really fun thoughts, bringing me back to reality.

"Nah. I really need to find Carrie."

A large predatory smile from Coyote. "Then Carrie we shall find."

The warehouse wasn't really a maze, just big boxes under one roof, each box having two or three doors. The junk scattered in each box though made negotiating through the rooms much like avoiding a demented child's Lego blocks scattered willy nilly.

"Willy nilly." I giggled. Coyote looked at me with cold calculation that cut through even my fogged up brain. "What? It's not like this should be news to you."

"Sit." Was all he said, motioning towards a random piece of unknown machinery.

"Woof!" I giggled at the role reversal, but I sat compliantly on a mostly horizontal surface. I admired the subtle grays and blacks along the machinery and floor. I was definitely feeling no pain.

"So now what, oh guiding light of fleas and lost children?"
Coyote flashed his very sharp teeth at me. "Pet me."
"Huh?"
"My fur is itchy and you have hands." He offered the side of his jaw to me with a slight tilt of his head.

I had to laugh, but did as instructed. Petting the proffered jaw and along his head behind the ears as he moved his head to get the best scratches for uncoordinated hands. His fur was very soft to the touch. I didn't feel any scabs or scars along the skin, like Rojo's dogs usually had. Coyote leaned into the petting harder. I was happy to accommodate. I was pretty sure he wasn't going to snap or bite my hand if I petted too hard.

"Ewww… damn mutt, you're drooling."

"Shhhh. Keep scratching." He rolled an eye at me, his tail thumping happily. "How do you feel?" Coyote asked after a couple more minutes of scratching.

"Feel?" I asked. I thought for a moment the lethargy and haze of the pot was starting to fade.

"Fuck! My high! You took it. Damn it! I had a good toke going." I glared at the damn dog, pushing him away and standing up.

Coyote stretched his front paws out and yawned widely. I could almost hear his back pop. I had a really good look at those sharp canines again. I clenched my jaw. "You are not going to intimidate me." I snapped.

"Good." He gave his body a shake, sending fur flying. The strands drifted down to add interesting patterns to the soot covered floor. I turned and looked at the ass of my jeans. Nothing. No soot and no dog fur. I looked back at Coyote.

"If I'm not stoned and not asleep, how the hell am I seeing you?"

"Magic." Was all he said with a smile. He was definitely laughing at me. Great.

I closed my eyes counting to ten then opened them up again. Nope, still there and I was still in a grungy fucked up warehouse with a talking mutt.

He nudged my hand. The cold nose was a real sensation. I sighed. Fine. Coyote nudged my hand again. I scratched behind his ears.

"You could have left the high in place, you know."

"You need to be thinking, not hazing." His eyes were closed in pleasure, making watching his lips move, speaking even weirder than it was already.

"Ok mutt, you got your scratches. Let's find Carrie."

It was his turn to sigh. At least he didn't pout. A pouting figment with a cold nose was going to be more than even I could handle at this point. With a flick of an ear, as if to say "I heard that." Coyote motioned me to follow him. We were back on our adventure.

Chapter Thirteen
Found

We moved on to a different part of the warehouse. The lights were off, though I could see. The room was almost pitch black. I was pretty sure Coyote would say "Magic" again if I asked him how this was happening. So I didn't. I'd already had my three impossible things happen to me today as it was. A few more might overload the system.

The original blast area was closer. The soot was thicker with particles still floating through the air, to add to the collecting debris on the floor. Here the walls were darker, showing scratch marks along the walls in a stark contrasting white. Made by what, or even who, I couldn't tell. All the regular lighting was gone. Fluorescent light bulbs crunched under my feet, the metal housings bent and twisted along the wall to my left.

The hallway had a few doors leading to gods knew where. Only one or two were intact. Most had been blown off their hinges, showing more burnt pot plants in melted plastic buckets. What a waste.

The good news, I could see a bright light at the end of the hall. I was pretty sure I wasn't dead so I had hopes we were close to our destination.

The bad news, I remembered all the late night horror flicks my sister's boyfriend and his cronies stayed up watching, drunk off their asses yelling at the screen when someone got killed. Then there were the movies that showed grotesque and violent ways to die they watched with rapt attention as if taking notes. Julio especially. That *esse* was a sick fuck.

I shivered. Whether from the dark or the memories, I wasn't really going to dwell on. There was a bump against my leg, which startled me enough to let out a yelp before I realized Coyote was having his fun at my expense. I glared down at him.

The damn thing dropped his jaw at me in canine laughter. *Bastardo*.

"I did not have parents. Rather hard to be a bastard." He replied.

"Luckily I wasn't questioning your parentage."

"Does this mean I get a point?"

I stopped for a second then had to laugh. "Point to you mutt."

"Coyote."

"Quite trying to scare the shit out of me and I'll call you by a proper name."

"Bastard is not my name either." He said primly.

"Now you're just being picky." I smiled as we continued. I wasn't nearly as scared as I had been, the company, though weird, was at least good.

"I am not good either. I am chaotic."

I had to think for a second. "Does that make you chaotic evil or good randomly?"

An ear flicked. "Both." Was his reply.

"How can you be both good and bad?"

"Practice."

I opened my mouth, then closed it. Rojo could do good, but mostly he had been a nasty man. I did not want Coyote turning loose his bad side. I shivered. One more body among those already in here wouldn't be news to anyone. I concentrated on the light ahead instead. Something more cheerful than a multiple personality dog with a really big bite that didn't worry about good or bad.

I approached the lit room with caution. I listened at the door before slinking around the frame. Coyote laughed at me and sauntered in. I kept my thoughts to myself, though I'm pretty sure he could still "hear" me. I got a flick of the ear for that one too.

The room looked like a bombed out bunker complete with warped industrial metal furniture, scorched black and twisted into odd forms, vaguely recognizable in post bombed sculpting.

I was about to leave this room when I noticed the pile in the corner wasn't furniture but a body. A body with bright blonde hair.

"Carrie!" I rushed forward breathing in huge gasping sobs. No No NO! Was all I could think as I slide on the concrete to roll the body over. I needed to see her face.

My hand touched her shoulder and she struggled to turn over. Her mouth was duct taped. Her hands and feet bound with zip ties. She was struggling wildly till she saw who it was and sobbed behind the duct tape in relief. Tears welled and tracked down her face, cutting through the soot and grime.

"Hey hey, hon, I'm here."

I tried to give her a hug, but she shook her head, moving her lips under the duct tape while trying to shake the tears from her cheek. She hated crying the way most people hated paying taxes.

I grabbed one edge of the duct tape. "Ready for me to rip?"
She nodded fervently.

I ripped the duct tape off, wincing at the sound, but tried for levity. "No need for a waxing this week, chica!"

"Oh my fucking god! Get me out of this please, Autumn!" He voice was barely a whisper. She didn't even try for a comeback. Now I knew she was scared. I didn't ask any questions, but got to work getting her freed.

I pulled the lighter out of my pocket and went after the zip ties. I got the feet first. If we had to leave quickly, I wanted her able to get up and moving. Then on to her hands. The edges of her skin, where the ties had been, were dark red and ridged. Someone had not only been thorough, but cruel. I had to aim the flame very carefully so as not to catch her skin.

"Damn girl! Who the fuck did you piss off."

Carrie sobbed, looking away. I looked up, stopping.

"Don't stop!" she hissed. "He might come back!"

"Who?" I relit the lighter, trying by will make the plastic melt faster.

"Karl. The Klingon." I looked at her startled. Stopping for a sec before starting again.

"You were right." Her voice wasn't even close to normal. She sucked in a breath trying not to sob.

"Damn we are in a bad situation, if you're admitting that."

"Bitch!" She giggled, but there were still tears rolling down her cheek. "The four of us saw you had left and Daniel got worried. We headed down to the pot forest when the explosion hit." She tried to wipe a cheek but was still tied.

"Daniel and Jeremy waited till the fire was minimal then ran towards the explosion point."

"Leaving Karl in charge of you?"

"Bastard!" She snarled. "Brought me here then put a gun to my head. Made me zip tie my ankles then he did my wrists." She started to shake. "He promised he would be back and what he did to the other girls was nothing to what he had planned for me." Her eyes were huge. She yanked her wrists away for a moment to dig heels into her eyes to keep from crying. She took a deep breath, her generous mouth edging to a thin line.

"I don't want to be here when he finishes killing Daniel and Jeremy."

I nodded and started burning the wrist zip tie again.

"We're going to be looong gone before that bastard has a chance to realize you're missing."

I tugged on the last strand. Carrie hissed rubbing her wrists but struggling to get to her feet as fast as possible. Her ankles weren't any better, possibly worse. I slipped an arm around her waist to help her up, and slung her right arm over my shoulder.

I was thinking furiously. There were two to four doors per room in this place. I looked for Coyote, but he had managed to disappear again somewhere among the finding and freeing of Carrie.

"Do you know which way he went?"

"Yeah, out that door." She gestured to the door behind us. The one to my left as I had entered the room.

"Oh good. We're going out this door then." I nodded to the one I had just come through. I was pretty sure we could back track to a side hallway.

"That going to take us out of here?"

"Not exactly."

"What?! Autumn, please, I don't want to be here anymore!"

"If we leave now, Drombal will be waiting for us and a really small cell. Anything we say will be used against us as our fault." I swallowed. "We need evidence that Karl and the hippie were neck deep in nefarious shit."

"Which means we need to hit the vaults." Carrie sighed unhappily connecting the dots.

"Let's go and get our get out of jail card."

"Drombal is going to be pissed." Carrie and I shared the same smile. We both liked this idea.

Carrie was not moving fast. "Sorry feet are still asleep." We were talking in hushed whispers. The hallway was still dark, but the light from the room behind us illuminated enough we didn't run into the downed and twisted furniture.

"Usually they are up behind your ears, so this has got to be a first."

"Fuck you!" she hissed while giggling.

"Point to me!"

I found the door I was looking for. The door was solid steel and still intact. This looked to be about the right place for the room with the broken statues and machinery. Good hiding places in case someone else was coming through there. The room after that should be where the vaults were.

I had Carrie sag against the wall while I pushed against the door. Locked. Of course it was. I glared at the door, shoving my hands in the hoodie in frustration. Lighter was there, key pouch was there, and the lock picks. Lock picks? "Oh fuck! He is going to be so pissed at me." I whispered, pulling the picks out. I knelt in front of the door to get a better view.

"Thought you left yours at home." Carrie asked. She had seen me use picks on several different occasions, but I usually didn't bring them while buying. Too many pat downs and I hated losing a good set to some thug copping a feel while patting me down. I brought out the picks mostly for when we did a little B&E to get the money we were owed. Like any working girl, neither of us could afford to be stiffed.

"I did. These are Comanche's."

"Comanche!" She let out a strangled squeal. "How the hell did you steal those from him!"

"Chica, I've had a hell of a night." I said grinning up at her before turning back to the lock at hand.

"Sexy tongue." Carrie said snidely. I couldn't talk and pick. Nor flip her off in the middle of picking. The tongue, sticking out, was a force of habit that I was going to break after this night though.

"Open sesame." I whispered, turning the knob. The door opened almost anticlimactically into a large open room with machinery and broken statuary. I sagged in relief. Not safe but getting closer to getting out of here with our hides intact. The picks were tucked back in my hoodie for further safekeeping.

"Now for the treasures!"

I laughed. Carrie never had a rough childhood except to choose whether she wanted whole grain toast or wheat for breakfast, but damn the girl was quick to pick up on the important things.

"Yes, do tell how you were going to pick a safe lock." Said a dry voice from behind us.

I got up with a helping hand from Carrie. She squeezed my hand in warning.

"Dude, if I could pick locks I would not be in this hell hole of a pot farm with its multiple dead bodies." I said laconically, turning slowly. "And good morning Agent Lozano." I said with a smile.

Daniel was standing in the middle of the hallway, his gun out and pointing at us in a very steady hand. "Carrie seems to think you can pick locks and you were on your knees." The gun was lowered, but the eyes never left mine.

"This door had metal wedged into it and required nimble fingers. Carrie's fingers are nimbler than mine, but Karl managed to do some damage from zip tying her. As for picking locks, I picked a bus locker with my stuff in it using a driver's license. Carrie's been impressed ever since, convinced I'm the next Houdini."

"Houdini usually had help. And I've noticed she's not that easy to impress."

"True dat!"

Daniel looked like he had had a rough day as well. Hair mused and tie off kilter. Jeremy was nowhere to be seen. "We're moving."

"What, no questions as to how Carrie was zip tied or where I was at?"

"Would it do anything but piss me off?"

I licked my lips, thinking. "Probably not."

"Then you can fill me in later. Right now, we're heading to a different room."

"One with vaults."

He narrowed his eyes, but gave a curt nod. He turned his back to us and started walking through the hallway.

"Did I mention I got to cop a feel on his butt earlier." Carrie whispered loudly as we meekly walked through the door.

Daniel only twitched a little.

"Was it firm?" I asked with a wink.

"Very!"

"If you two would be quiet, we might not run into bad guys for the rest of this night." Daniel said over his shoulder. His voice mild, but there was a growl in there.

Carrie got her meek and mild face on while I helped her to walk again.

That's my girl. I thought. Stupid college girls. We're just stupid college kids at the wrong place at the wrong time. I was really hoping Daniel was going to buy that, but my hopes weren't high.

Chapter Fourteen
Out in the Open

We walked into a much bigger warehouse office room and stopped. The decoration was bombed out Berlin, prior to that I think it had been empty. There was nothing but scorch marks all over with embedded pieces of metal in the concrete walls. There seemed to be some red gooey bits here and there as well. Marcus, I would bet. The only things left standing were the other five safes spaced through the room every 5 feet. Daniel stopped a few steps into the room, jerking to a stop. I heard a safety click off. Daniel spun towards the sound, his hand going to his gun. He stopped turning with a frown at the other agent, noting the lack of Jeremy and the gun pointed at Carrie and I. ""Karl, where is…. They're with us." Daniel's voice held annoyance but he quit reaching for his gun.

Carrie clutched my arm. I was trying to breathe evenly though I was right there in the scared category with Carrie.

"Yeah, I know. Now put your weapon on the ground and hands up." Karl looked very self-satisfied.

Daniel shot me a look. I looked at him with a closed face. Not the time to say "I told you so." If we survived, I was going to call his ass up every damn day for the rest of my life and say that to him.

Daniel reached into his jacket to the shoulder holster. He pulled his gun out with two fingers. His left hand held up and away from his body.

"Toss it towards me." Karl said. Daniel complied, his face blank of any emotion.

"Where is Jeremy?" Daniel asked as if talking to a child.

Karl gave him a nasty smile. "He's a little tied up at the moment. Now on your knees, hands over your head."

Daniel lowered himself slowly to the ground. This part

never ended up well when an agent was on the ground.

"Now cross your legs over each other."

Daniel did as instructed.

I caught a glimpse of a furry tail just outside the door in the corner of my eye. I licked my lips. Hopefully, the cavalry was coming. Stalling was going to hurt.

"You might want to give him a pillow so he's at the right height to give you a BJ." I drawled at him. Karl moved faster than I had given him credit for. I didn't get my arm up fast enough to block the Glock stock to my cheek bone. Something caught on my lower lip, coming down causing my lip to split, bleeding profusely.

Even Daniel had been taken aback by the sudden violence. "No!" He shouted. Daniel tried to get up, but couldn't before Karl had a gun trained on him again.

Karl was breathing heavily, but not from exertion. "After I skull fuck you twenty ways to Sunday, bitch, I'm going to tie you on top of the fertilizer bomb awake and alive with the clock just out of reach. Just so you can see your death coming." He was trying for calm and failing.

"As long as it's the end of seeing your disappointing 3 inch dick, short stuff." I snapped. Karl was turning a very interesting shade of red.

"Autumn!" Daniel hissed.

"He's going to kill us as it is. Fucker is your killer."

"He's FBI." Daniel said glaring at me. I think it was just to remind Karl most things could still be forgiven and not trying to refute the obvious.

"Not to belabor the point, but he has a fucking gun on us!" I yelled, glaring back.

Karl cleared his throat. Daniel and I glared back at him for interrupting our argument.

"How did you peg me?" He was talking to me. Joy.

"Besides the beady eyes and the nasty vibes? The killer Daniel's been chasing wouldn't have rescued me out of the tanker he had just dropped me into." I snapped.

"Who rescued you?" Daniel asked. He knew it wasn't himself or Jeremy or Karl. That left very few options left on the chessboard, or a new player.

"Comanche."

"He's a killer!" Karl screamed at me, spittle sprayed as if to emphasize the point. His eyes were wide and bugging out of his skull.

"Probably." I agreed mildly. Didn't want to push him into shooting us unless that was the very last option to being skull fucked. "But not the women the FBI have accused him of. If he's killed, it's been in self-defense."

"You got that from him rescuing you?" Daniel interjected into the by play.

"And when I rescued him."

"Stockholm's Syndrome." Daniel dismissed with a wave of a finger from laced hands on top of his head.

"Not enough time." Said another voice, deep and vibrating. Comanche leaned casually against the doorframe behind Karl.

"My hero!" Breathed Carrie.

"Down girl! Down! I'm all out of wipes." I said, but my knees were weak in relief.

"I'll take his shirt." Carrie was definitely measuring the breadth of the shoulders with her eyes.

Karl moved forward, hitting me again on the same spot with his gun butt, sending both Carrie and I to the floor. I shook my head to see where Karl was standing, but he had moved behind us now. Fucker moved fast. I glared at him over my shoulder. I really wanted to run him over with a car. Repeatedly.

"You don't have a gun, Jason." Karl snapped.

"Seemed to have lost mine in a pool. But I don't need one to deal with you." Comanche shrugged, but he kept his eyes on Karl.

"Didn't want to leave bullets. Wanted to make this look like a heist fuck up, but, hey, I'll go with the flow." Karl said with a smile, raising his gun to take aim.

A gun went off with a large bang two feet from behind me. Carrie flinched, squeezing my fingers so hard I would have sworn they were going to break. There was a thud, but it wasn't Comanche. I turned to look. Karl was down and twitching. The gun dropped from his hand and Jeremy pulling up the wires from a taser. There was a new hole in the wall about 4 feet to the right of Comanche.

"Thank you, Jeremy." Comanche nodded to the tall FBI agent behind us. Nick was behind Jeremy with a gun out. Not trained on Jeremy, but on Karl.

Comanche moved into the room with Renniks and Cubby behind him.

Chapter Fifteen
We've Got Nothing

Daniel stood up and went to his gun, picking it up. He did a check on the barrel but did not put it up.

Both he and Comanche looked at each other, measuring.

"Going to be difficult going in, Jason?"

"You've got nothing on me."

"We have your DNA at the crime scenes and bite marks."

"Not my DNA, nor my teeth." Comanche said calmly. No, not Comanche… Jason was being pretty laid back with a man holding a gun on him.

"Your hair was at every scene. Long white hair." Daniel clarified motioning to Jason's thick braid.

"His hair is short." I said. Carrie and I had moved out of the line of site with a good sideline seat to watch the show. No popcorn but we could live with that.

Daniel didn't take his eyes from Jason. "What did you say?" As if he wasn't quite sure I was speaking English.

"Comanche's hair is short and dyed. Those are extensions. His roots are going to need a touch up in a few days or they will be really showing the black roots." I opened my hands trying to placate with fact. "So whoever's hair was on your victims, wasn't his."

"Short?" Daniel was not going to believe me. Jason's face was stone, not helping.

"Then where did the long hair come from and why does it have his DNA?" Daniel snapped.

"My grandfather cut his braid before he died. He gave it to me for luck. I cut my own braid off then dyed my hair white. My braid went into a bon fire. My grandfather's braid was in my desk, then vanished two weeks later."

"At the Bureau." Daniel said.

"At the Bureau." Comanche agreed.

"The shooting victims." Daniel said grimly.

"Check the gun calibers. The one he usually carries won't match. It's too big." Said Nick. "But Marcus carried several different types and those might."

"Marcus is a bit torn up to go and ask." I said dryly. That got me glares from all over the room. I shrugged. Try to be helpful and everyone gets mad at you. Sheesh.

I had a thought.

"Did Marcus carry a Desert Eagle?" I asked.

"No." Came from both Comanche and Nick.

"Desert Eagle."

"Both the old man hippie and the manager from the diner, were shot with a Desert Eagle .50." I looked at Renniks. "Ratface carries a short man's compensating gold plated Desert Eagle .50."

Renniks reached for his gun, but not before Comanche moved. He grabbed Renniks' wrist, forcing it up behind his back, slamming him into the concrete wall. Then he wrapped his free arm around Renniks' throat in a chokehold.

"Karl should have let me just shoot you when I had the chance." Renniks coughed in pain at Comanche.

"You tried to have me killed." Comanche said, in a very low, very reasonable tone. That seemed to scare Renniks even more as he started to really struggle. Much like a rat being held by a cougar. All squirm and squeal, only delaying the inevitable.

Renniks made more choking sounds, turning an almost alarming shade of purple.

"Hoss, if you kill him you'll do his time." Said Nick, who still hadn't moved any further into the room. Good line of sight and an exit nearby, I thought.

Comanche kept with the chokehold just long enough for Renniks to pass out. "Good point." Comanche laid the knocked out gunman on the floor.

Jeremy crossed the room to hand Comanche a pair of cuffs. Comanche nodded his thanks before turning the laid out Renniks face down and cuffing his limp wrists behind the back. Renniks was going to wake with a massive headache. I wanted to give him a swift kick in the balls, but that would just be redundant at this point. Maybe later when he could see the kick coming.

"*Bastardo*!" I said softly.

I looked at Nick who was still holding a gun, but not pointing it at any one. I got up leaving Carrie on her own for a moment to rifle through Karl's pockets. I found two phones, one disposable and one regular, another gun, an empty syringe and two detonators. I laid everything to the side as I found it. I flipped open one of the phones out of curiosity then slammed it shut and put it someplace safe.

Jeremy reached for that one, but I slipped it into my bra. He stopped with his hand a foot away from my boobs. He glared and I gave him a smile that could have frozen lava.

I opened the disposable first and called speed dial one. Renniks pocket started to ring Saturday Night Fever. I rolled my eyes, no accounting for taste. I picked up the second one and moved by Carrie. She raised an eyebrow, but it was Comanche who asked. "What are you thinking girl."

I looked Daniel square in the eye. "You're not going to like this next one."

I dialed the second phone. Nick's phone rang. A real phone, not disposable. Comanche stood up, looking at him coldly. At least the ring tone was more acceptable. Nickleback's "Leader of Men". Nick nodded, switched his grip to two fingers before tossing it to Comanche who caught it with one hand that engulfed the gun, making the Glock 21 look petite.

"Why?" Comanche growled.

Nick looked at Jeremy then back to Comanche. "Deep cover. The Bureau wanted to know who had gone rogue and who had not." Comanche nodded slowly. Seems he was taking Nick not being a hard-core drug-running killer pretty well. Jeremy pulled out his own phone and dialed a number. Nick's phone rang with that one as well. This time it was Daniel who looked like he was sucking on a lemon.

"Who here other than Ratface and us girls, isn't FBI?" I asked into the silence. Cubby raised his hand tentatively, but put it down when the other agents gave him a hard look.

Comanche laughed. "They aren't stupid."

Daniel glared at Jeremy. Jeremy shrugged and spread his hands in apology. "Sorry."

"We're going to have a chat when this is over."

"No one is going to like that one." Jeremy sighed, rubbing his damaged hand.

"Why us?" Carrie squeaked in the tense silence.

"Wrong place, wrong time, and you both have files." Said Jeremy, not unkindly. Carrie made a face at him. So much for trying to hit Asian bliss in a burnt out warehouse with multiple dead bodies for booty card box.

"Easy targets and we wouldn't be missed by too many people." I said bitterly, glaring at Daniel. He didn't even bother to deny it, nor did he look particularly apologetic.

Carrie and I looked at each other. She chewed a bottom lip, tilting her head to Daniel and crew. I shrugged.

"Are we under arrest?" I asked cautiously.

"No."

"But Autumn will never get into the DoJ with her record will she." Comanche said. Not really a question.

"Probably not." Jeremy said, and he did sound contrite at this.

I sucked in a breath like I had been punched in the gut. My dream.

"What's in the safes?" Carrie asked.

"Bank heists that Renniks and Darts stashed." Said Jeremy. Carrie and I looked at him.

"The man running the pot warehouse. The hippie." Jeremy clarified.

"Hippie dude was a thief?" Carrie sounded appalled. Pot grower was an acceptable job for old hippies but not bank robbing it seemed.

Jeremy squirmed slightly. "Darts wasn't in charge, but was an accomplice. Daniel and I were checking out not only the murders, but the bank heist. There were similarities in forensics we were trying to tie together."

"But nothing tying Karl to the actual heists."

Jeremy shook his head.

"What about the murders?"

"Only DNA we have is Comanche's or what we thought was Comanche's."

"And that has been compromised." I said.

"Yep."

"We'll need to run a full scan and do dental." Said Daniel.

I looked at Comanche. "Jeremy used to be your partner, didn't he?"

It was Nick who answered. "Yes."

Comanche raised an eyebrow, looking at his crewmember.

Nick shrugged. "I read the files before taking the assignment."

"And you knew Jeremy how?" I said looking at Comanche

"Academy." Comanche said.

"So when Carrie and I described Comanche and crew in the cars, you knew there were other players?"

"Something like that." Jeremy said blandly.

I could really fucking hate all of them.

"Can Karl be pinned with anything? Like attempted murder of Carrie, or me?"

"I'd be willing to testify to that!" Carrie spoke up, rubbing her raw wrists.

"It could be argued he was trying to save your life." Daniel had a sour look to his face. Even with us testifying, he would probably walk. Daniel knew this and so did we. Nothing concrete.

"What about the bodies?"

"What bodies?"

"The ones in the pond."

Daniel and Jeremy exchanged looks. Daniel cocked an eye at Comanche, who nodded. "About eight, I'd say."

"Fuck!" Nick blanched.

"Yours?" Daniel asked to Comanche.

"No." Comanche's voice dropped into a menacing rumble.

"Water clears out a lot of DNA." Jeremy sounded bitter. Sounded like he had another case that got watered down. "So even if it was Comanche's or not, we won't have a lot to work with."

"So there is no DNA that matches Karl?"

"That we know of." Daniel said thoughtfully. He was no longer ruling out Karl as a killer. Yay!

I narrowed my eyes.

"We followed the DNA for Comanche and a CODAS DNA database."

"I hear a but."

"If he framed Comanche, it was spot on. He may have planted other false information."

"Like the bite marks?"

"Like the bite marks." Daniel agreed.

"What about sperm?"

"None found."

"Thought Karl said… damn. Never mind." I sighed, looking at Karl's inert body with disgust.

"No you can't just give him an acid bath." Carrie stage whispered.

"Spoil sport." I muttered back.

"So what's in the safes?" Carrie asked.

"We think it's from the bank heists. Six heists, six vaults. Well five vaults now." Jeremy said.

"Just the bank heists?"

"We won't know until we get a bomb squad out here."

"Would there be anything in there tying Karl to the heists?"

"We won't know till we get them open." Jeremy said patiently. It was late and we were all frazzled, but Jeremy still had this cool calm aura going. How the hell, I don't know.

"Fuck!" Talk about a round robin of bullshit.

"Not now dear, too much soot. I might get dirty." Carrie giggled. Someone was feeling good again.

Chapter Sixteen
Following the Script

I put my hands back into my hoodie. My fingers running across the bundle of keys.

I licked my lips, thinking. One chance it seemed.

"If I can open the safes would you be willing to expunge our records?" I looked at Daniel.

"No." But he held up a hand stalling my protest. "But I might be able to get a court order to lock them for extenuating circumstances under juvenile." He said juvenile as if we were still 14. I gave him a saccharine smile. Laugh it up, *esse*, I thought.

"In writing." I looked at Carrie. She had her own highflying plans that FBI and police records would be an issue for. "For both of us." I said firmly.

"What, you have pick locks?" Daniel asked irritatedly.

"Nope, but Comanche does in his hair extensions." I said with a smile and a suggestive wink.

"That just sounds so wrong." Mount St. Carrie was jiggling with her chortling. She covered her mouth with both hands trying not to laugh out loud and failing miserably.

"Yeah, you're more useful when you smuggle full sandwiches in your bra at we go to the movies." I said dryly. "You're a sure thing, he's once in a murder it seems."

"Bitch!" She tried to smack my arm. Yet, even sitting next to her, she still couldn't connect a swing. If we survived this, I was going to make sure she got some punching time with aim in. Comanche was irritated. Either at Daniel and his dead body comment or me for just being…well me. Hard to tell.

"Can you two be serious for five minutes?" Daniel snapped. Bodies and money. He hated one and was good at finding the other. I nodded in apology. I could see how our levity would give him an ulcer.

"Yes or no?" I said to him.

"Last guy who tried to pick the locks got blown up." Nick said, edging back towards the other doorway. Someone had self-preservation in mind still.

"And I don't lend my picks to just any one." Said Comanche, with hooded eyes, his arms crossed over his smoke and soot smudged white shirt.

I gave Comanche a slow, sultry, cheesy smile "Aww, but baby I've already had my hands on your picks." I batted my eyes at him. Comanche coughed back a laugh and Jeremy looked slightly offended.

Daniel may have been offended, but he knew a good offer when he heard one. "I would prefer not to explode, but I really want to nail someone's hide to the wall for the bodies piling up."

"Wait! You're going to trust some pot seller to pick safes?" Nick snapped, affronted by Daniel's seemingly callous call.

"I think Autumn's had better than average training in opening safes." It was Daniel's turn for a sly smile. Getting a bit of his own back from the other agent.

Nick turned to look at Jeremy. Jeremy chewed his lower lip, flexing damaged fingers. But he too nodded.

"Fuck you all!" Nick exploded, but he didn't leave. He looked angry and scared with wide eyes, and rubbing sweating palms along his jeans. He had been here when Marcus went to pieces.

Comanche's turn to chuckle.

"What? No nay say from the other peanut gallery?" I asked.

"I've seen your files, and had a few run ins with Rojo's gang. If you're even half as good as Juan, these safes should be within your skill range." Shrugging a shoulder Daniel said, without sarcasm on the back handed compliment.

"Thaaaanks." My voice dripped sarcasm. "So that's a yes, Agent Lozano?"

"If we survive, you get your files locked."

"How about you put that in writing first?" I suggested, crossing my arms over my chest.

"Pen and paper." He put his gun up, holding out a hand.

I opened my mouth, then closed it, looking at Carrie. She shook her head. "Nothing in my bra either."

"That's a first." I said sarcastically.

"Ohh!" Carrie wound up for the cutting wound, but was cut off at the knees when Daniel growled. "Girls! Focus please." Carrie snapped her mouth closed, but I could see she was storing up for something later. I grinned wickedly. Game was always on no matter when or where it seemed.

"Seems we're sort of stuck at the moment." Daniel said tiredly. The night was starting to take its toll on everyone.

A voice spoke up behind Comanche. "I have paper." Cubby moved out from behind the huge man to stand next to him in the doorway, edging in while searching through his computer case. He pulled out a small pad of paper.

"I... I don't have a pen though." He said sheepishly. I smiled at him in thanks and took the pad.

"I have a pen." Jeremy said, reaching inside his suit jacket. Daniel narrowed his eyes at Jeremy, Carrie giggled. Nothing like watching partners work together. And I was betting Daniel did not want to actually have to do what he promised in passing. A bad idea when you needed to squeeze later on.

The paper and pen were handed over to Daniel. It took him a moment or two for each note. He handed them to me for review, certainly not for approval. I passed them on to Carrie. She looked over them for a moment.

"Pen please." She said looking up to Daniel. He jerked slightly with a puzzled look, but handed the pen over. She made a scribbling mark on each note.

"If you would be so kind as to initialize the change." Her voice was cool and professional.

Daniel took the returned note like a man being offered a possibly venomous snake. He looked at the changes. His mouth quirked up.

"Really?"

"Yes." Carrie said primly. I was fascinated. I had never seen her actually become "Professional" in demeanor or tone. Silly, slutty, frustrated, and cunning. But professional?! I think my skull was about to explode.

Daniel initialized without a quibble, handing the notes back to Carrie. She took them to Jeremy to sign as a witness. She tapped her teeth with the pen for a second then handed them to Nick to sign as well. Once signed the notes, notepad and pen went into her impressive cleavage.

"What? You don't want me to sign as well?" Comanche asked in an amused, lazy voice. He was definitely amused, wearing a half smile.

"Would love to." Carrie fluttered her eyes at him. "But even with Autumn's high endorsement of you…" She made that one sentence sound like we'd been fucking in the back room all night. "Until you're cleared, your signature would do more harm than good."

Comanche gave a low chuckle. "True." Comanche began to undo the red leather thong tying his braid.

"Don't worry, CJ." I said breezily, stepping up to the first safe. "I don't need the picks. Though I think you may want yours back." I held up his picks in one hand. Comanche dropped the lazy stance to feel along his braid. Yep, I had been light fingered enough to steal the picks from his hair. I smirked again and tossed them to him. He growled at me, which made my smile wider. Nothing like pulling the mask off the Lone Ranger.

"Thought you said you could open the safes." Daniel said grouchily, dragging a hand through his hair to tame the dark curly mess. He was somewhat successful. "I can." I grinned at him.

"Without picks?" Disbelief.

"Got something better." I pulled the velvet bag with keys from thin air. "The keys."

"Son of a bitch!" he breathed I saw a hand open and close in a fist. He breathed deeply, then straightened his tie and pulled the sleeves of his shirt cuffs to align them at the coat ends. "You could have said that first." He was successful in coming across as calm and collected… mostly.

"Not without our guarantee." I said. I dropped the bitchy slut routine. "Carrie and I needed that assurance." I nodded to the notes she had placed in her ample bosom. Daniel pursed his lips, blowing out his cheeks. But he nodded and motioned me to continue.

"Ok Carrie, I need a lovely assistant next to me and you'll just have to do for the moment." I motioned for my trustworthy side kick and distracting assistant.

"Umm, those things explode!" Carrie was not following script. I shot her a glare.

"Not like you're not used to a big bang."

"Yeah, but only when it's someone cumming on my face!" She shot back.

"Gross! Nasty girl." I wrinkled my nose in disgust. I was NOT going to wonder which of her many boyfriends or "Marks" might have.

"You bring it out in me." She cooed lecherously.

"Lalalalaala." I really was not going to go there.

"Carrie." We both jumped as Comanche spoke up. He looked slightly annoyed. Guess he didn't like the halftime show. "Stand next to Daniel and I'll be the pack mule for those oh so heavy keys."

"Smartass." I said with a smile. I turned back to the safe chewing a lip. This might still work.

Comanche moved next to me and Carrie went to hide behind Daniel. He'd only block about half the shrapnel, but depending on which half, she might still be a happy camper.

"How may I assist?" Comanche went from scary badass killer to professional FBI demeanor in the five steps he took from the doorway, passing Cubby to standing next to me.

"Hold out one of those massive paws for a moment."

"Woof!" he quoted. I snickered softly, but he did hold out a hand as requested. I emptied the bag of keys into his hand. There were eleven keys. Seven similar, three small and one bigger than the others. Choices, choices.

I tried all eleven in the first safe. Two fit. I moved down each safe marking which ones fit and which did not. Putting one key on top of each safe. The extra keys went into my hoodie pocket. Comanche said nothing. Yet. There was one extra "safe" key.

"Probably to the safe that went boom!" I muttered to myself.

Comanche looked at me oddly. But I shrugged. Some dialogs were just internal. No need to let all the voices out in the open.

"Ok. Everyone grab your socks, I'm about to attempt to open one of these bad boys. So say your prayers now." I said to the room in general. There were several sucked in breaths. "I need that pen and paper please." I said.

Carrie passed them to Daniel, who handed them to Comanche.

"Thank you my good secretary. Write the numbers I call out." I said, tilting my head to look up at him with a slight, sly smile. Comanche's lips twitched slightly, but he complied, his hands swallowing both pen and pad.

I kept my fingers light on the dial and closed my eyes. Taking a deep breath, I turned the safe until I felt a catch. This was delicate work that required intense concentration. My first number came out more a whisper.

"Again please?" Comanche asked, tilting an ear towards me. I opened my eyes blinking for a second.

"Right 32." I closed my eyes, ready for the left turn.

"How do you know if the safe is a right left right or a left right left opener?" He asked.

I shot him a glare. Why now did he have to become verbose? Interrupting in the midst of cracking a safe that could explode was not the best idea.

"I don't." I snapped, stalling his next question with a raised finger. "And I won't till I give it a full try. This" I motioned to the safe. "Is the preliminary finding. Once I have what I think are the numbers we'll give it a try one way and if it doesn't fucking open we'll go to the next way. Comprendo?"

"Crystal."

I could tell he was more amused than offended. I glared once more because it was going to take a moment to get a calm enough center to focus. This was fucked up to start with. Who the hell wires safes to explode? I stopped for a second staring at the safe.

"They're wired as booby traps." I whispered.

"What?" Daniel asked

"Whatever is in here, money, jewels, Jimmy Hoffa's body, the safes were wired as traps to kill someone or someones. Not to keep the information safe, but to kill." My voice dropped in horror. I knew my eyes were huge. I searched for Daniel's face. He got it in one.

It was his turn to lick his lips. "Still want to continue?" He asked. The man had ice water in his veins.

"Contract is a contract." I said, turning back to the safes. Damn damn damn. Yeah, I knew they could blow up without the key, but blowing someone up using a safe was vindictive overkill.

"What the fuck did you do to piss someone off this much?" I whispered to the safe, putting my hands back on the slightly cool metal.

Chapter Seventeen
He's a Murderer

I looked up for a moment at Comanche, enjoying the site of the craggy rugged giant not quite in control looking at me intensely. "About to open safe number one. Say your prayers to whoever your favorite deity is!" My voice carried to the room, but, hey, I wanted my last view to be something sexier than a death wired metal box.

I licked my lips, both tongue and lips dry, but my hands were rock steady. I turned the key disconnecting the charge, then turned the dial. Right, left, then right. There was a click.

"Open sesame." I whispered on an exhale. I grabbed the handle to turn and open.

"No! You fucking cunt, don't open that! You'll kill us all!" Karl was awake and swearing now.

"What are you afraid for us to find in here Klingon?" I glared over my shoulder. My hands were still on the vault, but the handle was unturned, still vibrating with adrenaline from not having exploded. It almost felt like the safe was vibrating and warm in response to being turned.

"Klingon?" Comanche asked.

"He reminded me of an early Star Trek Klingon." I said, glancing up at him, saving my glares for Karl. "That and it rhymed with Karl." I shrugged. Some jokes you just couldn't explain.

Comanche snickered softly. My head wasn't the only one to whip around and look at the big bad scary snickering like a school boy over his first view of a playboy centerfold. Oh! Looks like I wouldn't have to. A bonus for the night.

"It's all Jason's fault!" All eyes were on Karl as he started yelling, trying to stand. His hands made clinking noise as Karl moved them in agitation to help him stand without much luck.

Nick was having trouble holding him down. Jeremy came over and leaned on him. Karl was stocky and strong, but Jeremy was proving that the tall suit was covering more than just lanky skin and bones.

"That's nice, fuckhead, but we're still here for the main floor show." I snapped balling my hands into fists. I was shaking in anger, any calm from working the safes gone. Shot at, entombed, seeing dead bodies… I was ready to do some facial rearranging.

A large calloused hand landed on my shoulder, pulling me back to the safe. I had started to take steps towards Karl. For what I didn't know, but probably nothing good would have come of it. I snarled at Comanche, trying to shake off his hand and keep moving forward. He didn't even look fazed and I couldn't budge a foot more.

I considered throwing him over my shoulder, but one look up, and up, and up, and I knew that would just be even more futile, let alone humiliating for me. Comanche was probably used to pulling puppies up by the scruff of their necks on a regular bases. I settled for glaring and jutting out a chin in challenge. This set Karl off to more swearing and struggling, his suit coat flapping with his eyes bugging out, trying to shrug off the two men holding his shoulders down.

"Why is that Karl?" Daniel's voice was mild, though I could distinctly hear an edge to his voice.

Comanche pulled me back towards the safe, till I bumped into both the safe and him. He kept a hand on my shoulder, bending to whisper in my ear. "Stop." The voice was gravelly and low. I glared at him. Ok, so I wasn't smart enough to know he could squish me like a bug, but damn I was pissed. Comanche's lip twitched. Yeah, yeah, puppy thing. I got it. Didn't mean I didn't stop glaring.

Daniel stepped forward towards Karl, moving to the center of the room, his feet crunching on grit and debris. He didn't block Comanche or me from Karl's view, but he was redirecting the attention for a calmer mood.

"Karl! Talk to me. I am here." Daniel waved a hand at chest height to get Karl's focus on to him. Karl was torn between glaring at Comanche and giving attention to his former superior. In those few steps, Daniel went from just an agent to a Presence in the room. Daniel gave a smile that was almost pure predatory. Karl's attention was definitely on Daniel now.

My jaw almost dropped. He had been as disheveled and messy as the rest of us, but was able to pull off suave and in control in seconds.

"It's all Jason's fault!" Karl blurted out, not so much struggling now as trying to shout his intensity of belief.

"Fault? The murders?" Daniel gave Karl his full attention. "Why is that Karl?" Daniel's voice was smooth, conveying it was just the two of them talking. No one else mattered, reducing the room to just the two of them.

Karl's eyes burned with violence as he looked at Jason. "He," Karl motioned to Jason with his chin. "Killed my sister." his voice was low, with an intense hate that bordered on insanity.

Jason jerked behind me as if he had been gut punched. "I did not!" Jason looked sad and in real pain. The hand on my shoulder squeezed tight, forgetting the flesh and bone underneath. I flicked his hand with a finger. The hold loosened slightly, but did not let go.

Daniel looked between the two of them. "How did he kill her?"

"He got her killed in a car wreck!"

"Was he driving or did he hit her?"

"He killed her!"

Daniel frowned and looked at Jason. Jason had his head bowed in a memory.

"Jason?"

"She was driving home from a bar and hit a median divider, flipping her car onto the other side of oncoming traffic. She died three days later in a hospital from the injuries."

"Which you caused!" Karl shouted, trying to stand up again.

"I wasn't there. In her car or the car that hit her. Nor was I at the bar." Jason exchanged glare for glare with Karl, his hand starting to go into painful squeezing territory again.

"She died because of you!" Karl screamed, spittle and foam

flying from his mouth. As he rose on his knees. Nick was thrown off, causing Jeremy to shift from holding down just one shoulder to both. Jeremy's jaws clenched as he tried to keep Karl from standing, putting a knee in the man's back, making a grab for the handcuffs.

Daniel's eyes narrowed but he didn't intervene, yet. Nick got back to his feet and pulled out the tazer, going for a close up at the neck.

"Not yet, Nick." Daniel said mildly. Nick's nostrils flared, but he put the taser back into pocket. He growled something too soft for anyone other than Jeremy to hear, who only shot him an irritated look.

"Any clarification you can give us here, Jason?" Daniel said over the noise of the three FBI wrestling for control. The masculine grunting and swearing was almost reality TV show stopping worthy. I was waiting for the suits to be ripped off and the oil to come out. Nick had gorgeous arms.

I shot a look at Carrie. Her eyes were huge as she watched the struggle, edging back towards the door and Cubby. One of us had better sense of preservation it seemed. I was going to have to have my head checked after this. Seriously.

"Mary and I dated for a while. She was…" Jason hesitated then shrugged. "She was high strung. Very needy. I broke up with her the week before my grandfather died. I left for the funeral two days later. A few days after I returned, I heard she had died from driving drunk." His voice was intense with suppressed emotion. I squeezed one of the paws on my shoulder in sympathy. Death of family sucked no matter what.

"She went to your favorite bar thinking you would be there needing someone to hold your hand!" Karl screamed his head inches from the floor, angling his head awkwardly upwards. He was on his knees, but Jeremy had jerked the handcuffs to waist height, forcing Karl to bend or have his arms broken. Jeremy had won control.

I couldn't see Jason's face twist like he was sucking on a lemon, but I could hear the distaste strongly. "A man cannot be in two places at one time. And I did not choose to be with her at any bar at any time." Girl must have been a real piece of work.

Daniel tapped a finger to his lips. "So you blamed Jason for your sister's death." It really wasn't a question.

"Were you the one that tried to kill him by throwing him in the pond?" I asked.

"Not me. But I would have if I had the chance." Karl gave a sick almost happy smile. "To bad it didn't succeed." I swallowed. Scary man had become very scary, making me backup a step into Comanche. He was rock steady when I moved back, still holding my shoulders.

"Renniks." Said Nick. He was starting to sound like Jason in not using words.

"Got the drop on me." He was embarrassed. I would be too if a 5'7" skinny little asshole got the drop on me too.

Now I was really fucking confused. "But Nick had the tazer…"

"Yep. Nick carries an asp. He's been trained in baton hand to hand and doesn't need a taser, but FBI carry tasers."

"Karl gave Renniks the taser to get you out of the way." I said connecting the dots.

"Fucking incompetent piece of shit was supposed to knock you out so I could frame you for everything here! Not dump you in the pond." Karl tried to rise up again, but Jeremy pulled his wrists a little higher, causing Karl to grunt in pain and lower his body lowering back down.

"That's when you gave him the black eye."

"Little shit. Should have shot him." Karl's face twisted up again.

"Probably." I looked down at Karl with a smile full of teeth. "He'll turn on you faster than a crack whore sucking on a glass dick, to keep from getting life for killing."

"His word against mine. I'll never see the inside." Karl sneered right back at me.

I glared. Fucker was right.

"We can't pin Comanche's attempted murder on you, but we have a lot of dead bodies that one agent swears aren't Jason's."

"All the hair on them proves they are his. DNA can't be refuted!"

"Except when it isn't his DNA or hair." I said smugly.

"His hair was on all of the bodies. Can't fake that long hair native American crap!"

"Wasn't mine." Jason said sanguinely, his chest rumbling against my back like a kettle drum.

"Bullshit! Came from your desk!" Karl screamed, then paled. He tried to rise up again, but got yanked short for his efforts. His eyes widened, and his mouth opened and closed like a frogs. You could hear a pin drop. Daniel looked both satisfied and sad. Karl just looked sick, and he closed his mouth with a snap.

"Now can we pin him with the murders?" I asked.

"Maybe."

"Maybe?! Tampering with evidence? Contaminating a crime scene? That'll get you a few years even with being an FBI agent!" I snapped.

Daniel gave me a pitying look.

"Let me guess, what I've learned in school is nothing like reality in the courts." I said bitterly. I knew street rules, but legalities were still only being practiced in class from books. Comanche just gave me a pat on the shoulder. Thaaanks.

"A good lawyer could still get him off." Jeremy said with a hand on Karl's neck, the other holding the cuffs almost chest high. Jeremy wasn't taking any chances.

I guess I shouldn't either. I bit my lip hard. "Sure I can't just shoot him accidently." I muttered. "Rabid dog and all that."

Comanche snorted while Daniel just shot me a look, crossing his arms. Jeremy just laughed.

"She could say the gun went off while he tried to escape." Carrie spoke up.

"Do not encourage her." Daniel ran a hand over his face. "Even if it does sound like a really good idea." He muttered.

"Well then, let's see if the safes have anything useful." I said, turning back to the safe at hand.

Chapter Eighteen
Open Sesame!

"Well, I think we've made some excellent progress! Let's see what's behind door #1!" I put my hands back on the cool metal door of the safe and pulled the handle. I had felt the door click, but the explosion Marcus engendered was causing this door to stick.

"Come on you POS! Give me some loving." I growled. I tugged harder, feeling the damn thing finally give a little.

"Maybe you need something a little smaller? That one looks too big for you to handle." Came Carrie from the sidelines. I didn't even bother sticking out my tongue, just shot her a glare and kept pulling. There was a dirty joke in all of this I just knew.

The door gave with only a slight creak.

"Open Sesame!" I shouted, making Jason, who was still standing next to me jump. I chortled at the disgusted look he shot me. Always good when you can make the big guy jump in fear. I shot him an impish look. He was not amused.

The door swung open revealing cash, credit cards filling a shoebox, and safety deposit boxes. The boxes were mostly shiny and flat, but one was blockier than the others and old, like rusted on the outside with dust and prints in the dust old. That one had me curious. I was itching to see what was in that one. I doubted Daniel would let me indulge though. Spoil sport.

"The cash I can see, but the credit cards?" Came Jeremy.

"Probably prepaid cards filled to the max, or at least a decent amount." I said, offhandedly still admiring the old safety deposit box. Fuck it.

"Comanche. Sorry, Jason, could I borrow your picks again please." I put out a hand to him.

"And if I say no?"

I looked up startled. I hadn't even considered he would say no.

"Cubby do you have a paper clip in your man purse?"

"Umm… let me look?"

Jason laughed softly at me and handed over the picks from his pocket.

"No time to put 'em back in your hair?" I asked, sitting cross legged in front of the safe, pulling the old safety deposit box to me gently. I balanced it on the top of one knee while keeping most of the box in the safe.

"I need a few alone moments for some gentle touching." He said primly. Carrie and I both laughed at that one, but none of the other guys said anything. Daniel moved closer to see what I was doing.

"Think this is a good idea?" Jeremy asked. He couldn't see what I was doing exactly, but he knew I was up to something.

"If it explodes, hopefully you'll be safe enough and have enough information to get a prosecution for our former colleague."

I stopped with the picks halfway to the deposit box. "Shit. I didn't think these would be wired."

"Highly unlikely." Said Daniel. "The safes seemed to be the main focal point for that little bit of booby trapping."

"How do you know that?"

"I don't. I'm just going on a hunch on who might have done the wiring." He held up a hand. "Karl obviously didn't have the keys and couldn't get in. And, Darts, who had access to the safes and the warehouse probably set these up, but that is only a guess."

"Makes you wonder what Karl did to piss off old hippie dude." I said turning back to the deposit box. I put the picks down on my leg, rubbing my hands together, then gently cleaning the lock area with a thumb. I leaned closer blowing into the lock to help clear any residual dust.

"Ok… now to see what you delightfully sweet thing might hold." I purred. Jose had taught me how to pick most things, but it was my nimble and steady fingers with the picks that had made me useful to him. I took a deep breath and began. The lock was sweet and easy, opening up with only a few twists of the picks.

I opened the lid to one of the most beautiful pearl and sapphire necklaces I had ever seen.

Carrie sucked in her breath. "That is a very nice necklace."

I looked closer but without a jeweler's loupe, I could only guess at the carat weight on the sapphire. "That is as close to a 200 carat sapphire as you're going to see anytime soon." I touched the sapphire in pure admiration. It was beautiful, and if I took it, I'd have to have someone cut it much smaller, losing quite a bit to the cutting. I sighed heavily. Not mine. No touch.

I pulled the necklace from out of the safe to see what was underneath. I didn't recognize the paper currency or the coin, but the coins were gold. I hefted one in my hand. Solid gold it felt like. Another mental sigh. Too easy to trace. Not mine. No touch. I gave a sideways look at Daniel. Seems someone was rubbing off on me. Damn it.

Jason held out a hand for the coin. I handed it up to him. "1800's English Half Sovereigns."

We just all looked at him. "I liked coins as a kid." He said with an almost defensive shrug, handing the coin back to me.

"Ok then." I put everything back in the box and the box back into the safe. Standing up, I dusted off my hands and butt. "Let's see what's in door number 2!"

All the safes were the same. Money, lots of money, and lots of prepaid credit cards in boxes. Shoe boxes or beer boxes. Any box with the credit cards was full with money stacked around both the credit card boxes and the safety deposit boxes.

"All that money…" Carrie just let out a sigh.

"Would buy you way too many vibrators. You'd never make it to class." I said.

"But what a lovely time I would have! Would even have enough for a vibrator party! Ohhh, I could…"

"Lalalalala! Not listening!"

"Ladies. If you wouldn't, please."

"Sorry, Agent Lozano." I said meekly.

"Are we done?"

"Just about!" I put all the keys from the safe back into the bag. I collected the pad and pen from Comanche, pulling off the top sheet with the safe information putting it into the key bag. The remainder of the pad and pen went into my hoodie.

"Thank you!" Daniel said with a tip of an imaginary hat. "Time to get out of here I think."

"Forensics are going to hate you as it is." I commented over my shoulder as I went to help Carrie walk.

Jeremy and Nick got Karl on his feet. Nick stepped five feet back, pulling out a wicked looking small wand that he flicked into a much longer two foot stick. I wanted to rub an arm. Those fuckers hurt and broken bones when applied with enough force.

Comanche went over to the prone body of Renniks and tossed him over a shoulder like a sack of wet potatoes that were slightly crazy. Cubby clutched his laptop bag and followed tall guy out.

"And we're outta here!" I said, starting forward with Carrie hobbling next to me.

"Not so fast you two. We're going to need a statement from you both." Daniel said, collecting guns, needles and phones from the floor.

"And a ride." Comanche said, as he ducked under a doorsill. Daniel caught up to Comanche as he was walking slowly.

"We're going to have to take you in as well."

"Of course."

"In handcuffs." Daniel was trying for professional and courteous.

Comanche looked like he sucked on a lemon for a second, but nodded. "I'd have done the same to you."

"As long as it wasn't over your shoulder as well." Their voices got softer as Carrie and I lagged behind.

"How's the ankles?"

"Good actually. Figured you had something up your sleeve though."

I smiled. "How much padding do you have in the bra today?"

"None!"

"Got enough room for a few other things in there?"

Carrie smiled wickedly. She was quick.

"Just enough for a couple of semesters and maybe graduate school."

"Coins and gems?"

I shook my head. "Too distinctive."

"Damn!"

"No you can't take them for souvenirs either!"

"Kill joy."

"You wouldn't like being a prison bitch blowing some 300 pound cow and her other eight friends."

"Probably not." Carrie made a moue of disappointment over the necklace.

She slipped a hand into my hoodie front pocket pulling out a pad and pen. Comanche had pushed the pen down pretty hard leaving the numbers indentions very visible. She slipped them into her front pocket. Nowhere near as smooth as I could but not obviously fumbling either.

We were almost to the entrance. "Wait for it." I said out the side of my mouth.

"Owww!" She squealed as a foot dragged over the floor sill. Daniel looked back but I waved him forward out the front door. Cubby was holding the door for Comanche with Renniks. Daniel went through before Cubby let go.

I stopped and pulled the master key out of my sleeve and pressed it into Carrie's hand. "Good."

"Very." Carrie oozed confidence and smiled. We continued our carrying routine out the door.

"Damn girl, you have to lose some weight!"

"If you weren't as weak as a three day old mutt, you could have carried me!"

"Chica, not even Hercules could carry that ass of yours! Even with a promised blow job!"

"Fuck you!"

"I win!!" I fist pumped the dawning light of the sun, dropping Carrie on her ass. There were several headshakes from the others. Carrie just stood slowly, rubbing her generous backside.

Carrie and I giggled, but stopped when we saw the mess that Karl, or Renniks, presumably, had done while everyone else was inside distracted at one point or another. All the hoods of both cars and Comanche's truck were up. Nick was behind the wheel of the truck, making frustrated banging motions on the steering wheel. Comanche was peering into the truck with a look of irritation. Jeremy was in the car doing something similar. Daniel had his gun trained on Karl and Renniks who was just starting to come around.

"My purse!" Carrie put a hand to her hip, groping for her little leather purse, looked back at the warehouse and sighed, hobbling back up the steps inside.

"Whatever, Chica." I waved her off, turning towards the other side of the building.

"Hey!" Daniel motioned Jeremy out of the car. Jeremy came to stand beside him looking slightly confused, having missed the opening moves. Daniel handed him the gun.

Comanche looked up and saw the split happening. He motioned Cubby to follow Carrie.

Neither Carrie nor I stopped. She vanished inside and I was almost to the edge of the building.

Daniel caught up to me, grabbing my arm, just as I made it to the old hippie's truck. "Where are you going?" His hand was firm enough to stop me, but he let go as soon as I turned around.

"To get the truck the old man had or we get to walk a helluva long way home, *vato*."

"You have keys?"

"Nope!" I kept walking.

Daniel caught up with me again, stopping me with a hand on the arm. "Stop!"

"Why?" I waived my hands in the air, letting frustration creep in to my voice. "We can't all fit into Comanche's truck even if they do get it running."

"We don't know if the old man had any accomplices."

"With all the lights, not to mention the explosions going on, do you really think some one's not going to come and investigate this little rave of ours?" I motioned broadly to the warehouse that was missing chunks of roof and lights coming out of other parts.

"That isn't the point." Daniel was getting irritated. More so when I just smirked at him.

We both heard Comanche's truck rumble to life. I tilted my head and nodded. "Ok, now I'm impressed."

"We have a ride."

"Karl going to be the hood ornament?"

Daniel's lips twitched and there was definitely a spark of humor. "Sadly, no. We still need him to testify."

"Damn!" I said, gesturing with the flat of my hand. "He's bat shit crazy, you know."

Daniel nodded in agreement. "Probably. But we uphold the law."

I opened my mouth, closed it and tried again. "Of course. No dead bodies for us."

"Good girl!"

"See I can learn."

"With a few hard kicks to the ass perhaps?"

"*Bastardo!*"

"So does this mean I get a point?" He asked, laughingly. I conceded the point. I swear I could almost see his ears go fuzzy for a second. I wasn't even fazed by that shit any more.

Chapter Nineteen
Radar

Daniel made a call to Drombal. Drombal rounded up police cars, the fire department and all the trimmings. He got to puff his chest and look like a big shot, though he wasn't allowed to put Carrie and me in handcuffs. That was the only fly in his cherry pie.

"No one's bleeding." I said, following Daniel back around the corner to the others.

Jeremy raised an eyebrow.

"Singed, bruised and dented doesn't constitute bleeding." I said to his unasked question.

"Not to mention all the dead bodies we found inside." Daniel said dryly.

I crossed my arms shivering. "Ok, those too."

Daniel flipped out a phone. He stopped for a second. "How much pot were you and Carrie going to buy?"

"Pot? Us? Never!" I sounded indignant and shocked with wide-eyed innocent. I was good at doing this part.

Daniel just looked at me. "This is covered in the agreement." He said compressing his lips into a thin line.

"Anything I say will not be used against Carrie or me in a court of law?"

"Pretty much."

"No." My face went blank. "I don't trust you. Well, ok, to save my life maybe... But you'd hang us out to dry if you could nail us without the slightest twinge."

Daniel got a hard look. "Someone is selling pot laced with formaldehyde called "Zombie".

"The seller or the type of pot?"

"The pot. All we have for the seller is a dark sedan."

"Like what FBI guys like to drive? Or suburban dads?"

"Something like that."

I licked my lips then chewed the bottom lip. "Sigma Delta Ki."

"Excuse me?" Daniel frowned.

"One of the dads is either providing or selling as the main supplier using the frat as a cover."

"And you know this how?"

"Carrie and I were warned never to set foot at any of their frat parties or else." I said with real hate in my voice. My fists were clenched. Daniel reached a hand out to touch my arm.

"The "or else" not specified?"

"I ended up with a cracked jaw and Carrie had her hand broken." I said tightly.

"But you guys never dealt."

I smiled.

"So what makes you think the frat is the cover."

"After any party or gathering at the frat, there are cases you hear about from the hospital of brain dead partiers from smoking pot." I rubbed my jaw. "Pot should be fun not dangerous." I bit my tongue.

"Rojo was run over a few days after your sister's overdose death." Daniel changed the subject non-too subtly.

"Yes. Yes, he was." I smiled at this, but didn't raise to the bait.

"You don't happen to know who would do that, would you?"

"He was a *puto* with many enemies." I was still reminiscing on Rojo's screams.

"Jose said all of Rojo's money went missing about the same time."

I shook my head in mock regret. "No honor among thieves, it seems."

"You've been paying rent and tuition in cash."

"I put in a lot of hours waiting tables when not in class." I gave him a perky, but not so friendly smile. All lips, but nothing in my eyes. "I don't have credit cards or rich parents to pay my way, Agent Lozano."

"True. You do realize you have files. FBI and police."

I nodded.

"They are pretty extensive." Daniel continued. "We try to be thorough when checking out dangerous drug dealers."

"Dangerous? Us?!" I blurted out, disbelief that we were considered dangerous.

"Couple of people have died around Rojo. And you. Couple of witnesses."

"No hard evidence, just circumstantial." I countered. "And the witnesses were so nasty that they couldn't get a starving dog to trust them, I'm betting."

Daniel just smiled. "You would have made a damn good trial lawyer."

"Would have?" I said cautiously with narrowed eyes.

"The police have you two on radar. Selling or possession will nix any law enforcement career and having a record will get you barred from entering law school."

"Duly noted." I said. Daniel nodded and went to stand by Jeremy, talking softly. Jeremy was motioning towards the warehouse when Carrie came out of the warehouse, breathless, clutching both our purses, only slightly worse for wear with soot stains. Cubby was looking rather wide-eyed and blushing, and not looking anyone in the eye.

"What did you do? Stop for a post victory blow job?" I asked softly, the others pretty much ignoring us as usual.

"Hey, I needed something to calm my nerves! And I was fresh out of cigarettes." She giggled and adjusted her bra with a wink. I grinned. I'm betting Cubby was given a bribe or three to be quiet for a few weeks.

Distantly we heard sirens. The sun was just coming up over the horizon. I faced the light. "A new day dawns." I murmured.

Chapter Twenty
Circle of Trees

The phone rang late in the morning. But for Lozano, it was still early. Three hours of sleep after running, jumping and not being on fire counted as a late night. A hand reached automatically for the small phone. The hand wavered for a moment, as if the owner wasn't sure he should smack the damn thing or answer. The phone was saved from being tumbled off the nightstand and under the bed only because there was no snooze button.

"Lozano here." His voice was a groggy snarl. "You better be dead or dying."

"Agent Lozano?" The voice was breathy, young and male. Not Autumn or Carrie. At least one good thing so far.

"You better be dead or dying, kid." he repeated, still unhappy about the broken sleep.

"Um. No sir. I'm not. Dying that is. Or dead." The voice was stumbling trying to speak but failing in coherency.

"Stop." The voice on the other end stopped. Lozano swung his legs out of bed, sitting up. "Now. Why are you calling me?"

"We have a crime scene, sir."

"Yes you do. And you have a lot of competent people who should still be covering the scene and giving me another…" Daniel looked at the clock on the other nightstand. "3 hours of sleep."

"We, uh, I was told to call you."

"By whom." So he could rip off their nuts went unspoken.

"Director Carls, sir. He said he needed your eyes on the ground."

"Can't rip off his nuts." He said out loud, not thinking about who was on the other end of the phone till he heard the indrawn breath. Damn, Autumn was rubbing off on him.

"Sir?"

"Nothing, Agent… I'm going to go out on a limb, you're an agent here?"

"Yes sir! First day sir."

"Stop." Daniel ran a hand through his hair, then popped his neck, trying not to snarl into the phone.

"Err… yes sir!"

"Where does Agent Carls want me now?"

"At the greenhouse, sir."

Daniel pulled the phone away to look at it in disbelief.

"We have forensics there?"

"Yes sir, but Director Carls said you were the lead on this, and, well… we have more bodies, sir." The kid's voice dropped almost to a whisper. More bodies and the kid was green over the phone.

"We're on our way. It'll be about an hour, though." Daniel sighed and hung up. He dialed Jeremy's number. The phone rang once before being picked up.

"Agent Fier."

"More bodies." Was all Daniel said.

"Good morning Agent Lozano. I will be ready in 10."

"Makes one of us." Daniel hung up, putting his head in his hand for a moment, fumbling putting the phone on the table next to the bed. "I'm up, I'm up." He muttered to himself, more to convince his body to move then actually moving. He stood, stretched and stripped out of his boxers to head to the shower. The clock said noon.

Jeremy knocked on Daniel's hotel door. He only had to wait a couple of moments. Daniel answered mostly dressed; his tie half-undone. His eyes were bloodshot with dark circles. Jeremy held up cups wafting the smell of freshly brewed coffee, and a bag with golden arches. Daniel was not a morning person, whereas Jeremy could function on 3 hours of sleep and keep going. Even if it was the middle of the day. After a year as partners, Jeremy knew this. Coffee, good strong coffee, would make him at least reasonable until he woke up. Daniel may be able to walk like a cat, but Jeremy got even by being perky and efficient ten minutes after he opened his eyes.

Daniel eyed the McDonald's bag in near disgust, but nodded and let Jeremy in. Jeremy handed Daniel the cup with a circle and an x marked on the top. Daniel took a sip after eyeing the lid for half a second. His eyes closed in deep appreciation.

"There is a god." He breathed.

"Several depending on who you ask." Jeremy said with a grin.

"Shush. No semantics this early." Daniel took three more swallows, ignoring the scalding creamy liquid.

"Had them add two espresso shots to that. I was promised you'd be climbing the walls, or at least be animated, should you have survived after drinking this."

Daniel looked up sharply. His face haloed by the rising steam from the coffee cup. "There are more bodies. They had the new field agent call us."

"Was he compromising the forensics?"

"Probably."

"Send him far enough away upwind he might stop throwing up. We need anyone else?" Jeremy wasn't talking just field agents.

"Comanche. Shit." Daniel corrected himself. "Jason, will be facing questions today and probably for the next week. Nick is going to be debriefed for about as long. And we don't need the girls for this." Daniel gave a delicate shudder. He set the coffee cup on the dresser. He needed both hands to get his tie correct and he had had enough caffeine to finish this part.

"I dropped them off at their dorm room myself last night." Jeremy said blandly. Daniel glanced over, his hands stopping mid loop. "Don't trust Drombal?"

"In a word, no." Jeremy said opening up the McDonalds bag, pulling out muffins. The smell of ham and not butter filled the room. "He's got too big an axe to grind with them both."

"Me either." Daniel tightened the tie knot and adjusted. He cocked his head to look at his image, nodding. 'Professionally uptight,' came Autumn's laughing voice in his head. Daniel's lips narrowed.

"Think we're going to have to put them in protection?"

Jeremy asked delicately unwrapping one muffin before taking a bite.

"If it is just Drombal then no, but this…" Daniel made a motion as if he was encompassing more than just the warehouse case. "Feels bigger."

"Like how the hell did two small time dealers get lucky in finding the big selling warehouse?" Jeremy handed off one of the English muffins.

"That would be one of them. Still wonder who the hell Darts was, besides just the grower." Daniel bit into his like a man resigned to a fate slightly better than death, but just.

The day was bright, but not blistering hot yet. No clouds, so no rain to ruin the site. The breeze was soft and playful through his hair. Daniel looked up in disgust for a moment, flipping out his sunglasses to ward off the bright light.

Jeremy drove both of them to the warehouse. The time read 1:20 pm on the Impala dashboard. Daniel was not only awake and perky now, but he was writing notes on a notepad. Neither spoke much on the drive out. Daniel and Jeremy would make their notes separately, then compare and discuss later. Jeremy kept his questions lined up in his head until he could get to his computer later in the day. Both were looking forward to the case closing soon. Soon being relative considering the obligatory mountain of paperwork.

Jeremy pulled off the road. Daniel looked up from his notes.

"This place doesn't look any better with the sun up and all the cops here."

"Better than it did last night." Jeremy said. He rolled down the window to show his badge to a young looking man in uniform. His id was looked at, then the young man held up a finger and talked into the radio mike hooked on his shoulder.

"Send them out back." Came the crackling response.

"Gentlemen, if you will drive around back."

"Who do we ask for?"

"Director Carls is here and waiting for you."

Jeremy and Daniel traded looks. Carls didn't do field work as much anymore, but he did for the really big messy ones.

Daniel blew out air from his cheeks. "Much bigger then we first thought."

Director Carls was a slim, older man with receding hair and a lanky frame held in an almost unnaturally straight manner. No one called him "Ramrod" to his face any more, unless they were very old agents or wanted to see Alaska really badly. He was also very easy to spot among the milling brown uniforms in his understated grey suit.

Carls was deep in discussion with two people in lab coats. The man and woman both had unhappy looks, but they nodded and went back to the mounds of dirt and grass where shovels and sifting frames were being employed.

"Gentlemen. Good you can join us." His voice was a pleasant tenor, but his eyes were on the workers, not the agents.

"Sleep is overrated sir." Jeremy said with a straight face.

"Liar." Carls said in an easy manner and smile, pulling his thoughts away from the mounds of dirt to look at the agents directly this time.

"Well, maybe not for Daniel." They both laughed at Daniel who looked at both steadily. His morning personality was well noted.

"I've read the preliminary report. It looks like you had a very exciting night, and wrapped up a major drug center and FBI embarrassment."

The two agents waited for the other shoe.

"However, it looks like we have an even bigger issue now."

"How so?"

"The body count from inside the warehouse is at 14."

Daniel and Jeremy nodded. They knew it would be high, but that was not a reason to bring them back out. Carls continued. "It looks like we have at least another 15 to 20+ out back in the compost piles."

Daniel blinked a few times. That was double what they had expected.

"We found a couple of computers intact. I have a few people on that, but the decryption may take a bit."

Daniel tilted his head for a moment, a thought nagging at

him. "Have you talked to the computer geek Jason had on his team?"

"No, why?"

"Jason brought him along for a reason. He wasn't a shooter or a cracker jack. Just questionable life choices and friends. He was here for a reason."

Carl's regarded Daniel for a moment and gave a slow smile. "No, I haven't, but I will now. Take a look around. I need another pair of eyes while I call this in." Carls flipped his phone open and walked away from the hustle and bustle to make a few ballbusting calls.

"Brown noser." Jeremy said sideways in a sotto voice.

"Anything to keep my ass from the frozen north of Alaska." Daniel replied walking towards the expanding pits, where both brown uniformed police and CSI were digging and calling out to each other.

"Got another!"

"How far along?"

"Old. Bones are pitted." One of the lab coats came over putting on latex gloves. He motioned for one of the shifter teams to come over to the body site, grabbing a camera from the table set up with equipment. Daniel and Jeremy wandered over as the bones and dirt were removed carefully, sifted, then placed on a body bag. Buttons, laces, fibers and wallets, where there were any, were bagged and tagged.

Jeremy dipped his head looking past the compost area. Daniel was still in a discussion of bones and decomposition with and without insect help. He stood up brushing off his pant legs with an economy of motion before walking to a stand of trees. There were about 12 trees in plastic buckets set to the side and what looked to be the start of holes for the trees. The placement looked odd, though. After a moment Jeremy walked into the first stand of trees to confirm an idea.

Daniel wandered up to him. "What do you see?" He asked.

"Is it my imagination or are these trees in a circle?" Jeremy asked, turning around as he looked at the trees. There seemed to be two types. The most common a flowering tree with open branches while the other was straighter and less fragile, without flowers.

Daniel walked to each tree using Jeremy in the center as a reference. "It's not your imagination."

"Karl wouldn't have done this."

"Don't think Karl knew what a tree was unless it came as a toothpick."

Jeremy gave a lopsided smile. "Very true." He waived a hand to the side where there was one other tree, a flowering one, ten feet out from the circle they were in but centered between two other trees. "That tree hasn't been planted for long. The dirt's been turned up."

"There are other trees set to the side for more planting." Daniel commented thoughtfully. He walked over to another hole ten feet out from the inner circle and again set between two trees. "Jeremy, how much do you know about planting trees?"

"I grew up in San Francisco. The only trees I saw were in Muir Woods."

"City boy, eh?" Daniel looked up with a grin.

"Yep!" Jeremy gave him that easy smile.

"So nothing about planting a tree." Daniel pursed his lips thoughtfully.

"No. The only thing I know is the roots need to be covered. After that…" Jeremy shrugged, "you're asking the wrong person. Why?"

Daniel ran a tongue over his teeth then jumped into the hole. It was mid-thigh. "Does this seem a bit deep to you for a tree?"

"Covers the roots." Jeremy said, walking over.

"Yeah, and an extra three feet." They both turned to the freshly planted tree then at each other.

"Time to get a shovel." Jeremy held out a hand to pull him out.

"I'm thinking so." Daniel said taking the proffered hand with a sigh.

The freshly planted tree covered a woman's body, that was as close as forensics could tell, three maybe four months dead.

No id, just a dress, shoes, and some rusting cheap jewelry.

"We'll get this one bagged along with the others, Agent." The young woman who had been talking to Carls earlier said.

"Thank you. Any Id's showing up?"

"We've had maybe one hit with an ID. Left in the shirt pocket. Other than that, nothing." Her camera was clutched in both hands, her eyes wide. Daniel knew that look. This was a bad scene. She'd be having nightmares for a while. He patted her on the back and walked over to Carls and Jeremy.

"Good work you two." Carls said to Daniel as he joined them.

"Thank you sir."

"He means with Cubby." Jeremy supplied

"Oh?" Daniel looked between the two.

"With the trees and bodies as well. But Cubby agreed to help work with our people. They're hammering out a deal now."

Jeremy and Daniel exchanged another look. "Really?"

"If that kid ever held a gun, it was plastic and shot water. Boy can barely hold his dick while taking a piss."

Daniel nodded. "Was our assessment as well, sir."

"We're combing through all of the financials as well as personal effects and leads. Lozano, we'll need you to look over the financials as soon as your paper work on this has been finalized." Carls said, with a level look at the shorter agent.

"Of course sir."

"Agent Fier, you will be partnered with another and IA is going to be talking to you shortly." Carls looked over the partners shoulders, waiving someone over.

"How shortly sir?"

"Right now." Carls said. They turned to see three other agents coming up from behind. "I want to know where this got fucked up and how to keep this from happening again. And I don't like cowboys."

"Yes sir." They both said. Carls nodded to them both and walked back to the digging.

"I'll send you long johns." Daniel said in a sotto voice.

"Thanks." Jeremy said with gallows humor as his day had just turned to shit.

Chapter Twenty-One
Let Down

The trial was more theatrical than a movie. The twists and turns kept me on the edge of my seat and I had been there for the final act. Seems old hippie dude, Cory Darts, had at one time been a very good bank thief and a cousin to Karl. A very close cousin who had taught Karl how to rob banks and not get caught.

Karl had decided to play on both sides. Good and bad. He worked for the FBI, helping to look for robbers while having access to the top tools and latest bank schematics. This made it very easy for him and his cousin, with disposable help, to plan very quick, in and out heists on Karl's vacations. They never took more than a couple of million, and maybe a box or two each time. The security boxes were random, more like a bonus then actually deliberate. Cory's idea of playing with fate.

Cory's other side business had been blank credit cards for a few of the drug running cartel who liked his pot. The pot was more of a side business, while the credit card blanks and filling had become a better sideline. So much so he no longer needed bank heists as an income source.

Unfortunately, Karl started to develop a taste for pain. He liked hurting the people at the banks and disposing of the help once they were no longer useful. Cory helped by being able to provide a very out of the way warehouse with huge compost piles out back that could break down a body in 6 weeks.

We hadn't seen that portion of the warehouse, but the pictures were graphic in the amount of both old pitted bones and fresher bones found at the bottom of the excavations. Once Cory branched out into water garden plants, Karl had decided the pond could be stocked with bottom feeders like catfish and crayfish so he could pick up, and dispose of, an extra person or two when he had the urge.

Karl and his sister had been very close. Too close. Karl hadn't wanted her to date Jason as he was too brown skinned. Then, when she had been dumped and died in the car accident, it drove him over the edge. The framing of Jason took on a life of its own.

Then things got really weird. Carrie and I got a much closer look at the workings of the FBI. Apparently Jeremy and Nick had been best friends in college; both having gone into the FBI, although different departments. Nick got to hang out with bikers chugging beer with whisky chasers, as he passed on tips about gun and drug running to his handler, while Jeremy did bank and money laundering; eventually being paired up with Daniel. They made a very good team, following the money of gun and drug sales that Nick helped facilitate.

It was Nick who had started to notice a few of the bank heists had similarities, with vicious attacks on the tellers and hostages, and only two of the crew the same, but everyone else new. Every time. This piqued Nick's handler's interest enough, he started a chart with dates, times, group members past and present, and body injuries done in the heists.

Nick's handler and Karl had been in the same office. Karl had only seen the chart by accident walking by. He had been smart enough not to ask about it; instead of staying late one night to hack into the handler's computer. The handler later died due to fatal car poisoning. The chart never showed up on the handler's computer, having been removed prior.

Nick was left without a contact except his old friend Jeremy. The two put their heads together and started to profile; however, the profile was too expensive until they had more than hunches to work with.

This was the time when Jason was more of a courier than deep cover. Unlike Nick, he actually had an office he visited and was able to keep abreast of the office politics. When he had broken things off with Karl's sister, Karl had thrown a punch at him in the office, which resulted in Karl being suspended with pay for 2 weeks. During the two weeks, Jason had gone to a funeral; returning with his grandfather's braid and to the news of his ex-girlfriend's death. The braid then went missing and the bodies started to pile up. Karl used the hair as a way to frame Jason, a convenient scapegoat.

Jason was in the field when he heard the warrant for his arrest come through. He had just made it out of the hotel he had been living in; stealing the drop money to fund his own investigation with at least three 'bad' guys with guns and a computer hacker: Marcus, Renniks, Nick and Cubby. Cubby had been good enough to find the old chart that had led Jason to Karl and Cory's hideout.

Cory had been shot by Karl on the day Jason had come to get information. Karl had made it to the back door just moments before Jason and crew had showed up, while Carrie and I were hiding in the warehouse. Karl had planned to come back and empty the one safe everything had been stored in, not knowing his cousin had gotten tired of all the dead bodies; having repacked all the heist monies into six safes with booby traps.

Carrie and I were key witnesses, but only to a very small portion. Much of the trial was centered around Daniel, Jeremy, Nick, and Cubby.

Daniel had managed to track the money sales, heist timeline and bodies to Karl; while Jeremy and Nick tag teamed on tracking the heists, card sales and pot shipments to Cory. Cubby testified about the hacking of Nick's handler and Karl's computers. He had also hacked Cory's home computer for spreadsheets on money accrued and sold from Cayman accounts.

Karl was freshly shorn and in very nice suits. He sat without saying much through most of the trial. His lawyer was very good and able to refute, or cast doubt on, almost all the evidence. The one piece he wasn't able to duck was the tissue samples of his last victim in the water pond. She had managed to scratch both him and Renniks. There was no way to explain why she had his DNA under her nails. Renniks turned state witness at this point. He sang about all the bodies he knew about in the warehouse. Seemed Karl had been a very busy boy. There were 49 bodies exhumed. Renniks could only positively ID 7 that he and Karl had killed in the last 10 months.

Renniks testified that Karl had recruited him to keep an eye on Nick and inform on his whereabouts. Nick had hooked up with Jason to monitor him for Jeremy, who was compiling information on both Jason and Karl, finding very different results than what Karl was presenting.

Marcus was the safe expert, but only due to the fact that he knew how to punch through a safe or vault panels from working a bit at a vault manufacturing company. He had not been prepared for keyed safes wired with explosives.

When it came time for Carrie and I to take the stand, we made sure to be very respectable in suits with skirts. Carrie took me shopping and found a very respectable, if dull, brown dupioni silk suit coat with long sleeves and mostly modest skirt, and a simple cream colored shirt. New jewelry and flats completed my ensemble.

Carrie wore a New York style dark blue pinstripe woman's suit with sensible pumps and her hair in a bun. Her impressive cleavage was modestly, and mostly, covered. Her earrings and rings were both smart looking star sapphires that matched the color of her suit; neither flashy nor gaudy. She could have been the poster girl for young urban professionals. The fact she was amazing on the stand helped too.

She pointed out logic flaws of the defense questioning and made suggestions for alternative ways in which Karl did not look quite so innocent. She had the judge and jury laughing a few times with her insightful comments.

She broke down once when Karl stood up and screamed at her, when she went into the harrowing detail of being tied up, beaten and threatened. Court had to be adjourned at that point. Eventually she was treated like a hostile witness instead of a dumb bimbo.

After Carrie took the stand, both sets of attorneys decided I should be asked very short, yes or no questions. This suited me fine. My delivery was definitely more matter-of-fact. Except when I described the body of Karl's last victim in the pool. I didn't try to keep the horror from my face or voice. The judge asked for clarification if I had seen bodies in the pool. Seemed yes was a little too short of an answer.

Drombal was brought in as a character witness against us. However he didn't have any hard evidence of pot dealing. And Carrie did bring up the restraining order. The DA also brought out our work history and GPA's. Not great, but for working girls holding a respectable waiting job or a retail job in Carrie's case, Drombal was once again left to slink away to try again another day. I smiled at him with my sweetest smile as he left the courtroom. He didn't stop on his way out, but there was a return snarl on his face. Carrie elbowed me whispering, "Stop teasing the animals!" Daniel shot me a look as well from the other side of the courtroom. Luckily, I wasn't anywhere near Karl to taunt him with just being alive. Maybe I could get an invitation for when he was scheduled to be put down.

I still wake up with nightmares. They're just different than from before the warehouse. It used to be Rojo was coming after me firing his compact AR15 before I could get the car in reverse to run him over. Now I see a tall brunette with closed eyes and dark hair floating in much clearer water. Sometimes, she opens her eyes at me and sometimes she just smiles, but every time I wake up crying with my fists bunched in the sheets.

There was no way I could have saved her, yet I still feel guilty and horrified. That could have been me had Jason and his crew not shown up when they had. Those nights, I can't get back to sleep so I start studying. This semester I'm sporting a 3.9 GPA. I study a lot.

After Renniks turned, and with Carries and my testimony, Karl would get the needle sometime in the next year or five. Renniks got 10 years with a chance for probation. Jason was cleared and Cubby was offered a job for the FBI working on a special unit's team.

"Good afternoon ladies." Daniel said from behind me in the court hallway.

"Shit!" Carrie jumped with a start, dribbling coffee from her travel mug on her hands.

I snickered and just sipped my chai; admiring my first French style manicure. I looked good! Professional even.

"How the fuck are you not jumping out of your skin!" She glared at me, trying to wipe her hands while holding on to her mug. Jeremy rescued her by taking the mug and handing her a handkerchief. He couldn't quite make the handkerchief appear out of thin air, but he was quick.

I turned to Daniel with a smile. "I don't listen for his footsteps, which he manages not to shuffle or clack on the tile, but his aftershave is very distinctive. Masculine and spicy." I said with a wink. I appreciated a good smelling man.

"I don't wear aftershave." He looked amused, but slightly superior. There was warmth in those lovely eyes of his, even if he was on the job.

"Then you have very strong deodorant, because there is a very definitive manly scent about you." I waggled my eyebrows suggestively.

Both he and Jeremy laughed.

"Point to you."

I just grinned and took another sip.

Jeremy was still being solicitous of Carrie and her sticky hands. She was trying to be very decorous and not get messy, but things were going downhill fast. I think she was slightly fumble fingered around Jeremy by accident and not on purpose.

I smiled slightly. I was pretty sure she had a major crush on him. She cleaned up her act since the greenhouse. She wasn't seeing anyone, nor making crude blow job jokes. Hopeless. Just hopeless, but it was her crush.

Daniel looked over my shoulder to Jeremy and Carrie with a rather blank face. He had caught on to her changed behavior too.

"So how can we meek and mild college students help you, agent Lozano?" I asked, to take a little of the scrutiny off Carrie trying not to make a fool of herself.

"The judge is ready to talk to the two of you about your files." Daniel said, straightening his tie, which was still impeccable. He had managed to look FBI professional no matter what the defense attorney had thrown at him.

"Sealed for good?"

"As sealed as a court can." He said with a slight shrug,

opening his hands.

"Damn." I took another sip to finish off the tea before throwing the disposable cup into the trash. Unlike Carrie, in the last three weeks, I hadn't quite picked up environmentally friendly habits and enthusiasm.

Daniel escorted us into the judge's office that was very crowded. Standing room only. Some of the people I knew and some I did not. Jason, Nick and Cubby were there, as well as the judge from the trial and two others. One man, was wearing the FBI look of short hair, and dark, unremarkable suit, with the stiff, ramrod straight, sitting or standing posture. The woman might have been his counterpart, but she wasn't FBI. Something… not FBI. The judge, with salt and pepper hair and an almost completely white beard, was in conversation with them when we walked in.

As we entered all eyes were on us. Carrie and I exchanged looks. Carrie took point with only a slight change to her face of vapid blond. I put on my happy collegiate face, moving slightly to the right and half a step back. Jeremy and Daniel were to the sides. I took a deep breath and let it out. This was not a hostile room, I told myself. We are NOT going to be jumped for the dope or cash we weren't carrying.

I touched Carrie's elbow. She looked back. I motioned with my chin to the chairs that had been left conspicuously open. She thinned her lips, but took the hint. We moved towards the chairs, but did not sit down, too many were standing to feel comfortable at the disadvantage of sitting.

The judge ended his discussion, moving to sit behind his very large dark wooden desk that was clear except for two files.

"Ladies, if you two would sit down please." The judge's voice was very deep and sonorous. Up close, I could see the eyes were a very dark shade of green. Green enough I was surprised he didn't have red hair instead of dark brown.

Carrie and I sat. Carrie leaned forward slightly, aiming her big guns just in case. I sat back, with arms akimbo, but hands touching at the fingertips. As the judge looked between the two of us and you could almost see the smoke coming from his ears. He looked to Daniel and then to Jason.

"I see what you mean by interesting pair of young women."

I wasn't sure if I should be amused or offended. Carrie chose to be amused and smiled brightly.

"So we have an agreement here signed for by Agent Lozano." He looked between the two of us seriously. I could tell by the timbre of his voice that something wasn't right. I leaned forward slightly with narrowed eyes. "This agreement is slightly outside of his jurisdiction."

"We paid for those files to be closed. On the stand, our testimony put away a freaking FBI serial killer your boys missed." I snapped. We bled for those files, damn if we hadn't paid for them in other ways as well.

The judge looked at me quelling. I looked back steadily.

"Your contribution to the case was indeed pivotal. Especially Ms. Reich. However, we have a few questions we want clarified." The unknown FBI man interjected smoothly. His hair was completely white, but smooth shaven.

"And you are?" Carrie asked, buttering her words with honey as she didn't quite bat her eyes.

"Assistant Director Carls."

"And your companion?" I asked, trying for sweet, but coming out brusquer then I planned.

"Agent Mia Rhodes."

"You're not FBI." I stated. I tilted my head at her. "Close but not uptight enough."

I heard a snicker from behind, but didn't turn to see which of the guys was laughing.

"Thanks." Her voice was dry but her eyes crinkled in amusement. "No. I'm with the CIA. Drug enforcement."

I nodded. That would make sense.

"So why are we having a pow wow on what should be a simple shut and throw the key away on to juvenile files?"

The judge exchanged looks with the new and definitely higher ranking people.

"We have a few questions we would like to ask in clarifying a few other things." Came Carls' response. He sat on the edge of the judge's desk, close enough for me to smell a spicy aftershave. Something expensive I bet, looking at his leather shoes and doing a quick calculation.

"How dependent on our response is the files being locked?" I asked cautiously. Something about Ms. Rhodes was making the hair on the back of my neck rise.

There was another exchange of looks.

"Somewhat but the files will be sealed." Jason said from behind. His voice a comforting rumble. Carls raised an eyebrow, but nodded with a sour expression. Seemed someone was back in good graces and with pull.

"I'd like to start with the question of who turned you on to Cory Darts." Ms. Rhodes said.

"This is covered under our written agreement?" I asked, facing her square on.

"Of course."

Carrie and I both pulled out tape recorders. "Would you be willing to state that again for the record Ms. Rhodes?" Carrie asked, setting the mini microphone of hers facing the CIA agent.

This time I could hear the laughter and it was definitely Jeremy's.

"I'd prefer that we weren't taped."

"And I prefer we weren't here at all." I stood up, smoothing down my skirt. "If you'd be so kind, your honor, and fulfill your obligation, we'll be on our way." I looked at the judge pointedly.

Carrie was on cue this time and followed suit. She stood, collecting her new monstrous blue leather woven bag.

"No wait!" Carls held out his hand, not quite jumping off the desk. "We really would like a few questions clarified and we will do it on tape." His gaze was steady and narrowed at Ms. Rhodes. You could tell she wasn't happy. She crossed her skinny arms over her chest, but nodded.

"So please if you will sit again, we can continue." Carls was putting the smooth charm back on as we slowly resumed our seats. He sat back on the corner of the desk and we brought our recorders back out.

Carrie nodded and I started. "So this is on the record as being covered under our written agreement with Agent Lozano for helping catch Agent Brennin on bank heists and multiple murders, while clearing the name of your Agent Jason… Errr, I don't know his last name."

"Running Buck." Came the rumbling reply.

"Thank you. Agent Jason Running Buck."

"Yes. All questions asked and answered will be covered under the agreement that your records will be sealed."

"And no prosecution or jail time for either of us." Carrie interjected.

"Or prosecution or jail time for helping us catch a serial killer." Ms. Rhodes finished. She shot Carls a look that could have melted steel.

"Jurisdiction issues?" I asked.

"Difference of opinions."

I frowned.

Carls clarified. "She thinks you should be locked up with Karl and Renniks while I'm of the opinion we would have lost more agents and a lot more people before Karl was caught."

I turned to regard Ms. Rhodes. "So why the hate?"

"We need to know who else knew of the greenhouse."

"But that's not the major question you want to ask."

"We will get to mine in a few. This is pertinent to the case."

"What, there are outside questions?"

"A few."

"Over?"

"Could you tell us who told you about the warehouse, Ms. Roberts?" The judge tried to move us along.

"Tony Jalisco." Carrie answered instead of me. I frowned.

"How did you meet him."

"At a party. One of the frat parties during rush."

"Have you seen Tony since the greenhouse incident."

"No." Carrie and I both answered. I licked my lips, frowning. Tony had been hot to get into bed with either one of us. Enough so that he had tried to bribe his way in with the greenhouse information. Tony had a slightly slimy feel when talking to him and very handsy. Carrie had seen a way to get out from doing small time dealing. She had taken a hit for the team. I took the information since he mostly spoke only Spanish.

There was a tapping behind us as of fingers on a keyboard. I shot a glance over my left shoulder. Cubby was deep into his square headed girlfriend's face, the odd part was both Jeremy and Jason were looking on as well. I looked quizzically.

"Can you describe him." Ms. Rhodes asked, drawing my attention back to her.

I stuck my tongue out of my teeth thinking. "Tall…ish"

"Not that tall. Only 5'8." Carrie interjected

"Seemed taller." I said with a shrug. "Boots with heels." I said, motioning towards boots on feet that weren't there.

"Added a couple of inches." Carrie nodded.

"Dark hair and dark brown eyes."

"Stocky with a small pot belly."

"Anything else?" Carls asked.

"He had scars and scabs on his hands." I said. "Small scars like you get from welding regularly."

"Anything?" Carls asked over our head.

"Tony Jalisco shows up a few times. With the descriptions we can narrow the field to three that might match the description." Jason said looking up from the screen in Cubby's lap.

Cubby turned the computer towards us. I had to turn in the chair on my knees to get a better look while leaning over the arm. Carrie only had to swivel at the hips a little.

"Third one down."

Carrie and I both looked. "Yep, that's him."

"Did you know he was in the Mexican Mafia?"

"No!" Carrie's eyes got huge.

I chewed the inside of my cheek, not saying anything. She looked at me. This time I squirmed.

"Umm… I might have guessed?" I sounded lame even to me.

"Autumn!" Carrie stuck out her chin with narrowed eyes. She was really pissed at me.

"What?! You wanted the bigger sale. We needed his information." I didn't shrug, but I did look her in the eyes.

"What if…" She started to get worked up.

"We already had the 'what if'." I said calmly.

That stopped her mid-sentence.

"I'm sorry, Carrie." I really was. She gave me a look while drumming her fingers. We would be talking about this later I could see, and she was not going to be nice. I sighed. I had this ass chewing coming, but I wasn't going to like it.

"How did you girls get information from him?"

Carrie and I exchanged looks.

"It is covered."

Carrie sighed, while I was trying not to giggle. Daniel stepped in helpfully.

"Same way you kept eyes on Drombal?"

"Yes." Carrie said.

"She kept him busy while I got the programs she wrote onto his phone and iPad. Every time he spoke, I took notes and translated." I said grinning.

"How long did it take you to get this information?" Carls asked. The room seemed strangely still.

"What kind of program did you use?" Ms. Rhodes, she was leaning forward with an avaricious look on her face.

"About a week. He was the courier. He made regular pick-ups and drop offs. The code changed weekly."

"So how did you get Darts to trust you?"

"They were going to be sending in a new courier as Tony was getting promoted. A chick."

"Name?"

"Never caught it. We got the information and went a day earlier then the *chica* who was supposed to be there."

Jason whistled. The stillness behind us went frozen.

"Ballsy." Daniel said.

"Desperate to not be small time dealers." I replied.

"You aren't afraid they would track this back to you?"

This time Carrie glared at me and I had the decency to look abashed.

"No." I said steadily, looking at Carrie. She had a challenging look.

"Tony was a well-known slut. Carrie would have been just another notch on his bed for a *gringo* bimbo."

"You didn't think Darts would say anything?"

"I had planned on saying we were the first of two sets of

chicas. They had two deals a week during peak times. Sometimes three." I said with a tilt of my head and a slight shrug.

"You were trying to fly under the radar."

"I looked and spoke the part."

"Carrie?"

"Erstwhile sidekick to throw off the *policia*."

"Not as well thought out as some of your other schemes it seems." Daniel said dryly.

I blushed. "No. This one might have come back to bite us hard. I was trying for optimism and Tony being too stoned and drunk to remember clearly what Carrie looked like, other than white and blond."

"You went to his place?"

"Hotel. He paid cash." Carrie said.

"How drunk did you get him?" Ms. Rhodes asked.

"Very." I said dryly. Carrie started to giggle.

Carls and Rhodes exchanged glances, which just made Carrie giggle harder, and I joined in on the giggling. It had been fucking funny at the time. Pun intended.

"What else is there to this?" Daniel spoke up from the back. He knew from experience that we were giggling too hard for our information to be that cut and dry.

"Tony was known as a tit man. He liked 'em big and bouncy. Didn't matter the size of the woman as long as the tits were huge. So Carrie got dressed up in a corset, showing off lots and lots and lots of cleavage."

"I could barely breathe!" She said primly. Her deep breath helped boost the girls a little higher, giving the judge, Carls, and Rhodes a sample viewing.

"You breathed well enough that you had nipple slip." I threw her a sidelong glance with a grin.

"Jealousy doesn't become you!" Carrie tried to huff haughtily, but started to laugh mid-sentence which made the girls start to jiggle. Again.

"Pfft!" I said derisively.

"Girls, if you would." Daniel interjected. There was more amusement but the professional in him won out.

"Yes, Agent Lozano!" we said in unison. I bet he rolled his eyes on that one. Carrie and I just giggled.

It took me a moment to stop giggling at the memory. I had to clear my throat twice to start again. "We laced Carrie's boobs and nipples with powdered Rohypnol mixed with powdered sugar and glitter. Sweet and shiny!"

"He was out in fifteen minutes." Carrie said smugly. "I let Autumn in and we set up his phone to give us GPS and download any messages so Autumn could translate. We also tagged his belt buckle for his whereabouts."

"Why not his shoes?"

"He had like 30 pairs." I said dismissively, with a wave of my hand. "More of a clothes horse than Paris Hilton." I shook my head, both amused and condescending. "But he always wore the same belt.

"Very ingenious." Ms. Rhodes said.

"Very." Carls said. Again that traded looks with the judge.

"Go ahead and ask." The judge said.

"Autumn." Ms. Rhodes said with a calm demeanor. "I'd like to ask you about Rojo..."

My hands went icy and the scars seemed to flare painfully all at once. "No." My voice choked and I could feel the blood leave my face.

"We know you couriered for him." She continued, trying for professionalism though irritation leaked through.

I said nothing, matching dead pan eyes with narrow eyed glaring.

"And your sister was one of his girlfriends who died of an overdose.

My nails were digging into the chair, the hard wood not giving underneath, bending my nails backwards painfully. I just didn't give a shit. The pain was helping me not to think.

"Could you tell us who his seller was?"

"No."

"Why not?"

I shook my head and glared at her. Her arms came uncrossed as she put one on her hip and the other open, inviting confidentiality, shifting from professional to confident. I wasn't buying it.

"This is ancient history. We could take down…"

"No."

"If I may, Ms. Rhodes." Daniel came to the front of the room next to Carls.

Rhodes grit her teeth and was about to argue with Daniel when I spoke up.

"Rojo's dead. His gang broke up after that and I believe you have most everyone in jail as it is. You don't need anything else from me." My voice was angry and growly. I know my face was reflecting the same.

"Just the main buyers and sellers." She snapped with a glare. So much for professionalism.

"I don't remember. It's been too long." I gave her a flat, unflinching stare.

"Were you there when Rojo died?" Daniel asked from left field.

"Yes."

"Did you drive the car?"

I smiled. Much like Coyote's smile. Teeth and lots of pulled back lip. "No. But I really wanted to." Yeah. I had really wanted to run the loco over. Many, many times. I could feel the raw hate coursing through my veins at the thought of Rojo.

"Do you know who did drive the car?"

I could have lied, but Daniel would have guessed, so I just looked at him without answering.

"Who was it Autumn?" Carls asked.

Him, I smiled at. "You're aunt I think. I wasn't really close enough to see, though, to be sure or confirm."

He glared. I smiled sweetly.

Daniel cleared his throat, bringing attention back to him. "Julio seemed to blame you for Rojo's death."

"He would. Rojo and I did not get along."

"Julio was under the impression you threatened to kill him as the ambulance drove up for your sister."

Antonio had to hold me back from clawing Rojo's eyes out. Julio had enjoyed slapping the shit out of me as I screamed curses at them both.

I nodded. "I did. And I would have, but someone else beat me to the punch."

"And you don't remember who or won't say, making you an accomplice."

"The person you want is now out of your jurisdiction Agent Lozano."

"How do you know this?"

"After Rojo got turned into a pancake and the car went for a wash, I went inside and poured bleach into every bag of coke in the house, then packed up every fucking wad of cash I could find. I handed 10k to Rojo's other girl and walked out with three duffle bags. The car came back and I climbed in. The driver and I split the cash, and I got dropped off at a bus station. Made my way here, got my GED, started community college, then a 4-year. When I ran out of cash, I started waiting tables and selling small time to make ends meet and make my tuition."

"And that's how you met Carrie."

"Not exactly, but close." My lips twitched.

"You left out quite a bit."

"Yes, yes I did. But I'll send you the memoir I pen in 10 years."

"You do that." Daniel nodded. "Ok… I think that is where we stand now your Honor."

"What?!" Rhodes was not happy.

"You are welcome to keep questioning her, ma'am, but you will just get pissed off as she gets more annoyed." He said blandly.

Carls opened his mouth, about to ask questions when the judge interrupted him.

"Ladies, would you kindly step outside. We need to discuss a few things."

Carrie and I looked at each other, but nodded, taking the hint and standing. Jeremy escorted us out the door and into a side room.

"We'll be right back." He said kindly to both of us, but was looking at Carrie, who blushed a dark pink at his attention.

"Thank you Agent Fier." I said with a smile.

I sat down in a rather comfortable brown leather

upholstered chair, putting my feet up on the low table. Carrie paced back and forth.

"You could have told me he was mafia!" She snapped.

"Would you have changed your mind?" I asked.

She stopped for a second then sighed, coming to sit down next to me in the other chair. "No, probably not. But you could have told me!"

"I *am* sorry, Carrie. I only guessed and didn't want to freak you out. You had the hard part as it was." I was both contrite and very honest. I couldn't have slept with Tony. Not wouldn't, but couldn't.

"Not even. The girls are well trained to get what they are told!" She said with a deep breath, raising her assets high.

"Down girls, down!" I laughed. "Better?"

"Yeah. But don't do that again!" She gave me a fierce look.

"I solemnly swear I will not not tell you if I guess someone we are about to tag and release is Mexican mafia again." I held up three fingers in a salute.

"Those are the wrong fingers."

"This one better?" I asked grinning.

"Bitch!"

We laughed. Friends still.

Chapter Twenty-Two
Dream Walk

We got our sealed files. We only heard a little of the shouting behind the closed door. Thirty minutes later we were ushered back in and shown our files were sealed and put into juvenile records.

The judge handed us both written documentation affirming this, with a "I don't want to see either of you again. At least not as potential sellers. Both of you are smart and creative. Something more constructive with your lives would be highly suggested."

"Yes, your honor." Carrie murmured, with lowered eyelashes.

"Hmmph." He wasn't buying the angelic innocent. He was a smart man.

I just grinned at my shiny new piece of paper. I was so having this framed. I never had a get out of jail free card before. The bureau also found a little extra in its slush fund to help out two poor college students who had helped them. Not much, but 10k would take us both through our last semesters.

Daniel did catch up with us right before we headed down the large marble steps in front of the courthouse.

"Autumn, Carrie." He stopped, looking for the right words. We waited patiently for a moment while he cleared his throat and adjusted his immaculate tie.

"If you don't tell us what you need, we'll start on the blow job jokes again." I said with humor at his expense.

He didn't even blush or look annoyed, rather concerned. Carrie and I exchanged glances.

"This is serious." I said.

"Seems so. He's not getting irritated with either of us now!" Carrie looked almost worried.

That seemed to give him an opening.

"Tony Jalisco was found dead two days ago along with five others we think we're couriers for the warehouse."

Both of us blanched.

"We would like to offer you protection." Daniel was leaning forward intensely.

"Witness protection?" Carrie asked warily.

"No. More like undercover cops watching you."

"Do we get to pick the officers?" Carrie asked, perking up.

"No dear. We're going to be bait." I said with a raised eyebrow at Daniel. He nodded, confirming. That was what was making him uncomfortable.

No wonder he was concerned, almost worried.

"Oh fuck!" Carrie wasn't slow, but sometimes she had to have the rose colored glasses peeled off with a crowbar.

"Since our options are 'yes to being watched' or 'dying without anyone knowing who did it', I guess we'll say yes." I wasn't bitter, just slightly disappointed.

"We'll try to make sure you aren't disturbed." Daniel had the decency to wince while saying this. Guilt will only take you so far after selling your own soul to the job.

"Or killed." I added sarcastically.

"Or killed." He continued calmly.

"Will you or Jeremy be on the detail?" Carrie asked, perking up at the thought

"FBI won't be in on this." Daniel said with a shake of his head.

I twigged to what was making him uncomfortable. "Drombal." I said flatly.

"Oh no!" Carrie was getting more than her glasses pried off. This one was going to happen without lube.

Daniel nodded and spread his hands trying to show he had done all he could.

"Leave Jeremy behind at least so he can make sure Drombal does what he is supposed to instead of getting us killed then nabbing the killers." I said hotly. Now I was getting angry.

"Drombal, has every reason to keep you two safe at the moment. You die and he can never live down the restraining order or give you enough rope to hang yourself as dealers. This way he looks the hero if you are rescued or if he can catch you red handed."

"And you'll leave Jeremy." I wasn't budging on this. Jeremy would keep Carrie safe and I was betting I could keep myself alive long enough to do some damage. Not safe but at least not a helpless victim.

Daniel grinned. One of the first I could remember seeing. His eyes lit up and could make a girl's knees go weak if he smiled more. "He actually asked to stay and help keep Drombal on a leash and an eye on you two."

"A close eye." Murmured Carrie. She was perking up once again.

"A very close eye." I leered at her. She mimed a punch at my shoulder.

"Carrie could you give Autumn and I a moment. Please?" Daniel asked.

This time it really was a request. Carrie gave a knowing grin and sauntered off to the waiting car and driver. The bureau had been very kind to assign to us for the entire trial.

I watched her saunter off with rolling hips and bouncing chest. The driver was keeping his eyes firmly on her. With a show like that who wouldn't?

"She really is a smart girl." Daniel said. Again with that smile. Be still my beating heart.

"Yep, she is." I was proud of her.

"The two of you could get into a lot of trouble." Daniel was turning serious again.

"More than we have now?" I was going to have to laugh at the twist my life had taken. Staying ahead of the Mexican Mafia was going to give me enough nightmares if I didn't try and find something to laugh at.

"You got lucky this time." He said, looking sideways at me.

"Yep. We had you and your intrepid friends to keep us safe." I said smiling, returning the sideways glance.

He ran a tongue over his teeth, then chewed a bottom lip. "If someone comes after you…"

"Hopefully Drombal will want to be a hero and not a cad."

"Autumn, try to be serious." Daniel said, irritatedly loosening his tie, trying not to glare at me. He was starting to lose his cool. Not that I was "trying" to push his buttons.

I sighed. "Daniel you are really cute and sexy and are very married to your job." His expression went from irritated to wide eyed startled. "Carrie and I hope to be you when we grow up, but with more sex in our lives. We want to do the right thing, not just fumble through getting by as small time dealers pushed into the big leagues." I leaned over and kissed him hard before stepping back.

"Trust us to do the right thing." I said with a smile, then turned back to the car.

Carrie was fist pumping me as I walked to her. My knees were weak. It had been a good kiss, but definitely a kiss goodbye. I was a little sad at this insightful revelation, but I would learn to live with it.

We didn't tell anyone about the cards Carrie had gone back into the warehouse, which would tide us over for a few years if spent thriftily. She had managed to stuff eight of the things in her bra and panties. Cubby had caught up with her just in time to see her adjust her bra next to safe number one. She had given him sad puppy eyes and a blowjob to help her find her purse and mine that Marcus had put somewhere. Both purses were under the front cash register desk where he had put them. He did accept the blow job though. One of his firsts I think. Carrie the humanitarian. I laughed when she told me.

We checked the totals the next day. Between 20 and 50k per card. I whistled. There was no way we could spend these like water without raising suspicion.

"No new car?"

"Not new, but you could probably get another blue POS, without raising too many eyebrows."

She got a cherry red bug circa 1969, with blue pin striping on the butt. Like owner, like car.

We both got small safety deposit boxes. I kept two cards on me. The key to my box was not kept on my key ring. Yes, I was paranoid. Carrie opted for something similar. She kept her bank key at the bottom of her always-filled condom box. I put mine inside my old ratty teddy bear of 19 years that was on the upper shelf with some of my favorite, but older, school books.

I piled on every last class I needed and rarely came out of the library or my room when not in class. I didn't have to work two jobs, just go to class and study. It was almost heaven.

Carrie did the same. I know she had some fun as she slipped out on the occasional weekends. I was not invited along, but wasn't offended.

I was stretching at 3 am, doing a bit of cramming before my final psych class' finale at noon the next day, when I saw Carrie being kissed by a rather tall slim man across the street. She looked like she was floating on air when she left his side to cross the street. Jeremy waited till she had entered the building before he turned and left. I just smiled. I was glad to see those two finally being able to get their hookup on.

Post-graduation was a bit of a letdown. Jeremy came to the graduation, but no one else did. He gave Carrie a kiss on the cheek and a bouquet of roses. She smiled so brilliantly up at him; I thought the lights went dim.

Jeremy gave me a hug and it was enough. I didn't ask how the others were. Jason had sent the occasional postcard from various parts of the country. Mostly a "Hi! Still alive and getting shot at" type card. I was glad to see he was keeping busy at work.

We never heard or saw anyone from the Mexican Mafia. After a few weeks, the plainclothes following us seemed to gradually disappear. I was less worried after we graduated. If we had been a hit priority, the hit would have already taken place. Mafia(s) usually didn't have a lot of patience for being crossed and letting people live.

Carrie had sent her impressive transcripts with a well-worded letter to apply for several analyst jobs both in the local police force and directly for the FBI. She also took two weeks to fly to Italy and be a *turista*. She sent back pictures of her and a few of her and Jeremy. They looked very happy together.

While she was out and about in Italy, I packed and tried to find things to keep me busy while waiting till she got back so she could figure out what she was going to do with her things.

She found her letter of acceptance for the FBI and the LAPD waiting for her, where I had put them, in the middle of her bed with a big pink bow and a box of dark chocolates. No accounting for taste, but she loved her chocolate dark and her wine white.

Myself, I was waffling between psych, investigator or being a lawyer when I realized that my transcripts to any of the collages of my choice were late. I would have to wait until the summer session started.

I had applied across the board for Criminal Justice master programs. I got back one acceptance. New Mexico State University. I looked up New Mexico and had to giggle at the state motto. *"Crescit eundo"* – It grows as it goes. I was just going to accept that at face value. I finished all the paperwork and moved down into a small apartment complex that rented to mainly students, readying myself for the summer session. I had seven weeks till the first class to actually enjoy sightseeing and laying out by the small pool in the new apartment complex.

The apartment was a studio. I didn't plan on having a roommate or company much so the small space was not an issue. Even with my bed, desk, the newly purchased couch for lounging on and a small TV, I rattled around the apartment trying to fill it with just me. I had never been on my own before without a roommate or *mi familia*. Thick carpet and beige walls... plain boring paint, but all mine. It was a new and an almost sinful enjoyment.

My second week there, I noticed the two cars and two different sets of plainclothes following me. Both sets had short hair and one set occasionally had a suit and tie on; the other not so much a suit, but khakis and neatly dressed. Not collegiate, but could blend in on campus or off.

The two sets kept well apart from each other. By the third week of being a tourist, the second most fun I had was running the two sets of trailers into each other and watch the sparks. By the fourth time, they just glared at each other and me. I would usually be sipping chai and just salute the glares.

By the fourth week we were all bored with each other. I didn't bother asking who they were and they weren't really the touchy feely type to come and chat me up. I started to ignore them though they couldn't give me the same courtesy. Oh well.

I had a feeling there was at least one or more I was missing and the ones I could see were for someone else's benefit if not mine. If there was someone else, they were very good. I never saw anyone odd more than twice, and New Mexico was not without its own set of freaks and geeks to watch.

The weather had been cool without being freezing cold during the winter months. This changed in one of those weird spring transitional weather things that happened come March. A snowstorm was incoming, hitting warmer air from the pacific. There was snow, rain and sleet alternating every few moments and fog. Lots and lots of fog.

I had holed up in my apartment with a good book and a bad reality TV rerun. I remember getting to the kissing scene and smiling nostalgically if sleepily. Next thing I know I'm in a dream. I knew it was a dream because everything was fuzzy on the edges and very banal. Being carpet and walls. My walls. My dreams had been either non-existent or nightmares of floating dead girls. This one was warm, but fuzzy, and a large dog was lying next to me. I turned to see Coyote nudging my hand with his nose. I petted him absent-mindedly.

"Thinking?" he asked.

"Trying not too actually."

"Rather hard to do." He rolled his head for that perfect spot behind an ear.

"Very." I murmured. Enjoying a dream without dead girls or murdering psychopaths.

"A degree in criminal justice is not relaxing."

"No, but I hope to do some good."

"You can't change the past."

"Not for me. For others."

"Not exactly a rich field."

I had to smile, and ruffled the fur between his ears. "I've seen rich people and how they live. Lies, smiles and lots of uppers to keep from being hollow." I said condescendingly.

"Not opinionated much are you."

"Never!" I laughed and he just did his huge grin thing.

"Thought of going into the FBI?"

"With my records?"

"They are sealed."

"The FBI could easily open them." I sighed heavily. "I would love to do some real good and not just…" I waved my hand towards the collage. I was being realistic.

"You are young yet. There are years of help to be had."

I snorted. "Therapy years for me I'm sure."

"Possibly." Came the bland reply. "Though your skill set is rather…unique."

The bed shook as Coyote jumped down from the bed.

"Put your shoes on, child." He looked at me over his shoulder coyly.

I didn't bother arguing about the weather outside as this was a dream, but did ask, "Where are we going?" as I sat up, searching for my Keds that had been casually tossed somewhere near the bed stand. The socks were in the dirty clothes so I had to find a clean pair in a drawer.

"I'm rather thirsty. How about a coke." He asked suggestively.

"It's your dream, Coyote." I grabbed for my purse.

"Leave the purse, just the change and your wallet."

"Going to get expensive on me are you?" I asked. "As long as you don't order the quail or peacock at the local haute dog restaurant we're good." Stuffing the change and ID wallet into my generous baggy front pockets.

"Let's go, mutt!" I chirped grabbing keys to lock the door behind us.

Coyote bounded out for all the world acting like a house broken Labrador being promised a throwing stick and a pond. We walked down the concrete outer hall towards the inner stairs where the lobby had a coke machine outside. The weather was all fog, wrapping the world in grey swirls of dream. I liked it. The sleet seeming to have stopped. I didn't notice if it was cold or not, but the fog was rather damp. This I didn't like so much.

No one else was walking around with us in my dream. I couldn't say I blamed them. I know I had fallen asleep around 11pm and a Tuesday night was really not a big party night anywhere, not even in dreams it seemed.

"You couldn't have made the weather nice and sunny?" I asked more from curiosity than caring.

Coyote just lolled his tongue at me as he bounded around. He seemed to be enjoying the damn fog and sleet. No accounting for taste. We made it to the coke machine and I put in dollar bills for a coke.

"Water."

"You said coke."

"And now I want you to get water."

I rolled my eyes, but pressed the water tab instead. Out rolled a plastic bottle of water with a solid thunk.

"Good, now pet me so we can get going." Coyote said nudging my hand impatiently.

I grabbed the water, stuffing it into the front hoodie pocket. "Look you. This is my dream and you don't get to be a dick in it."

Coyote lolled a tongue at me almost laughingly. I sighed and petted him. The world became distantly softer, fuzzier and more foggy. I giggled.

"Now we can go for a rather long walk."

"No more burnt out warehouses please." I said flexing fingers in warm fur.

"No. But do not let go of my fur."

"Why?" I was feeling very comfortable and floating, my hands stayed in the shaggy fur as directed.

"We're talking a walk through a dangerous neighborhood. Some of the people won't like you."

"Too Hispanic or too white?"

"Too human."

"Human?" My subconscious was being really weird tonight. Probably my anxieties about moving and the upcoming Master's classes. I'd review my dreams in the morning. Might even write this one down. I started giggling, thinking of how to describe the color tracers going by every time my eyes shifted from one object to the next. This was really weird.

I stopped and looked down at the hip high Coyote. "You slipped me something!"

I think I was outraged, though the high was really kinda cool.

"No, I just gave you back the stoned you had at the warehouse."

"Oh! You can store those?"

"I'm a god." Was his lofty response. I snickered.

"A god with fleas."

"Quiet, human, or I'll lick your face."

"Ewwwww!!" But I held on to Coyote, following him through landscapes oddly shaped and colored with muted earth tones. The sky seemed to change from fogged to clear. I saw the occasional form. Mostly person shaped. Some were totally painted in blue with white or black eyes. Some were painted in red with odd black symbols up and down their bodies. None approached us. There was a huge snake at one point following beside Coyote and then a rather large condor joined in. I could hear muttering, but it was like a conversation two rooms over. Low voices and with the occasional bit of laughter or yelling.

The scenery changed again. Here the moon was actually visible, not full but close, and very bright in what would be the midday position. Unlike at the apartment where the cloud and fog had blocked out everything that was ten feet in front of you. We were in a really rocky area with dirt, sand, and rocks of every size. The plants were more scrub then grass it seemed. There was a fire not too far ahead.

I could smell frying meat and something else. My stomach rumbled.

"Great, I have the munchies. My hips will never forgive you even if there is only dream eating." I inhaled deeply, salivating at the wonderful smell of grilling meat.

A shadow passed in front of the fire and I could hear a distinctive click of a gun safety coming off. I grabbed onto Coyote's fur tighter. It seems even in dreams I didn't react well to guns.

"Thought you said the dream hostiles wouldn't be coming near us." My voice was breathy but not scared. Yet. I was relying on the damn dog to protect me.

Coyote chuckled. The sound seemed to carry far enough

ahead that a person actually came into view, blocking the fire. A very tall someone. One I recognized!

"Hey, Jason! Damn, now this dream is getting better." I was smiling now. The dream was finally going in a direction I could get into.

Jason looked rather startled at seeing both Coyote and me. Seems the dream script wasn't being fed to him on cue.

"Coyote dragging you into dreams? If not I really hope this is just my subconscious giving me a nice thrill." I asked, eyeing him up and down. Yep, still yummy.

Jason just raised an eyebrow at me and put the huge Glock back in his side holster under the red flannel shirt that hung open over his black tee.

"Good evening, Autumn and Coyote. Would you like to come sit by my fire?" The invitation seemed a little formal for a dream, but hey, my subconscious was probably trying to say something. Not sure what but something!

"Certainly." Coyote was being very smooth. He shook his body, dislodging my hand. "You can let go now child." I just giggled and sat down in front of the fire to watch the flames jump up over the glowing wood coals. Coyote lay down beside me, nudging a limp hand with his cold nose. I gave him the obligatory petting he craved.

"She okay?" Jason squatted on the other side of me, concern written on his face. I just smiled up at him and went back to watching the fire.

"I gave her back the high I took at the warehouse." Coyote cocked his jaw for a better petting angle.

"When she slipped away from my crew." Jason looked up from the fire and the sizzling.

"Yes."

Jason had narrowed eyes and an angry expression. He was about to say something when I sort of started talking in a meandering way.

"I saw Coyote at the door and got up to follow him." I said dreamily. Jason shot one more glare back at Coyote who seemed unperturbed, before moving a large black skillet back over the fire grill. Whatever was in the pan started to sizzle, smelling very good.

"Hungry?" Jason asked after a few minutes of silence.

"Very! I've never had dream munchies."

"Dream munchies?"

"Yeah, fell asleep on the bed reading a book at the new place when Coyote showed up and we went on this walk. Weird people, but the snake and condor were pretty when they came walking with us for a bit. Not the Alice in Wonderland dream I always wanted when a kid. Though I have got to say, while I like the fire, a nice four poster bed would go better in front of a roaring fire then hard rocks."

Jason just about choked, his eyes going wide, almost dropping the two pronged fork he was moving food around with into the fire.

"Dream stoned, hmmm?" For some reason I didn't think he was talking to me.

"Easiest way to move through realms." Coyote replied. I went back to fire watching.

Jason got a couple of metal plates out, setting them to the side. He sliced up a rather large steak into two then spooned up what looked like fried potatoes from a foil covered container next to him. He sprinkled a little salt from another small container then handed me a plate with a fork and a hunting knife.

I looked at the hunting knife quizzically.

"All out of steak knives." He said to my look.

"That's ok. I'm just hoping to remember this dream so I can analyze my anxieties and weirdness tomorrow morning." I said, sawing into the steak. Juicy redness came out from the first slice. I put a bite of steak in my mouth and closed my eyes in bliss.

"Too under done?"

"Oh my gods! I am in love. This is perfect. Meaty juicy melty. Couldn't ask for better." I said swallowing, wiping my mouth on the sleeve of my hoody. Very good dream steak.

Jason grinned, handing over a square of paper towel. I nodded thanks and attacked the rest of the meal. The fried potatoes had been done in bacon grease, though I hadn't smelled any bacon cooking when we walked up. Crispy on the outside, while soft and fluffy on the inside. Crunchy and soft. Textural dichotomy. I was in stoner heaven between the melting rare steak and the pan fried potatoes.

Jason was finished before me as I was playing with my food as much as eating it. That and surreptitiously slipping Coyote a piece or two of steak.

"Coyote can get his own dinner." Jason said washing up his dish and the cooking dishes.

Coyote turned liquid puppy eyes on him. "Even a god needs sustenance occasionally."

Jason just snorted while I giggled and played with my food.

"How is Daniel doing?" Jason asked, casually drying his dish.

"Who?" I was chasing the last potato through salty red meat juice.

"Agent Lozano?"

"Not a clue. Haven't heard from him since the files were sealed."

This stopped Jason mid rub. He blinked a second.

"You kissed him pretty hard on the steps." Again the bland voice.

"Yep. Was good-bye." I said, enjoying the last sublime bite. I handed the plate to him over the fire. He took the plate right as I yelped from a flame licking the skin on the back of my hand, singing hair and hoodie, leaving a red welt on exposed skin.

"Ouch! Bad dream, bad!" I said hugging the pulsing hand close to my chest.

Jason dropped the plate into the small dishwaster tub and grabbed a small black kit next to his sleeping bag. He came to sit next to me, taking my hand in his. The dream did not make his hands any less large or warm. I did notice they were calloused, though oddly. Maybe it was just the muscles. Lots and lots of muscles. I giggled then winced from the raw burned spot being touched.

"Going to need to put some Neosporin on your hand and wrap it up." Jason said gently, but he glared at Coyote. Coyote gave the equivalent of a dog shrug.

"I did not suggest she hand the plate to you over a fire."

"But you are keeping her stoned."

"Nope. Letting nature take its course." Coyote stood and stretched, giving us a doggie grin before trotting out into the dark without a backwards glance.

"Leaving me to clean up the mess again." He said with an almost glare at the god's disappearing back side. We heard a yip of coyote laughter from the dark then nothing more.

I could see the muscles bunching in Jason's jaw fascinatingly. I reached up with my good hand, just touching. Warm and muscley, I giggled again. Jason shook his head, turning his attention from Coyote to my hand.

He pulled the hoodie sleeve up almost to my elbow turning my hand over and stopped. The cigarette burns stood out even in fire light. The knife cuts were mostly just white lines. Harder to see, but visible if you knew what to look for. He gave me a hooded look, and then continued with spreading the Neosporin on my hand and wrist. The wrapping took a few minutes longer as the burn went from the pinky to the edge of my hand down to my wrist, taking most of a wrap to cover. I was so fuzzy that the scars being seen weren't even fazing me.

Jason put everything back up into his medical kit with smooth precision. Replacing the kit by his sleeping bag, then coming to sit by me again. I enjoyed watching him. Very nice dream I thought. Erotic without being intense. Sigh. Too bad I couldn't get the dream to show up with a king size bed and him naked. Maybe next time. I went back to fire gazing.

"Autumn." Jason waived a hand in front of me, distracting me from the fire.

"Hmmm?"

"The scars. On your arm. Did you do those?" He was trying for a calm even voice and mostly succeeding.

I giggled. "Nope! Rojo hated it when you fucked up a sale or missed something he said. If you were close enough he burned you with a cigarette. If you were further and he had something to throw, he'd aim to hit you in the arm or leg. Forks, plates, knives, measuring scales. Well, if the scales didn't have anything on them that is." My mouth and brain weren't really connected at the moment, so the story sort of flowed out. "One time he was so mad at me he threw this really big knife he had been contemplating buying off some hombre who really needed to get a quick score but had no cash. I saw the throw and the knife coming at me and ducked barely in time. Instead of getting me, he hit Julio in the arm. Hard. The knife stuck at least an inch deep." I laughed at the memory. "I really thought Julio was going to draw down on that fucker, too."

"So these aren't yours?"

"Oh, they are mine… I just didn't do them to myself." I said dreamily, I was still lost in a memory of Julio and Rojo going at it. I had gotten back handed at the time, then hit with a belt and the belt buckle later for laughing, but damn it had been worth seeing Julio getting stuck like that. I grinned. I wasn't going to explain this to a dream. It was a location thing, would get fucked up in a stoned translation.

Jason let out a breath, smoothing down the hoodie sleeve. "It was a rough time for you." Not a question.

"Had its good points and some bad points. But I survived." I said looking at his really beautiful dark eyes. I definitely wanted a king-sized bed or at least soft grass in the next dream, damn it!

"Why was the kiss to Lozano goodbye?"

I tilted my head, looking at a really huge expanse of stars. Couldn't see those in a city. Too many lights.

"I really could fall into those stars." I murmured. Jason looked up and smiled.

"Aye. One of the reasons I like to come out here."

"I'll have to write you so you can tell me where that is. I'd like to visit a camping spot you've been to."

Jason just shook his head, but smiled. He leaned against one of the smaller boulders ringing his camp. I moved closer and put my head on his shoulder. I felt him tense up. He took another deep breath and moved an arm around my shoulders.

I had to remember what he had asked prior. "Lozano. Daniel. Kiss. Right. Umm… he is way too married to his job to even think twice about dating or even fucking someone as young and not "good" as I. That and he's too Hispanic."

"Too Hispanic?" That seemed to throw him.

"Rojo pimped out anything he wasn't nailing. But the guys liked the girls without scars. I had scars from him and Julio beating me as well as looking like a boy. Flat chested and short spiky hair."

"Kept you safe?"

"Mostly. There were a few times." I shook my head. "My sister had given me the best advice she could. "If you don't want to be there, close your eyes and go limp. It will be over as soon as he can get off." She was mostly right. I had to stop glaring at Julio and just act bored before he got tired of trying to make me scream." I shrugged. The haze helped that memory not hurt or make me furious as it usually did.

Jason's arm tightened around me.

"Don't get me wrong. I think Hispanic men are cute and Daniel rocked the suit and tie. But every time I've taken someone to bed that was Hispanic, I've had lousy just lying there sex. I can't do anything else it seems."

"Seen a therapist?"

I laughed. "College is a huge step for me. Therapy is for rich white people."

"Like Carrie."

"Carrie was my therapist a few times after some really bad sex. Best friend ever." I giggled at another thought. "You should have seen the first time she took me to an adult toy store and then showed me how to use the toys. Best orgasm ever. Need to find a man who can do the same thing."

Jason choked on laughter. It was a good rumbling sound in his chest.

"Do you miss her?"

"Yes and no. I miss having someone to talk with, but it's nice to be on my own. Second time I've ever lived without anyone else. I kinda like it." My eyes were getting heavy and Jason was very comfortable.

"Hey! I just remembered… How did you see me kiss Daniel?" I struggled to sit up without shrugging off his arm, to look at him.

Jason looked at me with a twinkle in his eyes and a slow smile. "I had wanted to say goodbye and that I would have liked to ask you out to coffee or dinner sometime when your schedule permitted."

"Damn." I sighed snuggling back down onto his chest.

"Damn?" I could tell this was not the response dream Jason had been hoping for.

"I really would have loved to hear that in real life rather than in a dream." I settled back down on his shoulder. "So not fair." I was pouting through a yawn.

Jason just laughed, his arm around me feeling good.

"Maybe in the morning I can ask you again." He rumbled into my hair.

"Maybe. I should say yes over the phone while jumping up and down where you can't see me, acting all cool while talking to you. Gotta keep up appearances you know." My voice was starting to slur as my eyes were drooping, I was struggling to keep them open.

"Yes, I do know." Jason kissed the top of my head, tucking me in closer. This was a really nice dream I thought, drifting off under a dark sky of bright stars and a dying fire, crackling low in front of us.

Chapter Twenty-Three
The Next Step

I woke to the smell of bacon and a bed that was both really hard, but felt soft on the skin. I frowned. The dream from last night was vivid. I stretched opening my eyes. The sun was just coming over the desert horizon, painting the sky line with vivid pinks and blues. Beautiful I thought, closing my eyes for another five minutes of snuggling on the sleeping blanket.

My eyes snapped open and I sat up with a jerk. Desert? Bacon? Coyote. Fuck! The night's dream came back to me in a rush. I looked around me. Jason was in front of a small brush-fueled fire with a rectangular grill set over it and anchored with stones that were no longer than his forearm. Supported on top of the grill was the huge black skillet from last night's dinner. Next to him was a slightly larger closed wooden box with two blue enameled metal plates on top. An impromptu table.

The stray thought that he had a nice profile in just a black tee and comfortable looking jeans molding to his long legs, floated through my mind. That and he was very comfortable to lean against too.

He looked up just then with a slow smile. I knew I had to look a mess and really disoriented. His hair was no longer in a braid but short. Well, relative to an ass long braid, but long for an agent. His current ponytail was to his shoulder with long black roots and white ends. The two tone looked good on him.

"Last night…"

"Yes?" he said with a grin.

I looked down. Nope, still clothed; in fact I was wearing his flannel shirt. I took a deep breath and listened to my body. No pain other than the hand I had burnt. Nothing that felt like sex had occurred, consensual or otherwise.

"We didn't have sex, if that is what you were worried

about." He said, concentrating on the bacon.

"Thank you for that, I was wondering. A girl thing. Not an insult." I stopped talking for a moment, prying my foot out of my mouth. Jason looked up with a warm melting smile. I just wanted to hide, but sucked in a deep breath because I really needed to know. "Could you answer the question of where the hell I am? Not to mention how much of last night was a dream?"

"For you most of it was a dream. For everyone else it was reality." He moved the bacon to a plate with a paper towel over it, then flipped open a small yellow plastic bubbled container next to the wooden box. Eggs were revealed to be inside. He cracked six of them into the bacon grease, to scramble them. The shells placed back into the plastic bubbles.

"Where. Where am I?" My mind was not working and I was having trouble accepting that reality and my dreams were the same. My hand throbbed in counterpoint to my thoughts.

"Lower Colorado bordering New Mexico and Texas."

I gaped at him.

"That's…"

"A long ways from where you were." He said, finishing up the eggs and spooning them on to the plates next to him.

"How did…" I was not tracking. I know I had a glazed look on my face.

Jason took pity, but he wasn't giving up the smile. "I called Lozano and asked where you were last seen yesterday." He brought the plates over, handing me a fork.

"He's keeping tabs?"

"You and Carrie. Though Carrie is very easy to track now that she's dating Jeremy." We both grinned at this.

"And he said?" I said, taking a bite. Damn this man could cook! Sexy and a good cook. Sigh. I know I made an idiot of myself last night. I would just have to deal. I shook my head slightly with a sour look.

"Too much salt?"

"Hmm?" I swallowed, nearly choking while shaking my head. Jason freed a hand to pound me on the back. Even gently pounding for him made me cough harder.

"No, no… breakfast is really good. Didn't know… err… well, that you could cook or that cooking over a fire was like good or anything."

"A culture shock?"

"Very." I took another bite. I pushed down my stupid anxiety of being a fool and concentrated on the food.

"Daniel said he had a team on you in New Mexico and that Rhodes did too."

"Keeping tabs or trying to get a hit man."

"Depending on who you ask, probably both."

I snorted in appreciation. "Good to be wanted."

"I suggested his team should be keeping better tabs on you and you probably weren't in your apartment."

"What did he say?" I looked up curiously.

"Don't know. He hasn't called me back yet." His eyes were crinkled with amusement.

"You're a real tease with information you know."

"I'm a good tease in many areas." He shot back. I stopped with my fork half way up.

"Are… are you flirting, Agent Running Buck?"

"Why yes, yes I am." Again that slow smile.

I grinned and blushed, finishing the bite on my raised fork. I was saved from answering when there was a chirp from Jason's back pocket. Jason put down his plate on a convenient flattish stone before pulling out the phone.

"Morning Lozano." He was smiling at me, but his voice was lazy and drawling to Daniel. I could tell he was having fun with this already. I couldn't hear Daniel's voice clearly, but I could hear the tone of someone having apoplexy on the other end.

"You don't say." Jason leaned over his plate and took a bite.

"Mmm…. uhmm." He nodded along, motioning me with his fork to keep eating. I did not want my breakfast getting cold. It really was very good. The floor show was pretty good, though, too.

"And her phone is still on the table?" This time his voice finally broke through Daniel's ranting. The voice went very quiet then almost calm. I could almost imagine him looking at the phone and something clicking into place.

"Certainly. Here she is." He handed the phone to me. I took the phone as if it were a live snake.

"Hello?" I said surreptitiously.

Silence for a good 5 seconds. "Where are you Autumn?" Daniel's voice was tight like he was really trying not to yell.

"Umm… I don't know. I woke up in camp with Jason. And a fire. With him cooking."

"Did he pick you up?"

"Nope."

"You're sure of this? He didn't slip something into a drink and bundle you into a car?"

"I didn't have company last night and pretty much every bar was closed due to the sleet and snow that came down last night. In Las Crusas. So, no, I wasn't given any date rape drug. Is that the fashion now for the FBI to get dates?" I said off handedly. I was only mildly irritated at being asked stupid questions. "Karl may have set a trend for you guys. You seem to be the one behind if so. You'll have to start working on your drug palming skills now, Agent Lozano."

Jason started choking as a bit of bacon went down the wrong pipe. It took him a moment to clear out his throat, turning his already tanned skin a slightly darker burnished shade. Not brown exactly, more ruddy and burnished. I was fascinated by the change.

Daniel's voice jerked my attention back to the phone, ignoring my comments on Karl the Klingon. "Then how the hell did you get to the Black Mesa State Park?!" That's 600 miles from where you were."

I cleared my throat. 600 miles?! Wow. No wonder he was busting a blood vessel. He must think his men really suck if I had left by normal means and given them all the slip. "Would you believe me if I told you a figment from the warehouse walked me here in about 10 minutes or so? Time was pretty fuzzy last night."

"Fuzzy? Were you taking drugs?! Thought you said to trust you?" Anger and betrayal chased through his voice.

"Fuck you!" I snapped, glaring into the phone. "I did NOT

take anything. Some damn dog walked into a dream, then walked me here. Ask your other fucking agent and see if I'm telling the truth, asshole!" My voice rose with each sentence. I tossed the phone back to Jason. My hands were shaking I was so mad. I couldn't even eat. I passed the plate over and got up. Jason looked on with concern, but was nodding to me while Daniel chewed on his ear.

It wasn't cold. Chilly yes, but not cold. I hugged the flannel shirt closer. Damn thing felt like it was dragging, it was so huge on me. I rolled the sleeves up then walked out of camp far enough I couldn't hear Jason talking. The sky was turning a pale blue as the sun crept higher, leaching color out.

I looked out at the very rugged terrain wondering how the hell I got here, while resenting Daniel even more. Fucker! I hadn't done anything stronger than aspirin. All I had to say was whoever was in charge of drug sellers in NMSU sucked. There were about 15 on campus and usually no less than two to three at any bar I had visited. I hadn't even felt the desire to smoke since Coyote had pulled the high from me in the warehouse, now that I think of it.

"You didn't need the smoke anymore." His voice came from next to me.

I glared sideways. Yep. Large panting yellow mutt. "Thanks asshole. I liked smoking."

"You would have cancer in another seven years and died within eleven."

My head snapped around so fast looking at him, the ground spun. "Fuck!"

Coyote only lolled a tongue. "You're welcome. Not to worry. Agent Lozano will get over his irritation. His superiors will always wonder though, giving you credit for slipping people hunting you."

"You going to be sticking around a while taunting me with weird shit from now on?" Did I have a brain aneurysm giving me hallucinations was the question I thought I should be asking.

Coyote yipped in amusement. Not sure if it was the question asked or the one unasked. "No, child. I won't be taunting you nor haunting you. Not till I need a pair of hands again." He nudged my hand for petting again. I obliged.

"Why me?" I tried not to whine, but I was being petulant and I knew it.

"It wasn't just you. There were many more involved. Some are even dead. Perhaps you should start with that." Coyote leaned into the petting, his body heavy against my leg.

"Thanks."

"Don't mention it." Was the sly response and sideways amused glance from half closed eyes.

Jason cleared his throat from behind me. I turned, startled, not hearing footsteps on dirt. Coyote took the distraction to lick my hands and saunter off.

"He say goodbye?" Jason motioned to Coyote. He had concern written all over his face. I wasn't used to someone feeling concern for me. It was… nice.

"Not sure."

Jason raised an eyebrow. "That one likes you."

"Lucky me." I said growly. Jason gave me a slow grin. "Are you going to do nothing but laugh at me for the rest of this… trip, CJ?"

"CJ?"

I blushed. I had thought of him as CJ since wandering off stoned with Coyote in the warehouse. "Jason."

"CJ?" He asked insistently.

"It's a stupid nickname I came up with at the warehouse. I'll just stick to Jason." That got me an inquiring look, but no questions.

"There's an FBI office not too far from here. Daniel would like to meet up with us to make sure I nor anyone else coerced you here."

I thought about this for a moment. "No."

Jason's jaw dropped. "No?" Like he didn't think he heard me correctly.

"No. I am not an agent and I am not under his jurisdiction. I'm not going to ruin my day or days with him asking me stupid questions he won't accept an answer to." My panties were still in a wad.

Jason's lips twitched into a smile that touched his eyes.

"I'll just call him up and tell him we won't be making it."

I sighed. "If you'll hand me the phone, I'll tell him myself." Time to take responsibility for my, sort of, actions.

Jason handed his phone to me. I looked it over then handed the damn thing back so he could unlock it and pull up Daniel's number.

Daniel picked up on the first ring. "Dammit Jason, you better have your ass in that ratty Jeep of yours with that girl in tow and not be dicking around in the sand."

"Sand really sucks to have sex in, Agent Lozano, so no we're not dicking around, but I sure as hell am not coming in either just because you want me to." I said with almost real pleasure to his snarl.

I could hear Daniel sucking wind between his teeth. "Autumn, we need to talk." This time his voice was professional and bland.

"I don't think you're going to believe me on anything I have to say, Agent Lozano, and since I do not work for you, you can come to Las Crusas and visit me for coffee. Don't think it's a date though because I'm asking Jason out as soon as I hang up with you." I pointed a finger at Jason as emphasis even though Daniel couldn't see the motion.

Jason grinned widely. Seemed he liked this idea.

"Autumn..." Daniel started again.

"No. I mean it. Come down to Las Crusas or don't bother trying to talk to me."

There was a heavy sigh. "Fine. I will see you and Jason tonight. That is if you two will be there."

"Of course... oh." Right, not in New Mexico at the moment. "Umm. I don't know where we'll be. I'll have Jason call you as soon as we have the day figured out."

"I will be talking to Jason soon then." He hung up.

I stared at the phone for a second then tossed it back to Jason.

"So..." I started.

"So where would you like to go?" He asked pocketing the phone into his back pocket while looking at me.

"How about coffee? Since we've already done dinner and

breakfast?"

He laughed. A deep rumble. He held out a hand to me. I took it after a moment's hesitation. Large warm and strong. I liked it. I smiled up at him.

"I think I know a good coffee shop on our way to Albuquerque." He twined his fingers through mine.

www.ingramcontent.com/pod-product-compliance
Lightning Source LLC
Chambersburg PA
CBHW070530100726
47907CB00004B/1051